WHAT HAPPENS AT THE LAKE

What Happens at the Lake
Edited by: Jessica Royer Ocken
Proofreading by: Elaine York, www.allusionpublishing.com,
Julia Griffis
Cover Model: Simone Curto
Photographer: Maurizio Montani
Cover designer: Sommer Stein, Perfect Pear Creative

WHAT HAPPENS AT THE LAKE

VI KEELAND

CHAPTER 1
Meet Paul Bunyan
Josie

Oh shit.

I shifted my rental car into park and got out to walk around to the back of the Ford Explorer. Frowning at the small dent on the bumper, I was at least glad the pushy agent had talked me into getting the extra insurance. Why was there a random pole sticking up here anyway? I sighed.

Whatever. I'd deal with it all tomorrow. It had been a long-enough day already. What should've been an eleven-hour drive here from New York City had taken fifteen because of a flat tire and standstill traffic in a few states, all while managing constant texts and calls from my ex, Noah. I turned to get back in the car, but stopped when I noticed something red sticking out from under the rear tire.

Was that...*a mailbox?*

Shoot. Guess this wasn't a random pole after all. I looked up at the house it belonged to and debated not knocking until tomorrow. But I was going to be here a while and didn't want to start out on the wrong foot with the neighbor. So I pulled the crushed metal box out from under the car, carried it up the driveway, and knocked on the front door.

When the door opened, I momentarily forgot why I was standing there.

Wow. Hot wasn't a strong-enough word. Green eyes with a hint of gray, square jaw with just the right amount of scruff, and a perfectly straight blade of a nose. Not to mention, he was super tall. Six three? Six four? His broad shoulders filled the entire doorway. He might've been the largest man I'd ever been this close to. I briefly wondered if he could buy shirts in a regular store. Noah wore an extra-large, and this man looked like he could squash my ex like a bug. That thought made me smile.

It did not, however, make Paul Bunyan smile. He folded his arms across his chest and looked down at the pummeled mailbox in my hands. "Something you want to tell me?" He lifted one brow.

"Ummm..." I held the box up. Why? I have no damn idea. But I felt the need to do something with my arms. "I think I hit your mailbox."

"You *think*?"

"No, no..." I nodded. "I definitely hit it. I meant I wasn't positive if it was yours."

"Where was the mailbox when you hit it?"

I turned and pointed to the grassy area at the end of the driveway, the same driveway I'd just walked up in order to get to the door. The lonely pole remained. "It was over there."

"And yet you're *confused* which house it belonged to?"

"I, uh..." Oh, this guy was a jerk. He didn't have to mock me. Things happen. Like car accidents. It wasn't like it was *that* big of a deal. I'd replace it. "Yes, I hit your mailbox. I apologize. It's been a long day, and I'm not such a great driver, and it's dark out. I was trying to back into my driveway, and well...driving backward isn't as easy as forward."

The man's eyes narrowed. "*Your* driveway?"

I pointed to the house to the right. "That one."

He stole a glance. "You're staying in that run-down shack?"

"Run-down?" I looked next door, but unlike this house, the porch light wasn't on, so I couldn't see too well. "The real estate agent said it needs some sprucing up."

The guy's lip curled. "Whatever you say..."

Great. Can't wait to see what the place looks like now. I shook my head. "Anyway, I'll replace your mailbox. Did you get it around here?"

He lifted his chin. "At Clifton's, the lumberyard down the road."

"I'll get a replacement first thing in the morning. Do you mind if I keep it until then, so I can make sure I get the right one?"

Paul Bunyan shrugged. "Whatever floats your boat."

"Alright, well..." I lifted a hand and waved awkwardly. "I'll see you tomorrow then."

I walked down the driveway, feeling his eyes on me, but I refused to turn back. Though once I got to my car, which still needed to be backed into the driveway next door, I had to face the house again, so I peeked up at the door. Sure enough, the grumpy giant remained standing there, watching. I waved awkwardly a second time, then slipped into the car and set the mangled mailbox on the passenger seat.

I glanced up at the house yet again after starting the engine. *Yup. Still watching.*

Great. He was probably waiting to be amused as I attempted to back into the driveway, since I'd confessed I wasn't the greatest driver. I didn't need that kind of pressure, so I decided to pull forward, turn around, and park head first. I'd just have to carry my bags a little farther. Except...now I was flustered. Between hitting the mailbox and this guy watching me, I accidentally put the car in reverse instead of drive and promptly hit the mailbox pole again. This time, I knocked it over.

Slamming on the brakes, I shut my eyes. *Fuck my life.* This trusting-my-instinct thing I'd started doing recently wasn't exactly working out as planned.

My throat tightened and my fingertips started to tingle—telltale signs of a full-blown anxiety attack coming on. That was the absolute last thing I needed, so I did what my new therapist had taught me to do. I squeezed my eyes shut and counted to ten while I focused on my breathing. I felt no better when my eyes flickered open, especially once I saw Mr. Bunyan still standing there. But I did feel compelled to say something. So I pressed the button to roll down the passenger window and waved.

"Sorry! I'll replace that, too!"

My new, not-so-friendly neighbor said nothing. I was pretty sure we weren't going to be besties, so no point in trying to smooth things over. I shifted the car into drive, double-checked that I was actually *in* drive before taking my foot off the brake, and managed to turn around and pull into the driveway next door without any other catastrophes.

Though when the headlights gave me my first good look at my new home away from home, I wondered if I had another catastrophe on my hands.

Oh no.

Two windows were boarded up with plywood, the garage door hung crooked, and half the shutters were missing from the house while the other half dangled. No amount of deep breaths were going to make this better. If the outside looked like this, I was terrified what I might find inside. There was a broken porch light hanging over the front door, so I left the headlights on when I got out so I could see.

The rusty lock I stuck the key into matched the condition of the rest of the house, so I'm not sure why I was so shocked when the key didn't turn. I jiggled the handle back and forth a few times. The lock felt like it wanted to turn, but needed a little convincing. So I put some weight behind it and...it moved. Oh, did it move alright.

Snap!

I closed my eyes. *Please, please, don't let it be broken.*

But of course, it was.

Shit.

Shit.

Double shiii-it!!!

What the heck was I going to do now?

I looked around at the house. Maybe the windows weren't locked on the first floor? Or I could pry off the wood covering what I assumed was a broken one. I spent the next ten minutes walking around the perimeter of the property, trying every window I could reach. Needless to say, the only luck I was having today was *shit luck*, so none were open. Back at the car, I flicked on the high beams to survey the rest of the house. The third window from the left on the second floor looked like it might be open a few inches. I considered driving the car onto the lawn so I could stand on the roof, but it looked like I still wouldn't be able to reach. Maybe I should call a locksmith? Though the last time I did that, it took more than three hours for the guy to come, and that was in bustling New York City, not this small town. I was dying to go to sleep.

I peered over at Paul Bunyan's house and nibbled on my lip. He wasn't the friendliest, but I only needed a ladder. My gut told me that was the easiest solution, and since my gut had gotten me into this mess, I figured it was its job to get me out. So I swallowed whatever pride I had left, traipsed back over to the neighbor's, and took a deep breath before knocking.

The tree-man opened again, and not surprisingly, he didn't bother to say hello.

"Hi again!" I chirped a bit too cheerily. "Could I possibly bother you for a ladder?"

His brows furrowed. "What for?"

I pointed next door. "I seem to have gotten myself into a little pickle. The key broke off in the lock." I held up the snapped-in-half proof from my keyring. "See? And I only have the one. None of the windows are open on the first floor, but it looks like there's one open on the second. If you have a ladder, I'm sure it won't take more than five minutes for me to bring it back."

The guy stared at me for a solid ten seconds. Then he brushed past me without saying a word. I had no idea if that meant I should follow, but that's what I did. Paul punched a code into the wall on the side of his garage and the door began to roll up. He ducked inside and grabbed a ladder.

"Front or back?" he grunted.

"Uh...front."

He hoisted the ladder onto his shoulder and marched across the lawn toward my place. I followed. "You don't have to carry it. I can do it."

6

The man of few words glanced at me and kept walking.

"*Oh...kay* then. I guess you'll carry it," I mumbled.

Next door, he surveyed the front of the house. Spotting the open window, he leaned the ladder up against the wooden shingles and started to climb.

Apparently he's also doing this for me...

I watched from below, silently appreciating the view of denim hugging a fine derriere. Maybe I was delirious after the long trip, but I couldn't help thinking a quarter would bounce off that firm thing, and I had a sudden hankering for a juicy, ripe peach.

I shook the ridiculous thoughts from my head as Paul "the Peach" Bunyan slid open the second-floor window and climbed inside. Two minutes later, he opened the front door.

I breathed a sigh of relief. "Thank you so much."

The towering man folded his arms across his chest while standing in the doorway—apparently a favorite stance of his—and looked down his nose at me. "How do I know you're really allowed to stay here?" he asked.

"Well, I own the house, so..."

He squinted. "When did you buy it? I didn't see any for sale sign."

"I didn't buy it. I inherited it. Fifteen years ago. From my father when he passed away."

"Who was the old lady that lived here then?"

"She was a tenant. My mom rented it to her after my dad died. I was only thirteen at the time."

"What happened to her?"

"Mrs. Wollman? She moved into an assisted-living facility last month. It became too much for her to live alone and take care of a house."

"I'll say..." He looked over his shoulder. "When was the last time you saw the place?"

"That would be never. This is my first time visiting Laurel Lake."

Paul glanced over his shoulder again and back at me. "Who's your contractor?"

I frowned. "Contractor? No one. I figured I'd fix the place up myself while I stay here."

His lip twitched. "This should be interesting."

I might've demolished his mailbox, and he might've carried a ladder over and climbed into my house so I could get in, but I wasn't going to let the sexy jerk ridicule me. I gripped my hips, and my eyes narrowed. "What's so interesting about me doing the work on the house myself?"

His bemused smile deepened. "It needs a little more than paint and throw pillows."

Now he was pissing me off. "I'll have you know, I'm very handy. I have a degree in *engineering*." I left off the fact that it was *pharmaceutical science* engineering.

"Whatever you say..."

"How about if I say thank you for the assistance this evening and you let me into my house?"

The jerk turned his body to make room for me to pass, though he didn't actually step out of the doorway. Mustering as much self-assuredness as possible, I straightened my back, raised my chin, and tried to ignore the tingles in my body as I shimmied past him and into the house.

Paul Bunyan flicked on the lights. I'd already decided that no matter what the inside of the house looked like, I wasn't going to give this man the satisfaction of seeing me react. But all the gumption in the world couldn't have masked what hit me when I got a look at the place. I gasped out loud.

Oh.

My.

God.

I blinked a few times, hoping I was imagining things. Maybe this was a bad dream? It had been a long day and I was tired, so perhaps I went inside the cute little house with the sparkling interior and took a nap... But nope, I wasn't dreaming. Newspapers were piled from floor to ceiling in one half of the kitchen. And the kitchen was *not* small. The stacks were a half-dozen rows deep, running probably fifteen feet in length and eight feet high. I was so shocked by the disturbing collection that it took me a moment to notice *the other half* of the kitchen. Cabinet doors—painted seafoam green—dangled from hinges. The tiled backsplash was missing half the tiles, and the sink was missing the faucet. And that was just what I could take in at first glance.

My mouth hung open. *A little sprucing up?* That's what the real estate agent had said. An arched doorway led to the living room. I made the mistake of peeking through, and the house started to spin a little. It looked just as bad in there, if not worse than the kitchen. There was no ceiling or walls! No damn sheetrock! Only planks of wood framing with wires hanging all over. Worse, stuff was piled high in that part of the house, too. At first I thought it was more newspapers, but when I leaned in for a closer look, I realized I was wrong.

"Are those VHS tapes?"

I guess I hadn't expected anyone to actually answer. In my stupefied state I'd forgotten all about Paul Bunyan, so I jumped when his voice boomed.

"Yep."

One word. *One damn syllable.* Yet I heard the amusement. That did it. The entirety of the day came to a boil. And the top was about to pop off this pot as I marched toward my jerk of a neighbor.

I stood toe to toe with him and jabbed my pointer into his chest. "You think this is funny? Do you?" It pissed me off that in the middle of my rage, I noticed how hard said chest was underneath my finger. The damn thing felt like a brick wall. *But no...just no.* I forced myself to ignore it and continue. "I drove fifteen hours in traffic, with my cell phone buzzing like an insistent mosquito at my ear, got a flat tire, the air conditioning in my rental broke, I hit your *stupid* mailbox, and then the key breaks off in the door. I had to slither over to the grumpy neighbor to borrow a ladder just so I can get in. And when I finally make it inside, the house is a shambles and clearly has been occupied by someone with a hoarding issue. And as if all of that's not enough, *not enough of a shitty day to kill a person's spirit*, then you *enjoying* this moment has pushed me over the edge." I pulled my finger from the human oak tree and jabbed it back in with each staccato word.

"I."

Jab.

"Am."

Jab.

"Done."

Jab.

"You."

Jab.

"Suck."

At least I'd managed to wipe the smirk from the guy's face. Though he didn't say a word. He just stood there staring at me. After a solid minute, he finally spoke.

"You staying here tonight?"

My eyes widened. "*Of course I'm staying here!*" I screamed like a lunatic. "*Where the hell else would I go?*"

He looked at me for a few heartbeats, then turned and walked out. I thought that was the end of things until I heard a car door opening. Ten seconds later, Paul Bunyan appeared in my doorway again *with my suitcases.*

I was rendered as speechless as when I'd walked into the house. The man set the bags down in the kitchen and disappeared again. A minute later he returned, this time with the blow-up bed I'd packed and a box. He added those to my suitcase pile and disappeared yet again. After two more trips, he caught my eyes and gave a curt nod. "You have a good night."

Then he was gone, door pulled shut behind him and all.

I shook my head as I looked around the house. What the heck had happened in the last fifteen minutes?

CHAPTER 2
America's Friendliest Town
Josie

"Hi. Do you deliver?"

The gray-haired man wearing a *Sam* nametag smiled. "Sure do. Where's it going?"

"About a mile away, on Rosewood Lane."

"Not a problem at all. I might be able to get you on the schedule for this afternoon, if you want."

"Oh, that would be great. Thank you so much."

"Do you know what you want delivered?"

"I have a list, mostly sheetrock and hardware and whatnot, but I thought I'd take a walk around to see if there's anything I might've forgotten."

He nodded. "You take your time. My name is Sam. I go on break in about a half hour, but I'll look for you before I go to see if we can't get you taken care of."

Now *this* was the kind of hospitality I'd expected when I arrived in Laurel Lake, not the reception I'd received from the grumpy guy next door. At least I hadn't seen him for the last two days. I'd gone over yesterday to tell him I'd ordered his replacement mailbox, but no one was home.

In the daylight, I was able to check out his house. Flower-boxes, pretty curtains, a wreath on the front door—it made me wonder if there was a Mrs. Bunyan. I couldn't imagine *him* decorating so nicely.

As I made my way up and down the aisles of the home-improvement store, my cell buzzed in my pocket. Digging it out, I tensed, expecting to see Noah's name on the screen yet again. To my delight, it was Nilda—the woman I wished was my mom. My shoulders relaxed as I swiped to answer.

"Hey, Nilda!"

"Hello, sweetheart. How are you?"

"I'm good."

"How's living in America's Friendliest Town?"

"Well, it's been interesting so far. The lake is gorgeous, so serene and peaceful. There are only houses on my side. The other side is protected state land, so when you stand out back, it looks like you're in the wilderness. All you see is a giant lake and big, old trees."

"That sounds like heaven."

"It is. The outside anyway. The inside...not so much. Dad's house was apparently occupied by a hoarder, and the place is pretty much falling apart. I spent yesterday filling a dumpster and still haven't gotten rid of all the newspapers and VHS tapes."

"Oh no. Are you staying somewhere else?"

I probably should've relocated with the condition the house was in, but I didn't want Nilda to worry. "It's livable. Just a little more work than I'd anticipated."

"It's a good thing my girl is the hardest worker I know."

I smiled. "How are you feeling? Have you gone to the doctor about that pain in your back?"

"I'm working on it."

"You said the same thing about the pain in your side a few years back, yet the only time you *actually went* to visit a doctor was when they took you out of the house on a stretcher because your appendix had burst. Do I need to call my mother on you?" There weren't too many things the esteemed Dr. Melanie Preston took an interest in, but she *loved* to bully people into seeking proper healthcare.

Nilda sighed. "I'll get an appointment soon. I promise. But speaking of Dr. Preston... Have you talked to your mother since your discharge?"

"She left me a voicemail, but I haven't called her back yet."

"I'm sure she's concerned."

I scoffed. "If she was concerned about how I was doing, she could've come to visit."

Nilda said nothing. In the twenty-five years I'd known her, she'd never once badmouthed my mother, even when she clearly deserved it. And it wasn't just because my mother was her employer, which she was. I doubted Nilda had ever talked crap about anyone. She was the kindest, most warm-hearted human on the planet. I owed her so much.

"Tell me about the people of Laurel Lake," Nilda said. "Are they worthy of the America's-Friendliest status?"

I could think of one person who didn't represent the title Laurel Lake had carried for the last seventeen years running. Then again, I'd thought of him a little too often over the last forty-eight hours. It was time I forgot all about Mr. Grumpy. I wasn't going to let one bad egg ruin the little town I'd fantasized about for most of my life.

"I haven't met that many people yet," I told Nilda. "But the guy at the home-improvement store is really sweet, and the lady at the coffee shop gave me a free cup yesterday when I told her I was new in town."

Nilda and I talked for the next fifteen minutes while I meandered through the electrical supply and heating sections, picking up various items I hadn't thought of when I'd made my shopping list. I wound up telling her about my neighbor, even though I'd told myself I was going to put him out of my head. Before we hung up, I reminded her to make a doctor's appointment, but I was pretty sure I'd have to call my mother and get her involved in a few days. In fact, I wouldn't put it past Nilda to *not* call the doctor just so I was forced to call Melanie. I'd never understood why she wanted me to have a relationship with my mother so badly, but I knew she meant well. After we hung up, I went to find Sam.

"I'm all ready to schedule the delivery," I said, holding out my list.

Sam perused it. "Our guys are only allowed to deliver to your driveway. Unless you're planning on using the sheetrock and wood right away, you might want to get a few tarps. They're calling for a little rain in the forecast over the next few days."

"Oh, good to know. Can you add that to my delivery, please?"

Sam winked. "You got it. And I'm going to set you up with George as your delivery driver. If you need anything carried in, he's good about that. Some of the guys are lazy and hide behind the rules."

"Thank you."

He picked up a clipboard and scanned some papers. "I can have that to you between one and four today. If for some reason you're not home, they'll pile it all up in the middle of the driveway."

"Okay. But I'll definitely be home. I have a bed coming too." I shook my head. "Thought I could get by on a blow-up mattress. But apparently my back figured out that I'm not a teenager anymore."

Sam smiled. "You and me both."

Hours later, I had my AirPods in while I watched a YouTube video on how to hang sheetrock when the kitchen table started to shake. I popped one earbud out and looked around. But I couldn't figure out what had caused it. Until *bang. Bang. Bang.* I jumped. *Jesus.* It must've been the delivery driver, but the pounding was a little aggressive.

However, the hostility made sense when I opened the front door and found Paul Bunyan on the other side. His lips were set in a grim line. I decided to counter with an equally over-the-top greeting, but mine was happy.

I smiled from ear to ear, putting all my pearly whites on full display. "Hi, neighbor. It's wonderful to see you."

He grunted a word I couldn't make out.

"What's that?" I cupped my ear. "I didn't catch what you barked."

He scowled. "Are you expecting a delivery?"

"I am. Why?"

"Because they dumped *your shit* in my driveway."

"What?" My mouth dropped open. "They couldn't have." I squeezed around the oak-tree-sized man who seemed to like to stand in doorways and peered over at his driveway. Sure enough, my delivery was there. And the truck was nowhere to be found.

"I don't know why they did that. I've been waiting all afternoon for that stuff to come."

Mr. Bunyan held up a yellow carbon-copy invoice. "I have an idea."

"What are you talking about?" I snatched the paper and scanned for the address. "Forty-four Rosewood Lane. They have the right address."

"They do, huh?"

"Yes."

He lifted his chin, gesturing behind me to the other side of the kitchen. I was confused at what he could possibly be showing me in *my* house to prove *his* point. Though my eyes widened when I caught on.

His dented mailbox.

His dented mailbox with the number painted on the side: Forty-four.

Oh shit.

"I..." My shoulders slumped. "I screwed up."

"You think?"

"I've walked by that mailbox so many times in the last two days, I guess the number unconsciously stuck in my brain." I shook my head. "I'll take care of it."

"How?"

"Just don't worry about it. It will be gone in an hour. Okay?"

His answer was a headshake. Mr. Happy turned and started to walk down my driveway. But then I thought of something.

"Hey, Paul?"

He stopped but didn't turn around. "Is that supposed to be me?"

I closed my eyes. *Shit.* "Sorry. I, umm...is that not your name?"

"No, it is not."

"What *is* your name?"

"Fox."

"Fox? Is your full name Foxton or Foxwell or something?"

"Just Fox."

"Okay, well, *Just Fox...* Did you happen to tip the

driver? Because it wasn't his fault that I gave the wrong house, and I don't want to stiff him."

Paul—or rather Fox—still had his back to me. Only now did he turn around and shake his head. "If I had *seen* them unloading onto my driveway, wouldn't I have told them they had the wrong house?"

"Oh." My face fell. "Sorry, I wasn't thinking."

"Shocker…"

My eyes bulged. "You don't have to be so rude! I made an honest mistake."

Fox kept walking. So I did the mature thing and stuck my tongue out at his back.

"I saw that," he said, already halfway back to his property.

Seriously? What the hell? Did the jerk have eyes in the back of his head? I bet those were jade green and lined with dark black lashes too, like the ones above his perpetual scowl. Nevertheless, I grabbed my sneakers and pulled them on before heading next door to drag my delivery over where it belonged.

I hadn't realized how much I'd ordered until I was looking at it up close. There was a lot of crap stacked on top of a big wooden pallet.

"Great," I muttered as I bent to lift the first piece of sheetrock. Unfortunately, not only had I misjudged the quantity of what I ordered, I'd misjudged the weight, too. A single piece of sheetrock had to be close to fifty pounds, not to mention that it was a heck of a lot taller than me. My feeble attempt to carry it was a joke, so I quickly resorted to holding one end and dragging it across the lawn. I'd made it about ten feet when my load suddenly went light. Mr. Friendly hoisted the sheetrock into the air, up over his head, and proceeded to take it next door like he was carrying five pounds. I had to jog to catch up to his giant strides.

"I can do it," I said.

"Where do you want it?"

"Umm... I guess in the driveway. The garage is packed with stuff the tenant left behind."

"They're calling for rain."

"I got a tarp."

"You need a pallet or the water will hit from the bottom."

"Oh. There's one at the bottom of the stuff they delivered."

"And that will help me now...how?"

Good point. I frowned and looked around, as if a wooden pallet was going to magically appear on my lawn.

"My truck should be unlocked," Fox grumbled. "Remote to open my garage is on the visor. There are a few wooden pallets leaning against the wall on the left side."

"Okay." I jogged next door while my surly neighbor waited with the sheetrock. Not surprisingly, his garage was immaculate, and the pallets were exactly where he'd said. I rushed back and set the wood down in the middle of the driveway.

Fox placed the sheetrock on top and headed back to the pile in his driveway.

"At least let me help you." I chased after him. "It'll be easier if we carry the sheetrock together."

He shook his head without looking my way. "No, it won't."

This time when he bent to pick up a piece of the sheetrock, he grabbed *two* sheets. I refused to let him do all the work, so I lifted the next one and began to drag it across the grass. By the time I made it to my driveway, Fox had made *two* trips carrying *two* pieces of sheetrock at once. The giant man didn't even break a damn sweat.

Fifteen minutes later, the big pile had been relocated to where it belonged. Fox gestured to the house.

"You hire a contractor yet?" he asked.

"No. I'm going to do it myself."

"You have a lot of experience hanging sheetrock?"

"No, but I'm watching YouTube videos to learn. It doesn't look that hard."

"Right. YouTube." He smirked. "That sounds like a solid plan."

My eyes narrowed. "What is your freaking problem?"

"Other than a busted mailbox and a bunch of shit I didn't order laying in my driveway when I pull in to park?"

I rolled my eyes. "Are you always such a Negative Nelly?"

"Realistic, not negative."

"You don't know me. Yet you're certain I'm not capable of doing repairs myself?"

"In order to hang sheetrock, you have to be able to *hold* sheetrock."

I narrowed my eyes. "You know, people in this town are supposed to be *friendly.*"

"And good neighbors should be seen not heard. We don't all get what we want."

"That saying is about *children,* not neighbors." I wiped a drip of perspiration from my forehead, noting that there still wasn't one tiny bead on Fox's stupid brow. "And why the hell aren't you sweating after carrying all that?"

"I exercise."

My arms flailed in the air. "Are you implying that I don't?"

Fox's eyes skimmed over my body before locking with mine. "Didn't say that."

The way my body reacted threw me off my game. "Whatever," I huffed. "Thank you for helping me carry everything."

"You're welcome." He paused. "Again."

The *again* ruined my attempt at a courteous exchange. Clearly this man wasn't capable of niceties. I flashed an obviously bogus smile. "You have a great day."

As seemed to be his signature move, Fox turned and walked away without a word. Who does that? Turns around without as much as a chin lift or a wave? *Someone I don't need in my life, that's who.*

Glancing over at my neighbor stalking back across his grass, I shook my head. *The guy really is a jerk.* My eyes dropped to his form-fitting jeans. *But damn...a jerk with a great ass.*

CHAPTER 3
Mr. Change
Fox

"*Jesus Christ,*" I mumbled to myself. "*What the hell is she doing now?*"

I should've never looked to my left as I drove past, should've never let curiosity get the best of me. But I did. And I stopped the damn truck too, watching through the big bay window at the front of my nutty new neighbor's house. The little spitfire blonde was balancing on a chair, which was on top of another chair, while doing something to the kitchen light. I should've taken my cell phone out of my pocket and dialed 9 and 1, just to be ready for what was about five seconds away from happening.

She wobbled as she stretched up, and my heart did the same. I ripped open my truck door, about to jump out, let myself into her house, and physically remove her from the unstable setup. But then the light she was fumbling with flickered on, and she fist pumped into the air. She climbed down, and I blew out a hot stream of breath, yanked the door back shut, and hit the gas before I could witness any other stupid shit happening over there.

On my way to the jobsite, I made my usual stop at Rita's Coffee Beanery. It used to be called just Rita's, but she'd added the yuppie-sounding *Beanery* when she gave the place a facelift a few years back. The Airbnb yuppies who came down in search of something that doesn't exist because of the dumb America's Friendliest Town moniker were more than willing to pay an extra buck fifty to buy overpriced coffee from a *beanery*.

"Morning." I nodded.

"How you doing, cutie pie?" Rita said. "You want your regular?"

"Yep."

"One black coffee and boring whole-wheat toast, coming right up." She punched some buttons on the register. "When am I going to be able to talk you into changing things up? My power shakes are pretty delicious. I'm like a magician. You won't even taste the kale in my cucumber and apple power smoothie."

"Not big on change."

She disappeared and came back with my usual foil-wrapped toast and large coffee. "I heard you got a new neighbor. Maybe you can make a friend."

This town should've been named America's Nosiest, not friendliest. I shook my head. "About as interested in new friends as I am your power smoothie." I held out my hand. "Now can I have my breakfast?"

Rita *tsk*ed. "You're lucky your mom's so sweet and you're such a looker, or no one would be nice to you at all, Fox Cassidy."

I offered a curt nod and dropped a five on the counter. "You have a good day, too, Rita."

At the jobsite, I found my motley crew inside the air-conditioned trailer. I pointed to my foreman, Porter, who was sitting on the corner of my assistant's desk, and scowled. "Why are you in here instead of out there doing your job?"

He flashed a cocky smile that got him a lot of tail, but didn't do shit for me. "It's not eight o'clock yet. I'm telling Opal about the future Mrs. Tobey. Went out on a date last night. I'm in love, I tell ya."

I walked past him and took a seat at my desk. "Are we still on nurses?"

Porter Tobey had worked for me for three years now. Year one he'd been on a teacher kick, dating only elementary-school teachers, said they were motherly and doting. Year two he'd moved on to flight attendants, which wasn't an easy thing to do considering our little town was forty-five minutes from the nearest airport. But he'd been dedicated and spent a lot of time at the airport bars, with an empty suitcase to look like a traveler and all. He liked flight attendants because they weren't doting—said he found their independence refreshing. Now it was nurses. There were more than a handful of those in Laurel Lake, and I wondered if the switch had anything to do with the long drive to the airport and skyrocketing gas prices.

"Nurses are so warm and caring." He sighed.

"How about the ladies at the unemployment office? How are they? Because that's where you're going to be spending your time—" I motioned to the door with two fingers. "—if you don't get your ass out of my office."

Porter stood. "You know, my lady nurse has a lot of friends. Maybe I can ask her to fix you up and we can double date. Might help get rid of the bad mood you've been in lately, you know, for the last three years."

"Out!"

Porter scurried out of the trailer, leaving just me and Opal. She shook her head. "You should be nicer to that boy. He looks up to you."

"He's twenty-seven, only six years younger than me. So he's not a boy. And he looks up to me because I got nine inches on him."

"He lost his father at a tender age. You're a role model."

"Then I'm helping by teaching him a solid work ethic." I pointed to the printer. "Speaking of work, think you can print me out the specs for the Franklin job?"

She looked at her watch. "After I call my mother. You might be able to bully Porter into starting before his shift begins, but you don't scare me."

I had the pleasure of listening to Opal discuss her mother's bunions for the next ten minutes. At promptly eight, she hung up, punched a few keys on the computer, and paper started to spit from the printer. Our desks were maybe ten feet apart, max. Opal walked the stack over. "Good morning, boss. Here are the Franklin specs."

"Thank you," I grumbled.

I read what she'd handed me, but Opal didn't move. Instead, she waited for me to look up again.

I sighed and lowered the papers. "Yes?"

She smiled. "I heard you have a new neighbor. Name's Josie."

"Jesus Christ. Is there anyone who doesn't know?"

"Reuben at the gas station said she's very pretty."

Blond hair, light blue eyes, and skin that made me wonder if it was as soft as it looked. But I wasn't about to give the town gossip anything more to talk about by sharing my opinions. I shrugged. "Didn't notice."

"She's a scientist, you know."

"You sure you got the right neighbor?"

"Lives in Mrs. Wollman's place—the old hoarder."

My brows pulled tight. "How did you know Mrs. Wollman was a hoarder?"

"Everyone in town knew that." Opal's eyes swept over my face. "Except you, apparently. Anyway, pretty girl's a doctor—not the kind you go to when you're not feeling well or break a bone, but one of those researcher types. Got a big job, develops new drugs for some pharmaceutical company."

Well, I hoped she was better at making pills than she was managing a construction project. "Good for her."

"And Frannie at the post office said her mail is forwarded for sixty days, not permanently."

"Doesn't the government have privacy rules Frannie should be following? Or does she open people's bills and letters and spread gossip about that, too?"

"She also gets holiday cards from Josie—Frannie, not the post office. Though obviously it must come through that channel to get to Frannie."

My brows drew together. "They know each other?"

"Nope. First time Frannie met her was when she came in to pick up her forwarded mail a few days ago."

"Yet she gets Christmas cards from her?"

"Not just Christmas, but Easter and Thanksgiving, too. They exchange cards for every holiday."

"What am I missing here? They don't know each other yet they swap holiday cards?"

"Yep."

"How does that work?"

"Don't quite understand it myself. But Frannie said they started exchanging cards a decade ago. Apparently a few hundred come through the post office with the same return address a few times a year. Dr. Josie sends a lot of cards to the people of Laurel Lake."

I figured Opal had to be missing a piece or two of the puzzle. The gossip chain had a chink in its links somewhere. Whatever, I had shit to do anyway. "What time is the tile delivery coming today?"

As usual, Opal ignored me. "Rachael at the supermarket said Josie stocked up on a lot of food. Apparently, she's not gluten free and eats plenty of carbs."

I tossed the papers in my hands into the air. "Seriously? What the fuck? Do you people all get together for a secret meeting to discuss the comings and goings in this town? Is there a camera you have hidden somewhere to tell you when someone enters?"

"Unlike you, some of us are friendly and like to get to know a bit about the new people who come around."

"I think it's more like you're all discussing other people's lives because you don't have one of your own." I moved my fingers to simulate walking. "Now, find out what time the tile is coming."

o o o

It was almost seven thirty by the time I stopped on my way home to pick up some dinner. The Laurel Lake Inn was a fancy restaurant by this town's standards; you didn't eat there dressed in dusty jeans and dirty work boots like I had on. But they made a bacon-wrapped pesto pork tenderloin that had me salivating even thinking about it, so I stopped in for takeout once a week. Usually I called in my order, but I'd forgotten my cell in the office and come straight from a jobsite.

"Hey, Syl. Can I get an order of the pork and mashed potatoes, please?"

"You got it, Fox. We're a little busy tonight. But I'll see if anyone else ordered the pork recently, and I'll pull their order for you. They can wait a few more minutes." She winked.

"Thanks. Appreciate that."

Sylvia disappeared into the kitchen, so I figured I'd step into the bar and have a cold beer. I made it three steps inside before I locked eyes with a certain blonde. Josie was a shit driver and couldn't carry more than five pounds, but damn, she was hard to look away from. She frowned when she saw me, which made me smile.

The restaurant might have been busy, but there were only two other people in the bar besides Josie and me. She had a plate of food in front of her and what looked like a glass of wine. I moseyed up and ordered a beer, trying my best not to look over, but that didn't last long. My eyes snagged on her hand on the glass, her left ring finger, in particular. It was bare. I'd noticed that the other day, too.

Josie spoke without looking up. "Heard a rumor you used to play in the NHL. Is that true?"

"Who'd you hear that from?"

"The nice lady at the post office."

Figures. That was how Frannie operated. She'd get you talking by offering information and then pry out bits and pieces of your life without you even realizing. I'd learned it long ago.

"The *nice lady* at the post office is a busybody who tells everyone's business out of turn."

"So does that mean you didn't play hockey?"

"I did."

She looked over and smiled. "I know. I googled you after she mentioned it."

"Why'd you ask me if you already knew the answer?"

She shrugged. "Were you any good?"

"Didn't Google tell you that?"

"The article I read said you were on the Olympic team."

"You know a lot of shitty professional athletes who make an Olympic team?"

"I don't know any shitty professional athletes at all."

I had to crack a smile at that. She was a wiseass. And pretty. But she also seemed like a lot of work. And that was the trifecta combination I kept far away from these days. So I sipped my beer and kept quiet.

"Are you ordering food, or did you just come for that beer?" she asked a few minutes later.

"I'm picking up takeout."

"The food is really good here."

I nodded. "The best Laurel Lake's got to offer. Trust me, I eat a lot of takeout."

"You don't like to cook?"

"Hate to clean up when the cooking's done. Easier to pick up something on the way home."

"I love to cook. I find it relaxing. But the oven at my house is broken. It was filled with newspapers from eight years ago, so I don't think Mrs. Wollman was much of a cook either. I'm getting a new one delivered tomorrow."

Sylvia walked in and put a hand on my shoulder. "Food's ready, Fox."

"Thanks. I'll be right there."

I would've liked to stick around, find out what else the good doctor liked to do, but that meant it was definitely time to go. Pulling a ten out of my pocket, I tossed it on the bar and waved to the bartender.

"Enjoy your meal," Josie said.

"You too. What time should I expect the delivery people tomorrow?"

Her cute little nose wrinkled. "Delivery people?"

"The new stove. Unless you managed to give the correct address this time."

She squinted at me. "Funny. But I think you'll be spared having to carry over an appliance."

I took one more look at her almond-shaped eyes and pouty pink mouth and thought to myself, *Shame*. I nodded. "Have a good night, doc."

"You, too. Wait. How did you know I was a doctor?"

I winked. "Rumor train runs in two directions."

CHAPTER 4

Deck the Walls
Josie

I'd become a regular at Lowell's, the small but well-stocked home-improvement store in town. Sam always remembered my name and asked me how construction was going, and the cashier had given me a twenty-percent-off coupon yesterday. Today was Saturday, so it was busier than usual even though it was rainy, and the people shopping looked more like homeowners than the contractors that had been around all week. I waited in line, scrolling on my phone, until someone tapped me on the shoulder.

"Excuse me. You wouldn't happen to be staying on Rosewood Lane, would you?"

I turned to find a woman who was probably in her early sixties, with bright makeup and an even brighter hot pink one-piece short set.

"Yes. How did you know that?"

The woman smiled. "Lucky guess. My friend described you, and, well, it's a small town, so it's not too hard to spot the new people." She extended her hand. "I'm Opal Rumsey. I believe my boss is your neighbor?"

"Fox?"

She nodded. "But don't hold that against me. Not everyone who works at Cassidy Construction is as grumpy as the boss."

I chuckled. "It's nice to meet you, Opal. I'm Josie."

"Rumor has it you're the owner of the place where you're staying."

"I am. I inherited it from my dad when he passed."

"I'm sorry for your loss."

"Thank you. It was a long time ago."

Opal nodded. "Most of us thought Mrs. Wollman was the owner, she'd been there so long."

"My parents actually grew up in Laurel Lake."

"Really? What were their names?"

"Henry and Melanie Preston. Actually, my mother's maiden name was Melanie Langone. My dad would've been seventy this year. My mom is sixty-eight. My parents had me later in life."

"Can't say the name is familiar." She twirled a lock of hair and winked. "Then again, I'm *a lot* younger than your parents. Did they go to school here in town?"

"My dad was born and raised in Laurel Lake. My mom's family moved here after she graduated high school. But she had a younger brother."

"Then you know who would probably know them?"

"Who?"

"Bernadette and Bettina Macon. Twin sisters. Born and raised here in Laurel Lake. They turned sixty-nine last week. Bernadette was a school teacher in town before she retired, so she knows even more people than me."

"Oh, I know Bettina Macon." I shook my head. "Well, not *know her, know her,* but we exchange holiday cards."

"Her too? I'm starting to feel left out. My friend Frannie said you guys exchange cards. Were they friends of your family or something?"

I smiled. "No. It's kind of a long story, but I send a lot of holiday cards."

"*Can I help the next person in line?*" the cashier yelled.

I'd been chatting away and hadn't even noticed it was my turn. I stepped up to the counter, and Opal followed right behind me.

"Well, we're going to be done here in two shakes of a lamb's tail," Opal said. "But I'd like to hear your long story. What do you say we have some lunch? Bernadette and Bettina's little sister, Rita, owns the coffee shop in town, and Bernadette works the counter on Saturdays so Rita can spend time with her babies in the afternoon. The shop sells these little finger sandwiches that are made fresh a few times a day. Absolutely delicious. I like them because they're small, so I don't have to pick just one. Anyway, I can introduce you to Bernadette, we can see if she remembers your daddy, and you can tell me your holiday card story."

"Umm... Sure." I shrugged. "Why not? That sounds like fun."

My new friend Opal drove a bright yellow Volkswagen bug. Light rain started to fall as we went to the parking lot. We took separate cars, but I followed behind her to Rita's. On the way, I couldn't help but think this was something I'd *never* do in New York City—agree to have lunch with a virtual stranger. Being down here had me letting my guard down, accepting a friendly person as just being friendly, not having an ulterior motive. The vibe was so different.

When we arrived at Rita's, the girl at the counter said Bernadette was on break and would be back in a little while. Opal and I ordered iced coffees and four different types of the finger sandwiches. We took seats toward the back of the shop on a comfy leather couch and matching oversized chair. The place reminded me of something out of *Friends*. Warm and cozy. A place where you'd meet your crew to catch up on stories.

"I'm all ears." Opal sipped her coffee and picked up one of the sandwiches. "Tell me your holiday card story, and if your story is good and we have time before Bernadette gets back, I'll tell you about the time she had a little too much to drink, fell down, and got her high heel stuck in her panties on the way back up."

I chuckled. "I might have to bolster my story a little to make sure I get to hear yours."

Opal's eyes twinkled. "Something tells me your story will be more than enough. Go on, now. Let's hear why everyone in this town except me gets a Christmas card from you."

"Well, I grew up in the suburbs of New Jersey. When I was little, my dad used to tell me all these amazing stories about growing up in Laurel Lake. Two years before he died was the first time the town was named *America's Friendliest* by *People* magazine. He was so proud that he told everyone who would listen. Laurel Lake became this mythical, sort of magical place to me. He always promised we'd visit, but my mom is a very successful neurosurgeon, and she works a lot. We'd planned to come a few times, but something would always pop up for her and we'd have to cancel. My dad died very unexpectedly when I was thirteen—cardiac arrest in his sleep. We'd never made it down."

Opal covered her heart with her hand. "Oh, that's terrible. Such a young age to lose your father."

"It was definitely tough. My dad was my best friend. I was never too close with my mom. My parents were a very odd couple—Dad laughed a lot, told tall tales, and had a warm and loving way about him. My mom, on the other hand, is a bit cold—sort of detached and all business, even to me. Her career always came first, and she wasn't home a lot. To be honest, I never really understood their pairing. But for whatever reason, my dad was over the moon about my mom. He worshiped the ground she walked on." I paused and sipped my iced coffee. "Anyway, back to the cards. After my dad died, I started spending a lot of time at my best friend Chloe's house. Chloe was one of seven kids, and they didn't have that much money, but they all loved Christmas. Every year in late November, they would decorate their house with Christmas cards from the prior year hung on strings. They draped them on every wall in the kitchen and living room. My house was done up for the holidays by a professional decorating team that came in and made everything perfect. I once asked my mother if I could put some homemade ornaments on the tree, and she told me to put them on the little tree in Nilda's room. Nilda was our live-in housekeeper who also kept an eye on me because my mother was rarely home."

I nibbled on a sandwich before I continued. "Fast forward five years to when I turned eighteen, and I went away to college and got my own studio apartment in New York. I couldn't wait to decorate for Christmas that first year—my way, not my mom's way. So I got five boxes of Christmas cards, fifty in total, and sent them out to all my friends. I think I received one back. In hindsight, most eighteen-year-olds are either too broke to send cards or too wrapped up in their lives to take the time to do it. It made me sad, though, because I'd wanted to hang the cards from string like Chloe's family did. The following year, I came up with the idea to send cards to strangers and ask them to send one back. The morning after Thanksgiving, I took a picture of myself smiling in front of my Christmas tree. I hand wrote a message in each card saying I wanted to collect cards to decorate my house, and I hoped they'd send me one. I had the Laurel Lake phone book in a box with my dad's things, so I decided to mail the cards to people who lived here. I figured if they were America's friendliest people, I'd have a better shot of getting a card in return. That year, I sent out fifty cards and got forty-one back. I got *one* from my friends the year before, yet *forty-one* from complete strangers. I hung them from string on all of the walls of my little apartment."

"I love that!" Opal said. "Your dad's people took care of you after he couldn't any longer."

"I never thought of it that way, but yeah, I guess they did." I sipped. "I still had the cards hanging up in March, so I decided to send Easter cards to the forty-one people who had sent me a Christmas card. The next holiday season, I sent fifty new cards to random people from that phone book, and close to the same number reciprocated. Over the years, I've continued to send to the old ones and add new. I think I receive about nine-hundred cards for Christmas now, and a little less for the smaller holidays, like Fourth of July. I go in alphabetical order in the Laurel Lake phone book. I'm up to the Ns now. Some get returned because the book I'm using is outdated, but I enjoy doing it."

"Makes sense why I haven't had the pleasure of receiving one from you, then. My last name is Rumsey."

I smiled. "I've sort of become pen pals with a few of the residents of Laurel Lake. I've exchanged letters in the cards with some. They tell me what's going on in their lives, and I do the same. I've never met any of them, yet I feel like they're old friends."

"That's wonderful. I'm surprised it took you so long to visit."

I sighed. "Yeah. It shouldn't have. Unfortunately, I followed in my mom's footsteps and spent a lot of years in school and working too much."

"I hear it's *Doctor* Preston."

I shook my head. "Dr. Preston is my mother. I'm just Josie."

"We've only met and I can already tell you're far from *just Josie,* sweetheart."

"That's kind of you to say."

Opal finished off one of the finger sandwiches. "So what finally brought you to Laurel Lake now?"

I looked down. "I...had a mental-health crisis and thought it would be best to get out of the city for a while."

"Pardon my ignorance, but I'm not sure what that means. A mental-health crisis?"

"Basically, I had a nervous breakdown. Everything has a new term these days, doesn't it?"

Opal reached out and covered my hand with hers. "I'm so sorry. Are you feeling okay now?"

I smiled sadly. "I am. I spent a month in an inpatient facility getting treatment. When I got out, I went home to a pile of mail waiting for me in my apartment. One was a letter from the real estate agent who had been collecting rent from the woman renting my dad's old house. She said Mrs. Wollman had moved out. I didn't feel ready to go back to work yet, so it seemed like the perfect opportunity to get out of the city and finally see the town my dad loved so much."

Opal squeezed my hand. "Well, you've come to the right place. Our lake has healing powers."

"It really is beautiful. There's a serenity here that you can't find in New York City."

Opal nodded. "Can I ask you a personal question, Josie?"

I chuckled. "More personal than me telling you I recently spent time in a psych ward?"

She smiled. "Are you single?"

My eyes dropped to my left hand. It was a lot lighter these days without the giant rock I'd worn for almost a year. "I am."

She leaned closer, like she was telling me a secret. "So is your neighbor, Fox Cassidy. You two would make a very cute couple."

"Oh gosh." I chuckled. "Fox and I have met. I don't think he's my biggest fan."

She waved me off. "Eh. Whatever he did to give you that idea is just Fox being Fox. The man is a coconut. Hard shell on the outside, but soft and sweet on the inside."

My brows shot up. "Fox? Soft and sweet inside?"

Opal smiled. "I know. Hard to believe, right? But it's the truth. Trust me, I've been working for him for a long time."

"What is it that Fox does?"

"He's a builder, mostly commercial stuff. But he also coaches a hockey team—a team for people with disabilities. Many of the kids have cerebral palsy or Down syndrome. A few have competed in the Special Olympics and Paralympics. And he does all that work for free. Without telling people about it, too, I might add."

"Wow, really?"

"Yep. Stick around long enough, and I'm sure you'll get to meet some of them. On the weekends I sometimes see him having lunch with guys on the team, or he'll be out running in the street with one or two he's giving extra training to."

Huh. I never would've guessed Mr. Grumpy Pants was so giving. Though it did kind of make sense with the way he'd carried my suitcases in, even after I'd smashed his mailbox. And the way he'd hauled over all of my sheetrock when I'd had it delivered to the wrong address. There was a gentleman buried underneath that grunting exterior. It reminded me of something my dad used to say, something I hadn't thought of in a long time. *"Boys speak. A gentleman doesn't have to; he acts."*

A few minutes later, an older woman wearing a black polo with Rita's Beanery embroidered on it walked over to our table. She tied a long apron around her waist as she spoke. "Hey, Opal. How you doing? Katie told me you were looking for me."

"Oh hi, Bernadette. I want to introduce you to someone. This is Josie Preston. Her momma and daddy lived here in Laurel Lake. He's a year older than you, and she's two years younger, so I thought you might know them."

"Oh?" Bernadette looked over at me and winked. "Is your dad forty-nine too?"

Opal scoffed. "You've got varicose veins older than forty-nine."

Bernadette waved Opal off, then tapped her finger to her lip. "Preston. Preston. Your dad wouldn't be Henry Preston, would he?"

I smiled. "He is. And my mom was Melanie Langone."

"Your mom I don't recall. But oh my gosh, Henry Preston. I haven't heard that name in years." She gazed off like she was visualizing a memory. "Handsome Henry. He played the snare drum in the marching band. Had those pretty bright blue eyes. All the cheerleaders had a crush on him, but he was kind of oblivious about it. He was voted best looking in our class yearbook."

"Really? Wow. He never mentioned that."

Bernadette looked into my eyes. "You've got the same peepers."

I smiled. "People have always told me I look like my dad."

"How is your pop doing?"

"He passed away a long time ago."

Her face fell. "I'm so sorry. I didn't hear."

"Thank you."

"Josie is staying over on Rosewood Lane," Opal said. "The house old Mrs. Wollman lived in."

"The hoarder? That's right. I forgot the Prestons owned that house."

"My dad left it to me when he died."

"Are you in town for a while?"

I nodded.

"You know who you should meet? Tommy Miller. He was your dad's best friend. Lives over on Lilac Street, a block from your place. The two of them always had a fishing pole in their hands and a smile on their faces when we were kids."

"Oh, I've heard a lot of stories about Tommy."

"He still lives here. Same house. Same thick head of curly red hair. Same jokes he's been telling for the better part of half a century. I bet you he has a lot of stories about your dad back in the day. Maybe he'll know your momma, too."

"I'd love to meet him."

"How about I make that happen? Say next Sunday afternoon at two at my place? A week from tomorrow. I'll host a barbecue. I'll ask Tommy who else I should invite that you might want to meet."

"Oh, I don't want you to go to all that trouble..."

"It's no trouble at all. This is what this little town is all about. We look for reasons to sit around the lake, drink spiked tea, and tell the same good stories over and over. When we find a person who hasn't heard them all before, that's reason enough to celebrate."

I laughed. "Okay then. I'll bake some desserts."

Bernadette nodded toward the front. "I need to get back behind the counter so Katie can take her break. But leave me your phone number before you go, just in case Tommy can't make it or something."

I held up my cell. "Want me to text you so you have it?"

She chuckled. "I've still got one of those flip phones. No idea how to text. But you can write it down on a piece of paper, and I'll add it to my phone book for safe keeping."

I smiled. "Okay."

"I'll see you next weekend, then."

"Looking forward to it. Thank you, Bernadette."

Opal and I watched Bernadette walk away. As she reached the counter, the front door opened and none other than my grumpy neighbor walked in. He shook the rain from his hair and stepped up to place his order. I hadn't even realized I was staring until Opal spoke. "Saw him at a wedding a few months back. His hair was slicked back like an old-time movie star. Even I couldn't peel my eyes away. I get it."

I shook my head. "Oh. I wasn't looking at Fox that way."

"No?" Opal grinned.

"I'm just surprised he doesn't have an umbrella. He seems so organized."

"Uh-huh."

I tried to ignore the sexy jerk standing at the counter, but it was next to impossible to not steal glances, even after Opal had called me out. While Fox waited for Bernadette to pour his coffee, he scanned the coffee shop. When his gaze found Opal and me, he frowned and shook his head.

"Hey, boss!" Opal yelled and wiggled her fingers.

Fox nodded like it was painful to offer even that much acknowledgment and went back to watching his coffee be made. He was out the door a few seconds later, paper cup in hand.

Opal smiled from ear to ear. "He likes you."

"Umm... What part of that brief interaction gave you that idea? The scowl when he spotted me or the way he ran out the door like there was something contagious in here he might catch?"

Opal's smile widened. "Both."

CHAPTER 5

YouTube
Josie

I took a step back and admired my hard work with a glass of cold lemonade. I'd hung *two* pieces of sheetrock in the living room after getting back from lunch with Opal today. It wasn't much, but it gave me a sense of accomplishment.

A knock interrupted my pat on the back. The front door was open, leaving only the rickety old metal screen separating me from Mr. Grumpy.

"Oh no. Please tell me Amazon didn't deliver the boxes I've been waiting for all day to your place. I swear I checked the address three times."

Fox held something up. *An umbrella?* "You forgot this at Rita's. Opal dropped it by my place and asked me to give it to you."

I walked to the door and opened it, though I could've taken the umbrella through the giant hole in the screen. "Oh, thank you."

He held it out. "Not sure why she couldn't bring it to you when she was right next door."

I suspected I knew the reason. Opal had big plans for me and Fox.

He didn't let go when I reached for the umbrella. "She's the town gossip. You might want to watch what you say to her if you don't want fifty people knowing your business by morning."

"I don't know why you would say such a thing," I said, eyes wide. "By the way, it's really sweet that you donate your time coaching a special-needs hockey team."

Fox rolled his eyes, but a hint of a smile played at the corner of his mouth.

I pointed to his face. "What was that?"

He swiped at his cheek. "What?"

"I think that was *almost* an expression of happiness, though I can't be sure. Maybe you're actually in pain."

A full-fledged smile spread across Fox's handsome face. The sight was pretty damn spectacular.

"Now was that so hard?" I asked. "You must realize you're a large man. The scowl you wear all the time makes you very intimidating. When you smile, it softens your entire look."

"Maybe I don't want to look soft."

I rolled my eyes. "Whatever, Mr. Grumpy. Thanks for returning my umbrella. Oh, and I saw my garbage cans were out at the curb this morning, but I hadn't put them there. Did you?"

He shrugged. "Needed to be done."

"Well, thank you again."

Fox turned and took a few steps. As per usual, without saying goodbye or anything. But before he stepped off the porch, he turned back. "Why are you here?"

"You mean in Laurel Lake? I'm fixing up the house."

"The town gossip told me you have a good job. Why

not hire someone to fix up the place? You'd be able to make it back renting the house out."

"I needed a project to keep myself busy."

"Why not keep yourself busy at work?"

"I...I took a leave of absence."

Fox squinted. "Why?"

I sighed. "If you must know, I had a bit of a mental breakdown."

His eyes roamed my face, like he was trying to gauge my sincerity. After a moment, he softened. "Sorry."

"It's okay. It wasn't your fault."

Fox looked back into the house. "You've made some progress in there."

I nodded, gesturing to the living room. "Even hung my first pieces of sheetrock today."

Fox glanced behind me again. "You hung that yourself?"

"Yep."

He walked into the living room, perusing the walls. "You want the good news or the bad news first?"

I joined him to stare at the wall. "What are you talking about?"

"Well, the good news is that you did a pretty decent job. Screws are eight inches apart on the edges and sixteen in the center. You didn't sink them so far into the rock that it would make spackling time consuming. Looks good."

I stood taller. "Thank you. I learned it all from You-Tube videos."

"I'm guessing you only watched one on walls, though, not ceilings?"

"I figured I'd watch some on ceilings when I got to that. But you're making me nervous now, what's the bad news?"

Fox pointed up. "Ceiling gets done before the walls."

My eyes bulged. "Please tell me you're joking."

"The wall pieces are installed after because they help support the ceiling." Fox put his hands together to form a T. "You also butt the wall sheets flush against the ceiling so there isn't a gap to fill before taping the corners."

My lips pursed. "Damn it. Those two pieces took me all afternoon."

"At least you didn't do the entire room. It's pretty easy to take down."

I sighed. "I guess I'll be watching YouTube videos tonight instead of the last episode of *Love is Blind*. I saved it as a reward to myself and planned to add some vodka to my lemonade for the occasion."

"What's *Love is Blind*?"

"It's a reality TV show where a whole bunch of single people get to know each other behind walls. They don't see each other until after they've fallen in love and he's proposed."

"That sounds ridiculous."

"Don't be so judgy. What do you watch?"

"The news. Sports."

"No wonder you have a perpetual scowl on your face. You might not have noticed, but the world is depressing."

Fox's lip quirked. "I'll tell you what. You watch your dumb show, and I'll come by tomorrow morning and show you how to hang the ceiling so you don't have to watch YouTube videos."

My eyes narrowed. "What's the catch?"

"What do you mean, catch?"

"I mean, why are you being so nice now when you've been a jerk since the minute I arrived?"

"Maybe I'm just being neighborly. After all, this is America's Friendliest Town, right?"

That last part was clearly sarcasm. "It's because I told you I had a breakdown, isn't it? You're afraid if you're not nice, you might come home and find me rocking on the lawn or something."

His lip twitched again. "Does the reason matter?"

I thought about it, then shrugged. "Not really. Hanging the two pieces I managed to put up took me six hours. I've been trying not to think about how long the ceiling would take."

Fox nodded. "Eight o'clock work?"

"I'll have coffee waiting."

"I like whole-wheat toast too."

I smiled. "I'll see what I can do."

He walked toward the door, opened the screen, and kept walking—across the lawn and in through his front door. The man really needed to learn how to say goodbye.

CHAPTER 6
Piña Colada
Fox

She smelled like damn summer.

And it pissed me off.

Plus, I was tired from a shitty night's sleep. I'd tossed and turned thinking about Little Miss Home Improvement wearing nothing but a pair of denim short overalls and work boots—no shirt, no socks, definitely no bra or underwear. I probably could've put myself out of my misery with a quick jerkoff, but I'd refused to give in and do that while thinking about the annoying damn neighbor. So instead I'd stared at the ceiling, angrily flipping from left to right every five minutes.

Josie hopped down from the last two steps on the ladder. "Can I ask you something?"

"What?"

"Are you always this grumpy in the morning?"

"I'm not grumpy."

"No? So this is what? Your idea of a sparkling personality? I asked if your coffee was okay, and you grunted at me."

"That wasn't a grunt. That was a yes."

Josie made a short, deep noise that sounded like a pig.

I arched a brow. "Is that supposed to be me?"

She made the sound again, this time adding some monkeylike arm movements and jumping around. "*Gronk.*"

"Cute."

She jumped again. "*Gronk. Gronk.*"

I tried not to react, but she was just too damn adorable.

Josie pointed at my face. "There it is again. The elusive Mr. Grumpy Pants smile. It's kind of...dare I say... *nice.*" She made an exaggerated gasping sound and covered her mouth. "Oh no. I hope it's not too painful."

"Alright, wiseass. I get the point. How about you take your oinking ass out front and grab one of the small two by fours I left on the porch? I'll show you how to make an easy support to hold up the drywall while it gets screwed into the ceiling."

Josie strutted to the door. The woman was wearing a white tank top and long, pale pink, flowy skirt to do construction. It looked like she was going on a picnic date, rather than hanging sheetrock—though the tank top hugged her in all the right places, and there was something about her collarbone that I couldn't drag my eyes away from. Porter was damn lucky she didn't work for me, or I might make her getup our official company uniform. I had a feeling the outfit might make an appearance in my late-night fantasies this evening, rather than the overalls. She bent to pick up the wood out front, and the top of her tank gaped open, giving me a clear view down her shirt. I forced my head in the other direction, though my eyes managed to slant and continue looking.

"Jesus Christ," I grumbled to myself. "I need to get the fuck out of here."

She returned with a foot-long block of wood and held it out to me. "Here you go."

I shook my head. "Not me. *You*. Grab the screw gun and climb up that ladder."

"Okay!" She was a little too chipper this early in the morning for my liking. Once she was at the top, she looked down. "What now?"

I pointed. "Now you take that two by four and screw it to that stud. About three quarters of an inch from the bottom of that joist."

"What's a joist?"

"It's the horizontal beam at the top of the wall. You're going to hang the two by four parallel to that joist so you can rest the sheetrock on it while you screw it into the ceiling."

"Oh! Smart. Okay." She did what I instructed then moved the ladder around the room, putting up the other two by fours. When she was done, she jumped down from the ladder and clapped her hands together. "Now what?"

"Now you go make me another cup of coffee and some whole-wheat toast, and I'll get the sheetrock hung on the ceiling."

"What? No. I'll do it."

"You're not going to be able to hold a fifty-pound piece of sheetrock over your head with one hand while you screw it in with the other."

"How do you know?"

I looked her up and down. "Because you're five foot nothing with a fancy manicure."

"What do my nails have to do with anything?"

"If you did any kind of physical labor, they wouldn't look like that. Hell, I bet you don't even do dishes."

Josie's eyes widened. Her hands flew to her curvy little hips. *"Excuse me?* I'll have you know I do dishes. I even have a new kitchen faucet—which I installed *myself* the other day. And I might not be the size of an oak tree like you or do manual labor for a living, but I do Pilates five days a week *and* I use twelve-pound dumbbells to do the Jennifer Aniston arm workout four days a week."

"A whole twelve pounds, huh?"

She scowled. "Don't mock me."

"Just being realistic."

"No, you're being *a jerk.* I should've watched the You-Tube videos. At least there the people doing the teaching can't insult the students. Can you possibly just tell me what to do and I'll do it?"

I shrugged. "Okay. Go out front and grab one of the boards, then carry it up the ladder. Start in the corner. Lean one side of the sheetrock on the two by four you put up and square the edge to fill the corner as much as you can. Then screw it to the ceiling beams."

"Fine."

Josie marched out to the driveway. I watched from the house as she struggled to lift the sheetrock from the pile. It went against everything in me to stand here and not help. After a few seconds, she set the board back down in the pile and returned to the kitchen. I thought she was going to admit defeat, but instead she rustled inside a plastic Lowell's bag on the table and pulled out a Gorilla Gripper—a tool that latched onto the sheetrock and allowed you to carry it with a handle. It made lugging boards a hell of a lot easier. A lot of my guys used gadgets like that.

Josie chucked me a feisty grin on her way back out. This time, she managed to lift the sheetrock, but it still wasn't easy for her to haul into the house, even though it was only twenty steps. There was no way in hell she was going to get that thing up the ladder and screwed into the ceiling on her own. She made it as far as the second rung before the ladder started to tip. If I hadn't been standing here to grab it, she'd be on the floor wearing a sheetrock blanket.

"Can I do it now?" I said.

"I'm capable. It's just going to take me a bit."

I gripped my hips. "How about this... We agree that you're capable, but we also agree that it will take me a hell of a lot less time to get the ceiling done, and I have shit to do."

She chewed on her pouty lip. "Alright. But *only* because you have a time constraint."

I took the board from her hands. "*Right.*"

Over the next half hour, I threw four boards of sheetrock up on the ceiling. Josie watched, eager to help whenever possible. At one point, a cell phone rang from atop a box on the other side of the room. Josie ignored it. But a few minutes later, it started to ring again. This time she walked over and checked the screen. "Do you mind if I answer this?"

"Do whatever you need to do."

Josie stepped from the living room into the kitchen. The house wasn't that big, so it was impossible to not overhear the conversation. One side at least.

"Hello, Mother."

Quiet.

"Oh no. Is she okay?"

I held off drilling in the last screw, so I didn't interrupt her conversation. It sounded important.

"Will they keep her overnight?"

She sighed.

"Alright, well that's good at least. I've been bugging her to go to the doctor. Thank God you were home when she fell."

There were a few minutes of silence. When Josie spoke again, she raised her voice. "I wasn't on *vacation*, Mom. I was in a mental-health facility. And you know that because I left you a message the day I went in."

Silence.

"No, actually there is a difference. A vacation is very different. You know what, I have to go. Please tell Nilda I'll call her tonight, when she's done in the emergency room." She swiped to hang up without saying goodbye.

After thirty seconds of shaking her head and staring at her phone, she seemed to remember I was there. "Sorry about that," she said. "Do you need me to hand you any-thing?"

I shook my head and debated saying something. But she looked pretty upset. "You okay?"

"Fine."

I waited another minute. "You want to talk about it?"

"Talk? I think you've said ten words to me since we met. And most of them were insults."

"Some people say I'm a better listener than talker..."

"No. It's okay. But thanks."

A minute passed, and she still seemed pretty riled up from the call. "God forbid my perfect mother have a child who isn't perfect. It's the first time I've spoken to the wom-an since I checked myself into a mental-health facility, and she asks me how *vacation* was. *Vacation*! You know, like I was sipping a margarita and lying on the beach instead of having my shoelaces removed from my sneakers as a safety precaution."

"Some people pretend things aren't happening be-cause they can't deal with them."

Josie huffed. "Not my mother. She's capable of dealing with anything."

"Maybe that's what she wants you to think."

When she didn't respond right away, I drilled the last screw in on the board and climbed down from the ladder. Josie was still stewing as I went outside, grabbed another slab of sheetrock, and screwed that one in too. The woman might be a shit driver, in over her head with this dilapidated house, and my dick had too big of an interest in her for my liking, but I wasn't a total asshole. It sounded like she'd had a rough time lately. So I took out my phone and texted Porter, asking him for something I didn't ask of many—a favor. Then I went about hanging the last of the ceiling.

Porter's truck rumbled to the curb just as I finished up. He had one of those obnoxious exhaust systems—the kind you paid extra for to wake up your neighbors when you left early in the morning. He knocked on the screen door while I was still up on the ladder.

I lifted my chin toward the door. "That's for me, if you could let him in."

"Oh," Josie said. "Sure."

From two rooms away, standing on top of a ladder, I still couldn't miss the way Porter's eyes lit up when he got a look at the woman answering the door. *Shit.* I should've seen that coming. Josie was his type—she had a pulse. Porter flashed a smile that made too many women drop their panties, but his dimples only made the muscle in my jaw flex. I hurried to sink the last of the screws, but Porter already had Josie's hand lifted to his lips by the time I climbed down and got my ass into the kitchen.

"Down, boy. I invited you here to work, not act like you're in a singles bar."

Porter's eyes gleamed. "I was introducing myself to the lovely lady."

I lifted my chin. "Josie, this is Porter. Porter—Josie. Now get to work."

Josie's forehead wrinkled. "Work?"

"Porter's an idiot who chases anything in a skirt, but he's a damn good spackler. He can start the ceiling while I get the wall boards up."

"Oh, you don't have to do that. I can handle it. The ceiling was more than enough."

"We got it."

"But..."

I motioned to my employee. "There's another ladder in my garage. Should be some wood you can use as a plank, too."

"On it, boss."

Porter disappeared. Meanwhile, Josie stared at me like I had two heads.

"What?" I asked.

"I don't get you. You act like I'm a pain in your ass just for breathing, yet you're going to help me."

"You *are* a pain in my ass."

"So why are you helping me?"

"Fuck if I know. It just feels like the right thing to do."

Josie contemplated my answer for a minute, then a smile crept onto her face.

"What?" I asked.

"Opal is right. You're a coconut."

"What the hell does that mean?"

"Nothing." She smiled. "Except I really want a piña colada now."

CHAPTER 7
Not Interested
Fox

"So what's Josie's deal?" Two hours later, Porter hopped down from the ladder. He wiped the spackle from his hands onto his jeans.

I glanced over and went back to measuring for the last piece of sheetrock that needed to be hung on the walls. "There is no deal."

"You're not interested in her?"

My jaw flexed. "Nope."

"Then why are we over here on a Sunday morning working on her living room when the high school job is running a week behind? If we were going to put in overtime, it would make more sense to be laying the oak floor in the gymnasium."

"Let me manage my business, and you manage yours."

Porter stuffed his hands into his pockets. "Don't have any business to manage. Opal said Josie hit your mailbox."

I looked up at the ceiling and shook my head. Did the whole, entire town need to gossip? "Why the hell is Opal talking to you about my mailbox?"

"Remember that time I accidentally backed into the address sign at the office? The bed of my pickup was full with boxes of cabinets for the Woodward job so I couldn't see so good."

"What about it?"

"You almost fired me, you were so pissed."

"So?"

"So your best employee almost gets *fired* for hitting a sign, and some woman you just met gets her living room done on a Sunday?"

"Shut up and finish spackling."

"I am done, at least until Josie gets back from the store with the joint tape I need to do that corner."

I looked up at the ceiling. Sure enough, everything was finished except that one edge. I gestured to the giant can of spackle on the floor. "Start the walls."

"No more left."

"There's a full bucket in my garage."

"I thought you only wanted me to do the ceiling?"

"Just start the damn walls."

Porter took his time moseying over to my place. He came back with the bucket in one hand and a Pop-Tart in the other.

"Don't you ever get any flavors except brown sugar cinnamon?"

"Don't you ever *ask* to go into someone's kitchen and raid the cabinets?"

He ignored me and continued to chomp away at the Pop-Tart. "So you wouldn't mind if I asked Josie out? She's freaking hot, man."

I didn't like the knot I felt in my stomach even thinking about Porter laying a finger on Josie, but I'd never hear the end of it if I warded him off. "I'm not her keeper."

"Great."

Since the sheetrock was done and I wasn't half as fast as Porter when it came to spackling, I decided to go next door and get a few fans to help the drying process. The humidity on the lake in July kept everything wet for days. While I was there, I got a call from a subcontractor I'd been trying to reach all week. By the time I returned to the neighbor's, Josie was back from the store. And fucking Porter was already making moves.

He stood behind Josie real close, his hand covering hers as he guided the spackle knife around the wall. I felt like punching him.

"Hey, boss." The fucker grinned. "Josie's a real natural. Painting landscapes is also one of her hobbies, same as me."

"Oh yeah?" I gritted out between clenched teeth.

"I'm not very good," Josie said. "And I haven't done it in years."

"That's a shame," Porter drawled. "Maybe you should change that. The lake at sunset makes a beautiful subject."

She smiled. "I'm sure it does."

"I have an extra easel. I can drop it by one day..."

"Oh, I don't want you to go out of your way."

"It's no trouble at all."

I'd had to give Porter the all clear to keep the town's rumor mill quiet, but I didn't need to stand here and watch him spin his stupid web. I cleared my throat. "I've got it from here, Porter. Thanks for the hand."

He frowned. "I still need to finish three walls."

"I can handle it."

"But I'm quicker."

"If you want to work today, you can head over to the high school job we're backed up on. I was planning on waiting until the HVAC system went in to catch up, so there was some air when the temps hit ninety like it's supposed to today. But if you're itching to work..."

Porter held his hands up. "I'm good."

"Alright then." I nodded. "I'll see you tomorrow."

He took his time collecting his shit, then walked over to Josie. "It was very nice meeting you."

"You, too, Porter. Thanks so much for helping out. I really appreciate it."

"Anytime. I mean that. You need a hand with anything around here, just give a holler. In fact, let me give you my number in case you want to reach me."

"Oh. Okay." Josie walked into the kitchen, grabbed her phone from the table, and handed it to Porter. He grinned as he typed in his number, then used her phone to call his. "Now I have your number, too."

"Thanks again."

"Maybe I'll stop by with that easel sometime soon."

She smiled politely, but didn't encourage him. My *not* employee of the month tipped his baseball hat to me on his way out. "Have a good one, boss."

"Yep. Later."

Once he was gone, I went about spackling the living room.

"What can I do?" Josie said.

"Nothing. This is the last of it for today."

She looked around the room. "I can't believe you got all this done in only a few hours. This would've taken me weeks, at least."

"It's what I do."

She sat on the ladder. "How did you go from hockey to contractor?"

"Blew out my knee. Wasn't even thirty yet. Needed something to do with the rest of my life."

"Oh, that's terrible. Was it during a game?"

I looked away. "Nope."

Josie was quiet for a minute. I could tell she was waiting for me to say more. "How did you learn to do everything?" She grinned. "I bet it was YouTube videos, right?"

I chuckled. "My father was a contractor. I worked for him from the time I was twelve. He wanted me to have a backup plan in case things didn't work out with hockey. I was convinced I was going to be a superstar, so I thought it was unnecessary. Turned out he was right after all."

"I wanted to be a ballerina when I was little."

"Oh yeah? You're a good dancer then?"

"No. I'm terrible." She laughed. "I have no idea why I just told you that."

An energetic knock on the old metal screen door made Josie jump. I hadn't heard anyone come up the driveway either.

"Is this Forty-Six Rosewood?"

"Yes?"

"I have a dumpster delivery. You want it in the driveway?"

"Oh. Yes, I'm sorry. Let me move my car for you."

Josie grabbed her keys and went outside. When she came back, the sound of a backup alarm chirped as the delivery truck positioned a small dumpster up the driveway in reverse.

"What's the dumpster for?" I asked.

She motioned to the newspaper piles in the kitchen. "The rest of this. There's also a full room of magazines on the second floor. I misjudged how much junk was in here when I filled the first one I ordered last week. The VHS tapes from the living room filled almost three quarters of it."

I looked at my watch. I'd told the subcontractor who'd called earlier that I'd meet him over at the Franklin jobsite to show him all the things his guys had done half ass. But I still had an hour. "I can give you a hand for a little while."

"Oh gosh, no. You've done so much already. I can handle it on my own."

"I'm here, and it'll go quicker with two. Plus, having this paper all over the place is a fire hazard. I don't want my place catching flames from yours."

Josie smirked. "You don't fool me, Fox Cassidy. All the excuses you make up can't hide the fact that you're a decent guy down deep."

If she only knew how indecent my thoughts about her were last night...

Rather than debate, I walked over to one of the stacks of newspapers and grabbed two arms full. The delivery guy was finishing offloading the dumpster when I walked outside. I tossed the first heap in while Josie signed the paperwork. After that, we got into a rhythm going back and forth. The sun was blazing hot, so by the third or fourth trip we were both pretty sweaty. Josie's white tank top clung to her, and every time she lifted her arms to grab a stack of newspapers, she flashed creamy skin that I fantasized about sinking my teeth into.

She wasn't my type, at least not in the non-physical sense. I liked women who didn't question why I wasn't up for talking, women who wanted one thing from me—and it wasn't to get to know me with my clothes on. Divorcées in their forties fit the bill nicely, preferably ones who were still bitter about men and not ready to find another husband. They also tended to know what they liked in bed and were comfortable making sure they got it. Simple. I liked it that way.

Which Josie was definitely *not*. She was the kind searching for something—a fairytale she still believed in. And not the original Grimm ones either.

She reached up to grab another pile of papers, and a bead of sweat slid down the hollow of her back as I walked up behind her. I salivated at the thought of licking the salty drop from her skin. I couldn't tear my eyes away, at least not until she turned and caught me. I jerked my head, trying to play it off like I hadn't been staring, and wound up banging into the kitchen table. A box teetered before falling to the floor. I tried to grab it but missed, and the top popped off as it landed on its side. Some of the contents sprayed across the kitchen.

"Shit. Sorry." I bent down and gathered up the stuff that had fallen out. It looked like a bunch of Christmas cards. Hundreds. "Mrs. Wollman hoarded cards too?"

Josie knelt down and grabbed one that had skated across the room. She added it to the collection in the box. "These are mine actually."

I felt my eyebrows scrunch up. "You brought a box of used Christmas cards with you from New York?"

"Yes."

I looked over into the box again. "How many years' worth you got in here?"

"Just one."

"People sent you this many cards? I don't think this many people live in this town."

She smiled. "Actually, they do. I'm only up to N."

"Huh?"

Josie placed the lid back on the box and stood with it in her hands. "Nothing."

I shrugged. "If you say so..."

I went back to relocating newspaper piles to the dumpster. On my second trip, I noticed another card sticking halfway out from underneath the stove. It was open, so when I picked it up, I couldn't help but see what was written on the inside.

Happy Holidays!

Tom and Renee Dwyer

What the fuck?

Josie came into the kitchen after her latest trip to the dumpster and found me staring at the card.

"Where did you get this?" I asked.

"The card?"

"Yes..."

She peered over and read the inside. "Oh, Tom and Renee. They're really nice. They live here in Laurel Lake. Do you know them?"

"You tend to know people when you get engaged to their daughter."

"I didn't realize you were engaged."

I caught her eye. "I'm not. Evie is dead."

CHAPTER 8
A Lifetime Ago
Fox

Five years ago

Am I seeing things?

No one was ever in the rink at this hour, and definitely not anyone doing *that*. I leaned against the plastic barrier for a closer look, making sure I wasn't imagining her. But no, that was most definitely a woman on the ice. And she was most definitely...*changing her underwear*. She had on a tennis skirt and cropped top, not even any tights in the freezing-cold place. I watched as a tiny piece of red material fell to the ice and she lifted one knee and stepped into what looked like a pair of black panties, three times the size. She shimmied them up her legs, scooped the red fabric from the ice, skated to the sideline, and tossed them over the boards into the penalty box.

I stayed quiet, curious what she'd do next. The pretty redhead seemed lost in her own world as she skated to one corner of the rink. She took a deep breath, stood tall staring straight ahead for a long time, and then began to skate

backward with determination. When she got three quarters of the way to my side of the ice, she looped forward
and leaped into the air. Her body twisted and rotated so
fast, I lost count of how many turns she'd done. As she de-
scended, we locked eyes and her focus broke. She landed
hard on her ass.

Shit.

I bolted out onto the ice. Luckily I was already laced
up. I leaned down to help her, but she pushed my hands
away.

"What the hell were you doing, just standing there?"
she demanded.

"I didn't want to interrupt."

She brushed ice from her ass and climbed to her feet.
She was going to have a nice bruise later.

"That was some move you did there."

"It would've been, if you hadn't scared the crap out of
me. How did you get in here, anyway?"

"I have a key."

"Oh. Well, can you give me another fifteen minutes
before you start resurfacing? I really need to nail this
move."

"Resurfacing?"

"You're the maintenance guy, right?"

I smiled. It had been a few years since I'd walked anywhere near a rink and someone didn't recognize me. Especially a few miles from my hometown, no less. But I decided to play along. "Yeah, I can give you another fifteen."

"Thanks."

She skated back to the other side of the rink, leaned
over with her hands on her knees, and shut her eyes for
a while before getting into position again. Then she did
the same move, except this time it didn't seem like she got

in as many rotations as she had on the last pass. Though at least she stuck the landing. I was impressed, but she looked annoyed with herself. I'd watched figure skating on TV before, and this woman seemed as good as any of them. She repeated the trick once more and landed looking unhappy again.

Taking a deep breath, she glared over at me. "Do you have to watch me like that?"

"Are you training for a competition?"

"I'm training for the Olympic qualifiers."

"Won't you have people watching you when you try out?"

"Yes, but I'll have things down by then. You're making me nervous."

I liked watching her, and it was also past the time I'd blocked off the rink to do my workout, but I appreciated her determination. "No problem."

Though when I went into the office, I turned on the security monitor and pressed the button to bring up the interior cameras. Kicking my feet up on the desk, I clasped my hands behind my head and watched the woman do her trick five more times before nailing it on the sixth. Her turns were so fast, I couldn't always count, but the fist pump and smile on her face told me she'd done it. I zoomed in the camera and found myself smiling back at her, though she obviously couldn't see me. *Damn, she's gorgeous.* She started to jump around on the ice, doing some sort of quirky celebratory dance with her arms flailing all around. When she was done, she skated off and stepped into the penalty box. She glanced around the arena, probably to see if I was still lurking, then bent and grabbed something. I couldn't see behind the boards, but the way she was wiggling around, I was pretty certain she was changing her underwear again. Strange. But show me an athlete who didn't do weird shit.

A few minutes later, she appeared in the doorway of the office. I hadn't yet turned off the monitor. She leaned in and looked at the screen.

"You were watching me?"

"You nailed your move. Congratulations."

"I told you that you watching me made me nervous."

"You *knowing* I was watching you made you nervous. Can't be nervous about something you don't know about." I shrugged. "Also, if you skate a little faster, you'll be able to get more height on your jump and you probably won't cut it so close when you come down."

"I was skating as fast as I can."

"No, you weren't. You start out that way but then back off because your nerves get to you. You gotta go balls out."

She squinted at me. "Does the boss know you sit around watching people instead of working?"

I smiled. "I think he'd be okay with it."

She tilted her head. "Maybe I should ask him?"

"Maybe you should." I held her stare. "By the way, what's with the underwear change?"

Her eyes widened. "You watched me do that?"

"It's not like I was peeking through your bedroom window. You did it center ice."

"I *thought* I was alone."

"Were the other ones too restricting for all those flips or something?"

"No. They just weren't lucky."

"Come again?"

"The ones I put on are lucky, and I was pushing myself for an extra turn."

I didn't enter the rink before a game without tapping the gate three times, so lucky underwear made sense to me. It wasn't the objects, but the belief we held about them. Whatever worked.

I lifted my chin to her bag. "Are the underwear in your bag?"

"Yeah, why?"

"Can I borrow them?"

"What are you, some kind of a perv?"

"No. Just need a little extra luck."

"For what?"

"Hoping a pretty woman I met will say yes to going out with me."

"You're not referring to *me*, are you?"

"I am."

"You don't even know my name."

I extended a hand. "Fox. And you are?"

"Evie. But I'm not going out with you."

"Why not?"

"Because I don't even know you."

"Have coffee with me then. Here, right now. There's a vending machine near the locker rooms. Then you can get to know me, see that I'm a great guy, and say yes to dinner."

"I don't know..." She twisted her lips like it wasn't a hard no. "Don't you have to take care of the ice?"

I hadn't lied to her, just let her draw her own conclusions. I grabbed the clipboard that always hung on the wall and looked at the schedule. "No one else comes in until eight."

She looked over her shoulder at the empty arena. Her face changed, and I got the feeling the seesaw she'd been straddling was about to come down on the wrong side. I might've only met the woman, but I knew one thing about athletes: They love competition. So I changed my approach. "I'll tell you what. How about we race for it?"

"Race? You mean on the ice?"

I nodded. "If I beat you, you have coffee with me. Then it's up to me to charm you into dinner."

She laughed. "Are you serious? You know I'm a professional ice skater, right?"

"I do." I extended my hand. "But you don't know how well I skate."

She chuckled. "I think you're offering a losing bet."

"Do we have a deal anyway?"

"Sure. Why not?"

I stood. As I rose to full height, Evie almost looked concerned for the first time. She'd only seen me standing from a distance, and the rink was elevated from the surrounding surface.

"You're so tall."

I winked. "Longer legs make me a faster skater."

She smiled, still overconfident. "Whatever you say."

We walked side by side to the entrance and slipped off our plastic blade guards at the same time before stepping onto the ice. Evie skated backward to one side of the rink. "Do you want to take a warmup lap?"

I was too cocky for that. "No need."

She laughed. "Where are we skating to? The other side or the other side and back?"

I shrugged. "Your choice."

"Then let's go there and back. I'll count, and we go on three, okay?"

"You got it."

We both took our stances, leaning over with feet spread and skates digging into the ice, waiting for push off.

"You ready?" she said.

"Born ready."

She shook her head. "*One. Two...Three!*"

We blasted off, flying across the ice. I had to hand it to her. For a little thing, Evie gave me a decent run for my money on the way there. But I could cut a turn better than every man in the league, so I smoked her ass on the way back.

She bent over with her hands on her knees, panting. "How did you learn to skate so fast?"

"Years of practice."

I was about to remind her of our deal and show her the way to the coffee vending machine, when Neil, the *actual* guy responsible for resurfacing the ice, yelled from the side. "Morning, Cassidy!"

I waved. "Morning, Neil!"

I looked over at Evie. Her brows were pinched together. "I thought you said your name was Fox."

"It is. Cassidy is my last name."

"Fox...Cassidy? Like the hockey player?"

I grinned. "*Exactly* like him."

CHAPTER 9
Great Views
Josie

I could get used to this...

Shades of orange and purple reflected off the lake as the sun dipped toward the trees. As I watched from a lounge chair on the back deck, the serenity of the setting seemed to seep into my pores, helping my breaths grow slower and deeper.

Today had been one long day. But I'd gotten more done in the last twelve hours than in the last three months. The dumpster was full. The kitchen was finally free of newspapers. The living room had sheetrock and spackle, and three quarters of the magazines were gone from the second floor. Much of the work had been done compliments of my confusing neighbor, at least until he'd found a card from his dead fiancée's family and hightailed it out of here as fast as he could. It was a strange coincidence—a handful of cards fall from a box, and he happened to pick up *that* one? Then again, I suppose it would be a much stranger coincidence in a city like New York with eight-million people. In a town as small as Laurel Lake, the odds weren't all that astronomical.

More importantly, I'd just talked to Nilda, who was back home after a fall when her back spasmed. Thankfully, she was okay. I finished the last of the spiked lemonade in my glass, took in the beauty of the sky once more, and closed my eyes. After a few minutes I started to drift off, but footsteps in the distance snapped me alert. My eyes opened to find Fox standing on the end of his dock. He stared out at the lake, and I couldn't help but wonder if he was thinking about his dead fiancée. A few minutes passed, and I started to feel like an intruder, like these moments were supposed to be private, between him and the lake. So I got up quietly, attempting to slink into the house without him knowing I saw him. But three steps toward the door, the plank of wood underneath my foot gave way.

"Shit!" I screamed as I went down.

"Josie?" Fox's deep voice yelled. "Are you okay?"

So much for my slinking ability. I clutched my aching ankle and tried not to sound injured. "I'm fine! Just lost my footing!"

But a few seconds later, Fox appeared on my deck. "What happened?"

I waved him off. "I fell. It's no big deal."

He crouched down next to me and touched my ankle. I winced.

"Hurts to the touch?"

"A little."

"You have ice in the freezer?"

I shook my head. "I used it all to make my drink."

His lip twitched. "Hang on. I'll be right back."

Fox disappeared into his house, returning a minute later with an ice pack and a towel. He set it on the lounge chair I'd been sitting in, then leaned over and pulled one of my arms over his shoulder. His other arm wrapped around my waist and hoisted me up.

"Don't put any weight on it."

"Okay."

We hobbled over to the chair together. Fox guided me to sit, then crouched down and examined my foot.

"Does this hurt?" He pressed on the top.

"No."

"What about this?" He wiggled my toes.

"Doesn't hurt."

"Can you move your ankle?"

I grimaced as I attempted to roll it back and forth. "I can, but it hurts."

"Hopefully it's only sprained. Do you want to go to urgent care? There's one in town. I think it's open pretty late."

I shook my head. "No, I'm sure it's fine. I'll just keep off of it and ice it for a while."

He folded the ice pack into the towel and tied it around my ankle, like he did this every day.

"You're good at that."

He nodded. "A lifetime of playing hockey. Dozens of bangs, sprains, and breaks over the years."

"Oh, that's right."

"I'm going to grab something from the house to elevate your leg."

"Okay."

He came back with a pillow and stuffed it under my foot. "How's that feel?"

"Good. Thank you."

Nursing done, Fox knelt to check out the area of the deck my foot had crashed through. He pressed down on the surrounding wooden planks and shook his head. "These boards are all rotted through. It's pine, and even when it's treated, it's not the best wood for outdoor use. It's too soft. Should've used oak. Most people go with Trex or some other composite decking these days—looks like wood but without the rotting and fading." He smacked dirt from his hands and stood. "This whole thing needs to be replaced."

I sighed. "Great."

He eyed my glass of lemonade sitting on the table. "What's it spiked with?"

"Vodka."

"Got any lemonade without the alcohol?"

"I do. I made a whole pitcher. It's in the refrigerator. I added two shots of vodka directly to the glass, so the lemonade is just lemonade. Help yourself."

Fox took my almost-empty glass and disappeared into the house again. He came back with a refill for me and full glass for himself.

"Two shots looked like a lot, so I added one to yours."

I rolled my eyes. "Thanks, Dad."

It surprised me that he took a seat on the chair next to me. I didn't think he'd stick around after the way he'd bolted out of here earlier. But we sat side by side, silently looking out at the lake.

After a long time, Fox spoke softly. "I apologize for the abrupt way I left this morning."

"No need to apologize. You did so much for me today."

He nodded. Then seemed to get lost in his head. He sipped his lemonade and tilted the glass toward me. "How many of those have you had?"

"This is my third. But I have a pretty high tolerance for alcohol. It's genetics. Comes from my mother. She doesn't drink much, but when she does, she can knock back three or four dry martinis and be fine. My dad, on the other hand, had a few beers and would get giddy and slur his words."

"Is vodka your go-to?"

"It is, actually. I like dirty martinis best. But tonight I was in the mood for something sweet."

Fox sipped. "I would've taken you more for the wine type."

"What does that mean? What exactly is *the wine type*?"

"The kind who wears flowy skirts to sheetrock."

"It was one of the few things I had left that was clean. The washing machine is broken, just like everything else around here. I have a new one coming in a few days." I sighed. "The real estate agent said the place needed some sprucing up. I was expecting painting and new carpet. I didn't expect to be doing construction. Sorry I didn't pack my steel-toe work boots and Carhartts."

Fox squinted. "You have steel-toe work boots and Carhartts back home?"

"No." I grinned. "But I could've bought them and packed them if I'd known."

Fox chuckled into his lemonade.

The sun was almost gone now, but a lone golden streak sliced through the trees and marked a trail across the calm water of the lake. "It must be pretty incredible to live here and see this every night."

A stretch of silence fell between us. "It's been a while since I appreciated the view."

"Really? How come?"

"Just a lot of memories."

I assumed Fox meant memories with his fiancée. It was the second time today I'd dredged up his past. "I didn't get a chance to say it earlier, but I'm very sorry for your loss."

Fox caught my eyes but said nothing. I couldn't tell if he was upset I'd brought up the subject or just wasn't good at talking about it. I wasn't even sure how recently he'd lost her. He picked up his glass and chugged the rest of the lemonade. I thought he was doing it to get the hell out of here. As he swallowed, I noticed the way his throat worked. The bob of his Adam's apple made my insides feel tingly.

Great. The man is obviously struggling with the loss of his fiancée, and I'm ogling him as he does it.

When he finished, he held up his glass. "Still parched. Think I need another. You mind?"

"Not at all."

He eyed my still-full drink and left it behind. When he came back out, he knocked back another long swig.

"So how do you know Evie's father?" he asked.

"Evie?"

"Evie Dwyer," he said. "Tom is her father. Renee is her stepmother and grew up in Laurel Lake."

Oh! Evie. Fox's fiancée.

"It's sort of a long story."

He shrugged. "Got nowhere to go at the moment."

I spent the next ten minutes telling Fox the story I'd shared with Opal the other day—about my friend Chloe and her family hanging Christmas cards from strings, and how cards from the amazing people of Laurel Lake adorned my walls for most of the year.

Fox just stared at me.

"You think I'm a weirdo, don't you?"

"Yep."

I laughed. "You were supposed to say *'Not at all. I think it's a heartwarming story.'*"

"I'm not much for lying."

"Remind me not to ask you if I look like I gained a few pounds."

Fox did a quick sweep over my body. His gaze lingered for a heartbeat or two at my cleavage before making its way up again. "No worries there. You look pretty good to me."

Was hard-ass Fox giving me a compliment and, *gasp*, flirting?

No matter, I didn't even get to fully enjoy the moment before he went and ruined it.

"So what made you take a slip-on shoe vacation?"

I was confused until I remembered I'd complained to him about my mother describing my stay in a mental hospital, where they'd taken my shoelaces when I arrived, as a *vacation.*

I probably should've been insulted that he was poking fun. But instead I found myself smiling. It was oddly refreshing that someone didn't feel the need to tread lightly on the subject. People didn't tease someone about things they felt bad about.

"Since you asked so nicely, I was struggling with depression and anxiety. It started with my work. I'm a principal scientist at Kolax and Hahm Pharmaceuticals. I develop new medicines for cancer treatments. One of the drugs I developed went into phase-three clinical trials, which is when it's tested on a large number of people. AMERL7 was supposed to produce tumor regression in patients with brain cancer. It had showed a lot of promise during the earlier phases. But when we went wide, we discovered it

77

had an interaction with the chicken pox vaccine. Fourteen children died because they participated in my trial."

Fox's face dropped. "Shit."

"Yeah. It hit me hard, and I couldn't move past it. I tried for a few months. By the time I checked myself in, I was spending twenty-three hours a day in bed. I was physically exhausted from depression."

"I'm sorry."

"There were other factors, too. Like I was supposed to get married in August."

"Next month?"

I nodded.

"What happened?"

"My ex-fiancé, Noah, is an orthopedic-surgery resident. He works a ton of hours. I was feeling really lost after everything happened in the trial and started having trouble sleeping. One night, he was supposed to get off at midnight but didn't come home. I texted him, and he said he'd just gotten out of an emergency surgery and had to stay because someone had called in sick. I decided to surprise him and deliver him dinner."

"Uh-oh."

"Yeah. I was the one who got the surprise. When I went to the desk on the surgical floor, another resident told me Noah had left a little while ago. I figured someone must've come in and he didn't want to text me so late since I'd been having so much trouble sleeping. On my way back to my car, I noticed a Volvo parked in the hospital parking lot that looked like Noah's. When I got closer, I realized he was in it. He was sitting in the driver's seat with his head back and eyes closed. I *thought* he was so exhausted that he'd fallen asleep. It wasn't until I got to the door that I saw a head bobbing up and down."

"Jesus. I'm sorry."

"The worst part was that I stood there frozen and the asshole *finished*. I'm pissed at myself to this day that I didn't at least ruin the moment for him."

Fox smiled. "It sounds like you had a rough couple of months."

"I never thought I'd be someone who needed help."

"I think most people could use it at some point in their life and don't have the courage to ask for it. You're strong."

I smiled sadly. "Thank you for saying that."

"Are you better now? Or should I add another lock on my door because you become dangerous when unhinged?"

I wrinkled up my napkin and threw it at him. "You're such a jerk."

He smiled. "Seriously though, are you good?"

"I think so. I talk to a therapist over Zoom every other week. I suffered a trauma that left me with depression, but I don't have long-term clinical depression. I had never experienced anything like that, so I didn't know how to handle it."

"All kidding aside, I'm right next door, if you ever want to talk."

"Wow. Thank you. I got the impression you weren't much of a talker."

"I'm not. I might not listen or respond. But you can talk."

I smiled. "That sounds more like the neighbor I've come to know and dislike."

Fox smiled back and looked down at my foot. "How's the ankle feeling?"

"Much better."

"We should take the ice off for a little while." He leaned forward and untied the towel. His fingers brushed against my leg, and it felt like my skin caught fire. I jumped, surprised at the feeling. Fox pulled his hands away, holding them up. "Sorry. Did I hurt you?"

"No. I'm, uhh...just ticklish. That's all."

I got the feeling Fox might've seen through my excuse. But if he did, at least he didn't call me out. "How does it feel now?" he asked.

I rolled my ankle around. "Better. It's definitely only a sprain."

"You got lucky. Could've cracked it the way that board gave out." Fox glanced around the deck. "This is probably about four-hundred square feet. I'll get you some estimates to replace it when I'm over at the lumberyard this week."

"You don't have to do that."

"Not a big deal. I'll be over there anyway."

"Alright. Well, thank you." A mosquito landed on my arm. I smacked it off, but a second one had already landed on my leg. "Crap!" I whacked at it.

"Gets buggy out here after the sun sets. Lasts about an hour and then it clears up. Why don't I help you inside?"

I sat up and shifted my feet to the ground. "I can do it."

Fox stood, and the board under his feet made a creaking sound. "Shit. This thing's dangerous."

He stepped forward and leaned. I thought he was going to help me up like he did before. But instead, he scooped me into his arms.

I yelped. "This is worse! Now you're putting both our weight on the wood at once. We're definitely going to fall through."

He walked toward the house. "Better me than you."

"How so? Why is it better you get injured than me?"

"'Cause I can live with a broken ankle. Wouldn't be able to live with letting a lady break hers if I could stop it."

I'd never been the type to play damsel in distress, but I had to admit, it was kinda nice being carried by Paul Bunyan. I looked down as he fiddled with the sliding glass door to open it. "It's pretty high up here. You get a different perspective from this view. I'm always looking up at people."

"If you say so..."

Fox set me down on a chair in the kitchen. As soon as my ass hit the wood, my phone started buzzing. I frowned at the name flashing. *Noah*. My eyes jumped to Fox's face. Unfortunately, I wasn't the only one who'd read the name.

"My ex. He's upset I'm down here." I pushed *Ignore* and the phone quieted.

Fox's eyes narrowed. "Why the hell does he care where you are?"

"He wants me to forgive him. Give him another chance."

"Is that what you want?"

"No, definitely not. I'm not happy with the way things ended, but I've had a lot of time to think about the relationship we had. I realized I was settling into a life I thought I was supposed to have and not really the one I wanted, if that makes any sense."

Fox nodded. "It does." My cell started to buzz again. Fox and I read the name flashing at the same time. "Why don't you just tell him to stop calling?"

"I have. But he's persistent."

Fox held my eyes, but said nothing. Once again, I pushed *Ignore*. But ten seconds later, the damn phone started buzzing. The muscle in Fox's jaw flexed.

"You really want this guy to stop calling?"

"I haven't answered in a week now, but he keeps filling up my voicemail. At first I felt bad, but now it's gotten annoying."

Before I realized what he was doing, Fox swiped the phone off the table and pressed to answer on speaker-phone.

"Is this Noah?"

My eyes bulged.

"Who is this?" my ex snipped.

"This is the man telling you to stop harassing Josie. You need to stop calling her phone."

"*Who the hell is this?*"

"Are you listening to me? Josie doesn't want to talk to you. You fucked up. It's over. It's as simple as that."

"Put Josie on the damn phone!"

"Not gonna happen. Now, Josie's been trying to be nice, because she's a nice person. Me, I'm not so nice. So I'm gonna tell you straight up how it is. If you call her phone again, she's going to contact the police department and tell them she's being harassed. If you continue to harass her after that, I'm going to pay you a visit myself. I might be six four and two-hundred-and-fifty pounds, but trust me when I say you won't see me coming. One day you'll be walking to your car in the hospital parking lot in the dark and suddenly we'll meet."

"This is insane. Who the hell are you?"

"No more calls, Noah. You don't want to piss me off."

With that, Fox calmly ended the call. He set the phone back on the table. My eyes were still wide with shock, but as it wore off, I grinned. "That was freaking fantastic."

"Yeah? Thought you'd be pissed."

"I wish I could've seen the look on his face."

Fox smiled and lifted his chin in the direction of my foot. "I'm going to go. But ice that ankle once an hour until you go to bed."

"Okay." I stood, but he put his hand up.

"I'll lock it behind me."

"The bottom lock doesn't work. Only the top one. So I'll lock it behind you."

Fox didn't look happy, but he continued to the door. He stopped before opening it and looked down at me.

"By the way, you were right..."

"About what?"

His gaze shifted down from my face. He winked at my cleavage. "View from up here is pretty damn good."

CHAPTER 10

Presents and Premonitions
Josie

"Hello?"

"Hi, Josie?"

The voice was familiar, but I couldn't place it. "Yes?"

"It's Opal."

"Oh. Hi, Opal."

"Hope you don't mind, but I schmoozed Sam at the home-improvement store into giving me your number."

Yet again, it was apparent how different small-town life was from city life. I couldn't imagine the guy at the Home Depot on Twenty-Third Street even knowing my name, much less giving my telephone number to someone. If that happened back home, I'd probably get a restraining order. Yet here, it seemed perfectly normal.

"No problem. What's going on, Opal?"

"I was hoping you'd be up for lunch today. I have a little present for you."

"A present? For me?"

"Don't worry, it's not expensive or anything. But I'm guessing you're the type of person who doesn't judge value by a price tag. If I'm right, my gift is priceless."

"You have me intrigued now..."

"That's what I was hoping. One o'clock work okay?"

"Sure. Why not."

"Woodwards on Main Street. It's the little café on the same side as the Beanery."

"I know it. That's perfect. See you later, Opal."

My ankle was still pretty sore, so I left a little early for my lunch date and stopped at the small pharmacy in town to pick up an ACE bandage. The woman behind the counter smiled at me. "You must be Josie."

I should've been used to it by now, but it still caught me off guard when a stranger knew my name. "Yes. How did you know that?"

"My aunt Frannie mentioned you were in town. Plus, I recognize you from the picture you sent years back. I'm Lily Dunn. We exchange cards a few times a year."

I didn't remember all the names on my card list these days, but Lily's I did. Mostly because she had sent me one first. She and I were about the same age. Her aunt had told her about the card I sent, and Lily thought it was fun. She didn't receive a lot of cards herself, so she'd mailed me one, and I'd added her to my list.

"Lily, it's really great to meet you. You and your aunt were the first people I exchanged cards with. It's meant a lot to me over the years."

"Me too. I was looking forward to telling you a story in my next card. You're part of the reason my boyfriend and I got together."

"I am? How?"

"Mark was a friend of my older brother's in high school. I always had a secret crush on him, but he was three years older and my brother saw me as a little girl, so it was never going to happen. He went away to college and got engaged, and so did I. Over the years, he and my brother fell out of touch, but I always kept tabs on him on Facebook. Last year, my fiancé and I split, and then around Thanksgiving, I noticed Mark had changed his status from in a relationship to single. A few days later, your annual Christmas card showed up. I don't know why, but it got me thinking. Cards made you happy, so you took the bull by the horns and sent them out, hoping you'd get what you give. That afternoon, I decided to mail Mark a card. I wrote him a note and mentioned that I was single and wondered if he might be interested in meeting up sometime. He sent me back a card, and one thing led to another—we've been together since a little after New Year's when we met for dinner."

"I love that! Good for you, Lily. I've never thought of my cards as inspiring in any way, but I'm happy to have been a little part of you taking the chance."

Lily and I stood talking for another fifteen minutes, and by the time I left, it felt like I'd caught up with an old friend. I almost forgot to buy the ACE bandage I'd come for. Her story was exactly what I needed today, especially after I'd gone out back to look at the deck in daylight and realized not only was it rotted, but so was the dock at the edge of the water.

Opal was already seated at the café when I walked in. She waved animatedly, as if it were possible to miss a woman wearing a neon green top. It was the second time we'd met and the second bright outfit I'd seen her dressed in. Somehow the bold colors went with her personality.

She stood as I approached and wrapped me in a warm hug with a matching smile. "There she is…"

"Hi. Sorry if I'm a minute or two late. I stopped in at the pharmacy and met someone I've exchanged cards with. We started talking, and I lost track of time."

"Lily Dunn?"

"Yes, she was so nice."

Opal nodded. "Sweet girl. She's Frannie's niece. Glad she finally hooked that Mark Butler. Girl had been crazy about him since she was a kid."

I smiled thinking how Lily had just told me she'd had a *secret* crush on her brother's friend. Seemed there weren't actually too many secrets in Laurel Lake.

I shook out the cloth napkin on the table and draped it across my lap. Opal lifted a small bag from the floor and held it out. "For you."

I was curious, so I dug right into the tissue paper. "Oh my gosh. Is this what I think it is?" The phone book was a little thicker than the tattered one I had, but still less than fifty pages in total. I fanned through it with a smile.

"It's hot off the presses. No one even has it yet. The town used to be the one to put it out, but they stopped doing it seven or eight years back when they got hit with some budget cuts and lost the girl who updated it. My friend Margene started doing one instead, every other year as a fundraiser. She sells a bit of ad space inside and charges people ten dollars for the book. Last time she donated over two-thousand dollars to the animal shelter. I figured the one you had was your daddy's, so it had to be outdated by now."

"It definitely is. Mine is over twenty years old."

She pointed at the booklet. "That one has home addresses, home phone numbers, and the cell phones of just about every resident of Laurel Lake. Figured it would keep some of your cards from getting returned and wasting postage."

"Thank you, Opal. This means a lot to me."

"My number is in there, too. Anything you need, don't be afraid to use it."

As I slipped it back into the bag, the back cover caught my eye. There was a half-page ad for Cassidy Construction, most of which was Fox's face.

Opal noticed my staring. "He's not going to be happy when he sees that. The grump refuses to include his information in the book. Says anyone he wants to have his phone number already has it. A couple of months back, I told him I wanted to run a cheap ad and the money went to charity. I didn't mention where. He grumbled *fine*, so I took the liberty of putting his mug on the ad, along with his cell phone number. Figured it would attract more attention than a logo."

"Oh boy." I chuckled. "I would love to be a fly on the wall when he sees this."

"He'll fire me. Again. But then he'll realize he doesn't know any of the passwords for the software we use, and he'd have to answer the phones and be friendly to people. So he'll get over himself."

"Sounds like you really have his number."

"He wasn't too hard to crack."

"Maybe for you, but I find the man confusing as heck."

Opal smirked. "He spends a lot of time fighting the war inside of him—the one between good and evil. But one thing you can bet on, Fox Cassidy will always, in the end, do the right thing. These days, that pisses him off."

"These days? So he wasn't always so grumpy?"

"Nope."

"What made him that way?"

"The usual. Trying to change things that couldn't be changed, and instead, they wind up changing you. I think we all have things in our lives that turn us into different people. Sometimes it's for the better; sometimes it's for the worse. But we evolve and move on the best we can."

I certainly understood that. I wasn't the same person I'd been even a few months ago. I nodded. "That's very true."

"But I have a hunch there's another change coming for Fox Cassidy. A good one this time." Opal's eyes sparkled. "And for you, too."

CHAPTER 11
A Lifetime Ago
Fox

Four-and-a-half years ago

"I'm nervous."

I rubbed Evie's shoulders. "Of course you are. You wouldn't be the athlete you are if you took success for granted."

"What if I don't qualify?"

"There's no room for doubt right now. You gotta leave that shit on the table."

I'd flown to Atlanta last night after my game to be here for Evie's qualifier. We'd been pretty much inseparable the last six months, since the day I'd kicked her ass and won a date. Well, as inseparable as two professional athletes who spent twelve hours a day training could be. My team had already qualified, so Evie was carrying an added pressure. I had to fly back this afternoon, but I felt like she needed me here, especially since her mother was here, too. A not-too-successful former competitive ice skater herself, the woman was the mother of all controlling stage-mothers.

She was also a raging alcoholic and religious zealot—a combination that wasn't fun.

But speak of the devil.

Paula Dwyer marched over to the waiting area where Evie and I stood. I'd hoped she might oversleep this morning, after finding her in the bar three sheets to the wind when I arrived late last night. But no such luck.

"There you are. How's the leg this morning? Did you use the massage gun like your trainer told you to do? You know I didn't make the state competition years ago because I ignored my trainer's advice. You're twenty-five, a dinosaur in figure skating years. This is it for you. You screwed up all your other chances. It's now or never so you—"

Who the hell tells their kid they *screwed up* right before the biggest competition of their life? I put my hand up, interrupting. "Paula."

"What?"

"She's trying to stay calm."

Her mother frowned. "So now you're the figure-skating expert, are you? What do you know about pressure? You qualified with a *team*."

"Fox is right, Mom." Evie sighed. "I don't need to be reminded that this is my last chance."

"I was only trying to give you a pep talk." Paula dug into her purse and pulled out a flask. She twisted off the cap and took a long swig.

I kept my mouth shut and whispered to Evie, "Why don't you put your earbuds in and get in the zone?"

She nodded. For the next fifteen minutes, I watched the big screen while Evie quietly stretched and listened to music. Her coach was busy inside with one of his other skaters—a woman I'd met a few times at Evie's practices. My neck was a knot of tension as the woman took her place and started her routine. Everything seemed to be going great, until it wasn't.

She fell. I hadn't thought Evie was paying attention, but when I looked over, her eyes were glued to the screen. She swallowed. A few minutes later, Brian, her coach, emerged. He tamped down the look of disappointment on his face as he walked over to us.

"How you feeling, Evie?"

She plucked an earbud out. "Okay. Is it time?"

"Two more. But we should go inside and wait on deck."

Evie blew out a deep breath and nodded, looking to me.

I smiled and put my hands on her shoulders. "You got this. No hesitations. Leave it all on the ice. Balls out. You hear me?"

She nodded.

Her mother shouldered between us. "The Lord blessed us with these talents. Let's honor Him."

Evie bowed her head as her mother said some prayer. I believed in God and had said my share of pre-competition supplications, but breathing in alcohol fumes from the woman reciting the words just didn't sit right with me.

The next twenty minutes were torture as we waited. Thankfully, I managed to shake off Paula and sit by myself. When Evie opened the half door to skate onto the ice, I found myself tapping the bench next to me three times for luck.

The music started, sending my heart racing like someone had put paddles to my chest and fired up a shock. Evie's routine had some early tricks, so there wasn't even a chance to be lulled into a calm. My hands folded into fists, and my leg came off the seat each time she jumped. She was killing it so far, but her hardest trick was in the last pass. I held my breath as she got into position for the long trek across the ice. This was it. It was the playoffs, and the teams were tied up, with one shot on goal before the buzzer sounded.

Shoot and...

Evie flew up in the air and started to twist.

And twist.

And twist.

It looked like she had it, until she landed the tiniest bit off.

And crashed to the ground with a loud *crack*.

o o o

Two days later, I finally had twenty-four hours off.

I pulled to the curb in front of Paula Dwyer's rented house and turned the car off. Evie still lived with her mother, mostly because she was rarely home. She'd been training since she was eight years old. If she wasn't at the rink, she was traveling to one of the dozens of competitions she competed in to keep her national rank and squeak out a living—a living that supported both her and her mother.

Paula answered the door and threw her arms around my neck. "The Olympic athlete has arrived!"

I could smell the liquor on her breath at ten in the morning. But it wasn't my place to lecture a grown-ass woman.

"Hey, Paula. How you doing?"

"Just peachy." She stumbled back. "The gimp is in the kitchen."

Gimp. I was certain that word would offend anyone, particularly your daughter who'd cracked her ankle and

93

lost her shot at competition in the Olympics forever. Paula's sympathy drained in real time with the bottle. I walked past her without responding and headed for the kitchen.

Evie was slumped over the table, still wearing the red, white, and blue sweatshirt I'd helped put on her after her coach carried her off the ice two days ago. Her casted foot was propped up on the chair next to her.

I gently jostled her shoulder. "Hey. You okay?"

Her head lifted. She squinted, and a crooked smile spread wide across her face. "I thought you couldn't come until Saturday."

"It is Saturday."

"Oh." Her brows furrowed like she wasn't sure I was telling the truth. "What happened to Friday then?"

I picked up the empty glass next to her and sniffed. It stunk like her mother. "I'm guessing you drank it away."

She shrugged and her head fell back to the table. "Whatever."

I sighed and looked around the kitchen. The sink was piled high with dishes. There were two open pizza boxes on the counter, with a few day-old slices inside. And the garbage can was overflowing. I moved a Wendy's bag crumpled on top and looked deeper. Underneath was an empty handle of Tito's and a broken Jack Daniel's bottle. There were also a few juice and soda cans, which I guessed from the looks of things, had been the mixers.

Evie was already snoring, so I scooped her up from the table and carried her to her bedroom. That was no better. There were half-empty cups and plates strewn about, and laundry all over. The suitcase she'd had at the competition hadn't been opened yet.

I settled her into bed and took out the dirty dishes. I wasn't judging. Lord knows I'd had my share of benders after a tough loss. Hell, I knew some guys in the league who did it after every *game*. I hated that she had pain to numb at all. Though I wasn't sure what to do with myself while she slept it off. I straightened her room, did some laundry, and wound up cleaning the kitchen. The cabinets and refrigerator were nearly empty, so after a while I went to the supermarket. I could use the fresh air anyway.

When I returned, her mother was in the kitchen, but Evie was still knocked out. Paula sat at the table drinking while I put away the groceries I'd bought. When I was done, I took the seat across from her.

"She's taking it hard, huh?"

Paula lit a cigarette and blew the smoke in my face. "Of course she is. She blew her future. What is she going to do now?"

I shook my head. "She's twenty-five and healthy. Her ankle will heal. There's plenty she can do."

"Like what? Give ice skating lessons for minimum wage?"

"If that's what she wants to do and it makes her happy."

"How is she supposed to put food on our table doing that?"

Our. Evie had been this woman's meal ticket for long enough.

I'd been kicking around asking Evie to move in with me. We'd only been seeing each other six months, but it wasn't easy to find time to spend together when she lived in Chicago and I had forty-one road games a season. Plus, I thought it would do her good to be close to her father and his wife, rather than Paula.

"I'm going to ask Evie to come live in Laurel Lake with me."

"That will only do her harm."

"How so?"

"When you live life on a merry-go-round and it suddenly stops, you find a way to make it spin again."

"What does that mean?"

"You'll see. Me and my girl, we're cut from the same cloth."

CHAPTER 12
Jealous Much?
Fox

It was the fourth time I'd walked into the second-floor guest room this morning. I doubted I'd come in that many times over the last year. But the scenery from the window had recently changed, and it was pretty damn easy on the eyes. I had a bird's-eye view of the yard next door, where Josie was currently stretched out on a yoga mat, ass up, in what I thought might be called downward dog.

I sipped my coffee as I watched, feeling a bit like a dog myself. Yet I couldn't pry myself away. A few minutes later, though, it seemed the show was coming to an end. Josie rolled up the mat and disappeared inside. I had a shitload of things to get done today, and wasting time watching Little Miss Yoga Pants wasn't one of them. So I took a quick shower, grabbed my to-do list from the kitchen table, and headed out. But the pickup truck parked at the curb stopped me in my tracks after only a few steps.

Fucking Porter. What the hell was he doing over there?

And why did I suddenly feel a need to break something?

I mentally added another item to my to-do list: Get my ass over to the rink and whack some pucks with a stick. It was either that or get laid, and I wasn't much in the mood for what came before and after getting laid, namely polite conversation.

I stood on the porch for a few minutes, struggling to stop myself from going next door. There were a million reasons not to.

Shit to do.

Not interested—well, at least my head wasn't. My dick seemed eager enough.

Punching an employee was frowned upon. Though he wasn't at work at the moment...

I stared at my truck, trying to get my feet to walk toward it. But the fuckers wouldn't budge.

Then I heard a laugh, a feminine one that floated through the air and did things inside my chest that I didn't care for one bit. It was like someone had turned the heat up on the blood flowing through my veins. Warmth seeped into my upper body, giving me the sensation of being tucked under a flannel blanket next to a fire.

I shook the thought from my head. *Seriously. What the fuck has come over me?*

Pissed at myself, I forced one foot in front of the other and managed to climb into my truck and back out of the driveway.

Don't look. Don't look.

I gave myself a much-needed pep talk as I shifted the pickup into drive. But as I rolled past her mailbox, about to pass the big bay window, I realized I'd made a rookie mistake. *I should've gone the other way.* Because there was no way in hell I could stop myself from looking.

Porter's smiling face had me slamming on the brakes and pulling to the curb so fast that I completely forgot the mailbox. I hit it with a loud bang.

Fuck my life.

I got out of the car and walked around to the side. My truck had a decent dent on the rear quarter panel, and the mailbox was on the ground. Worse, Josie was on her way out with Porter in tow.

"Are you okay?" Her face displayed genuine concern.

"Yeah," I grumbled. "I'm fine."

"What happened?"

"I, uh, forgot something at the house. Went to turn around and missed the mailbox."

Josie's pink lips curved to a gloating smile. "It seems I'm not the only one capable of failing to see a bright red mail receptacle."

I frowned. "You could at least pretend you're not enjoying this."

Her smile widened. "Who, me? I'm not enjoying anything."

I'd somehow managed to forget all about the man standing behind her. Wishful thinking, I suppose. But once I noticed the smirk on his face, that's where I drew the line. I pointed to his mouth. "You, I'm not going to tolerate the smile from."

The fucker chuckled.

"What are you doing here anyway?" I snarled.

"Came by to drop off an easel for Josie."

"Where is it?"

Porter thumbed toward the house. "Inside."

"Then why are you still on my block? It's bad enough I have to see you all week."

The dumb-shit's smile widened. Was he really enjoying my insults, because I had plenty to hurl his way if he wanted...

"Josie invited me to stay for coffee."

I looked over at her. "Better watch it. I hired him for a set of extra hands on a job three years ago. I can't get him to stop coming back."

She shook her head with a smile. "Would you like to join us for coffee, too, Fox?"

While I hated the thought of the two of them alone together, I hated myself more for the way I'd been acting this morning. So I begrudgingly declined. "Got shit to do."

I turned to get back into my car, realizing I still had the mailbox in my hand. Scowling, I held it up without looking back. "I'll pick up one of these, too."

The rest of the morning I spent stewing while running errands. I went to get my oil changed, hit the nursery to pick up tomato plants I was late getting into the ground, stopped at the grocery store, and then went to the home-improvement store for a new showerhead to replace my leaky one. While I was there, I ordered Josie a new mailbox and stopped over in the decking section to get some prices for her rotted deck. I was gone more than three hours, so I didn't expect to see Porter's truck when I returned. Unfortunately for me, that wasn't the only thing I saw.

"What the hell are you doing?" I cut across my grass and met a shirtless Porter at the end of Josie's driveway. He tossed a pile of wood at the curb and wiped sweat from his forehead.

"What's it look like I'm doing? Getting rid of that rotted deck out back."

"But why?"

He shrugged. "I saw the ACE bandage around Josie's ankle, and she told me what happened the other night. I offered to give her a hand."

I had no right to feel territorial, but that didn't stop me from wanting to shove Porter into his car and finish the job myself.

"She's not one of your fuck buddies, Porter. You should leave her alone."

"I thought you weren't into her?"

I folded my arms across my chest. "I'm not. But she's been through a lot. She doesn't need a Porter Tobey hump-and-dump special right now."

"It's not like that. I like her."

I clenched my jaw so hard, I was surprised I didn't break a tooth. "Let me unload my truck and I'll give you a hand." *Translation: The sooner it's finished, the sooner you're out of here.*

"It's fine. I'm almost halfway done."

"I'll be over in a few."

I tossed the bags from the trunk in the house and quickly changed into some work clothes. Unlike lover boy, I wasn't going to be stupid and carry planks of wood wearing shorts, no shirt, and a pair of fucking flip-flops.

Next door, it appeared I was the only one who'd changed to do some work. Josie was still in the skin-tight yoga getup she'd been wearing early this morning. The only thing she'd changed was adding a pair of work gloves. I frowned, not because I didn't appreciate the outfit, but because I wasn't the only one doing the appreciating. Josie bent to pull up a plank, and Porter's eyes followed. I cleared my throat to give him the courtesy of knowing I was coming. He was lucky he got a warning and it wasn't my fist.

Josie leaned back, holding onto the plank, putting her weight behind it to try to pull the board up. I shook my head and went behind her.

"What do you think is going to happen when this comes up or snaps in half with you leaning like this?"

"I think there's going to be one less piece of rotted wood."

I pointed to the Adirondack chairs that sat at the edge of the lake. "Go sit."

"You can't tell me what to do like that."

"You hurt your ankle two days ago. You shouldn't be leaning on it, and definitely not hauling heavy wood out to the curb." I lifted my chin to Porter. "We'll finish it up."

"No, Fox. It's not that I don't appreciate all your help, because I do. You've been a lifesaver, if I'm being honest. But I don't like the tone you just spoke to me with." She tucked her chin and deepened her voice. *"Go sit!* I'm not a dog, you know."

I sighed. Here we go again. "How would you like me to ask, Josie?"

"I don't know. Just don't order me to do something. It's rude."

I took a deep inhale. "Fine. Why don't you go sit, and we'll finish this up so you don't make your ankle worse?"

She smiled. "That was very nice. But I think I'm good. I don't need to sit."

This woman made me nuts. Through the corner of my eye, I caught Porter with a shit-eating grin on his face. It looked like he was about to bust a gut laughing.

"What's so amusing?" I barked.

"Nothing, boss." Porter chuckled, but he was smart enough to get back to work, even if he wasn't technically working at the moment.

Over the next half hour, Porter and I ripped up the rest of the rotted deck and piled it at the curb. Well, technically, Josie hauled a few boards out too. When we were done, we were all sweating.

Josie took off her dirty work gloves and looked around. "You guys make everything seem so easy."

"This was nothing." Porter winked. "It keeps me in shape."

"Oh yeah? This week we have some concrete to break up and haul. I was going to bring a laborer in to help with the carryout. But if you want to keep in shape..."

Josie laughed. "Can I get you guys some lemonade or a beer or something? Maybe some lunch?"

Porter looked at his watch. "I'd love to stay and hang out, but I actually have to run. Can I take a raincheck?"

She smiled. "Of course. Thank you again for everything."

"I'll text you. Maybe I can take you out for that beer one night?"

Josie's eyes briefly shifted to me before she forced a smile. "Umm...sure."

Porter beamed. Meanwhile, I wondered what would cause more pain, broken fingers or knocked-in teeth. Though he was completely oblivious. He patted my shoulder. "I'll see you in the morning, boss."

Good riddance. I managed a nod.

Once the shirtless wonder was gone, Josie looked to me. "What about you? You want a beer or something to eat?"

I shrugged. "I'll take both."

She smiled. "Okay. I'm going to wash up and change. Then I'll make us some sandwiches and drinks. You want to come in and wait?"

"Think I'll get washed up myself."

"Okay. How about fifteen minutes? I'll bring the sandwiches to your deck, since you actually have one?"

"Sounds good."

I took a quick shower and got changed into shorts and a T-shirt. It was already hot as balls outside, and humidity made the air feel like molasses in the lungs. Usually the lake offered a breeze, but not today.

Out back, Josie floated over from next door wearing some pastel pink getup. She was freshly showered with wet hair slicked back into a ponytail, carrying two Coronas with lime wedges stuffed into the necks in one hand and a plate with sandwiches in the other. The smell of vanilla wafted onto the deck a few feet before her, and yet again, I found my eyes drifting down to her collarbone.

The view was pretty damn spectacular, and I didn't try to hide my watching.

She grinned as she stepped onto the deck. "Someone looks hungry."

You have no fucking idea. I took the plate and beer with a thanks and realized as Josie settled into the seat across from me at the table that it was the first time I'd had a woman back here in a long time. The women I did bring home spent most of the time in my bedroom. I wasn't much on morning-afters, so I usually didn't do sleepovers either. But I couldn't say I didn't like having something pretty to look at as I ate. If I were being honest, her company wasn't bad either. It was the string that came with getting involved with the type of woman Josie was that I wasn't much fond of.

"So guess what?" She lifted the beer to her lips.

"What?"

"Noah hasn't called in two days—not since you threatened to jump out of a bush and crush him like a bug when he least expected it."

"That's good."

"I was thinking about you while I was in the shower."

I arched a brow. "Oh yeah?"

She chuckled. "Not like that, dirty boy."

Shame. Because I've been thinking about you like that more often than not during my showers lately.

"What were you thinking, then?"

"You're kind of an enigma. Most men are like Porter. They do nice things for women because they want something in return. But not you. You're more like Superman. You swoop in when I need help and then disappear for days, turning back into grumpy Clark Kent."

"Trust me, I'm no hero. But you should be wary of guys who only do something because they want something in return."

She bit into her sandwich. "You mean guys like Porter? I don't know. I think if I ruled out men who wanted *something*, there would be very few left. Porter seems harmless enough, though he's not really my type."

I didn't like that I felt relieved to hear she wasn't interested in Porter. Nevertheless, I couldn't stop myself from poking around.

"What is your type?"

She shrugged. "I'm not sure I know anymore. I think I'm better at knowing what's not. Porter is nice enough, but he seems like a player."

My lip curved. "Good call."

"What about you? Do you have a type?"

"Yeah. Simple."

She laughed. "What does that mean, simple? Like a simpleton? Someone who is gullible?"

"No, not a simpleton. Just simple. As in, the opposite of complicated."

"So a no-strings-attached type deal? That's your type?"

"I'm not against strings. Just don't like the kind that tie me up in knots. And so we're clear, I mean figurative knots. Not the literal ones. Those I wouldn't mind."

Josie smiled. "Thanks for the clarification."

"You're welcome."

She looked out at the lake. I watched her face. She'd been enjoying the view but then seemed to think about something else, something less enjoyable.

"What do you want to know?" I asked.

Her brows tugged together. "How did you know I was going to ask you something?"

"You're not exactly a hard read."

"Oh really?"

I tilted the neck of my beer to her. "Really."

She pinched her eyes closed. "What am I thinking about now?"

"Didn't say I was a damn mind reader. Said I could see on your face when you're overanalyzing something."

"I *do* do that. It can be debilitating at times. In fact, my therapist gave me some tricks to try to stop doing it."

"What were you overanalyzing right now?"

She pointed to my chair. "Why you're sitting there."

"Number one: It's my house. Number two: I think most people sit when they're eating."

"Yes, but why you picked that particular seat. You were out here before me, so you could have sat in this chair or that chair. This chair has a beautiful view of the water.

106

Yet you didn't sit in it. I was wondering if it's because that was your regular spot or if you were thoughtful and left me the seat with the best view."

I stared at her. She was damn beautiful, especially framed by the lake. But the word *complicated* didn't begin to describe Josie Preston. The woman had analyzed why I picked a damn chair.

"Well..." she said. "Which is it? Is that your regular chair or did you leave me this one so I'd have the nicer view?"

There was a third possibility she'd failed to consider—that it didn't matter where I sat because my view was going to be pretty damn great with her across from me. But I wouldn't be sharing that tidbit.

I shook my head. "Stop overthinking and finish your sandwich."

We ate the rest in blissful silence, Josie enjoying her view and me stealing glances at mine. Not surprisingly, it wasn't me who spoke first.

"Do you ever swim in the lake?"

And there went the peace I'd been feeling. "No."

"Is the water contaminated?"

"Water is fine."

"Do you not know how to swim?"

"I know how to swim, Josie."

"Jeez." Her forehead and nose scrunched up in tandem. "You don't have to get so cranky. It was just a question."

"And I gave you an answer. Problem with you is, that's never enough."

"Sheesh. I didn't realize there was a problem with me. Thanks for letting me know."

She stood and folded her now-empty paper plate. "I can take a hint. Thank you again for all of your help today. And I'm sorry if I'm too chatty for your liking." She took a few steps away and turned back. "We can keep our friendship limited to you dragging my garbage cans to the curb when I forget. Thank you for doing that again yesterday. Oh, and I guess you watching me from the window while I do yoga. You seem to enjoy that more than talking to me."

CHAPTER 13
Small Town—Big Parties
Josie

Did I walk into the wrong backyard?

There were balloons, music, a half-dozen Yeti coolers, and a gaggle of men congregating by a smoking grill. This must be a birthday party. Or maybe a graduation celebration. I hadn't been able to find a number on the house when I pulled up, but to the left was six twelve and to the right six sixteen, so it had seemed only logical that this one was six fourteen.

I turned around to sneak out before someone realized I'd just crashed their party, when I heard my name.

"Josie! There you are!" Bernadette Macon pushed up on her tippy toes, flailing her arm around as she waved from the other side of the yard.

Oh Lord. I'm in the right place. But this was definitely not a *small get-together...*

I hesitated before walking to meet her in the middle of the yard. Bernadette swamped me in a hug like we were long-lost friends, rather than people who'd met at the coffee shop last week.

I smiled. "I thought I was at the wrong house. I didn't realize you were having a party today. For some reason, I thought it was just going to be us and Tommy Miller, maybe a few other friends."

She waved her hand around at the packed backyard and laughed. "This is a few other friends."

There had to be fifty people milling around. "I'm not sure I even know this many people," I said.

Bernadette hooked her arm with mine. "Well, you do now. All of these people are here to meet you. You've exchanged cards with a lot of them. When word got out you were the guest of honor today, my phone rang off the hook. It was fun being popular again."

When I looked around, all eyes were on me. It was a little overwhelming.

"What do you have here?" She pointed to the stuff I was carrying. "Does it need to go in the refrigerator? If it does, it might have to settle for sitting on top of the ice in one of the beer coolers. My fridge is stuffed with eight gigantic trays of Hawaiian macaroni salad. It's Troy Zimmerman's favorite. His wife passed away six months ago—God rest her soul—and the ladies are all on the hunt now. Not sure why they bothered, he's only going to have an eye for Georgina Mumford. She's got a big waddle."

"A waddle?"

Bernadette motioned to her neck. "Saggy skin. Troy's always had a thing for a woman with a waddle. His wife looked like a turkey in that regard."

I wasn't sure what to say to that, so I held up the boxes. "Uh. No. Nothing needs to be refrigerated. I made cupcakes and rainbow cookies."

"Good. Come on, let's put them inside and get you some wine to help settle your nerves. You look like my students always did when I'd spring a pop quiz on them in English class."

A few ladies were prepping food at the kitchen island. Just like in the yard, they all stopped what they were doing when I walked in.

"Now don't scare the poor girl away." Bernadette waved them off. "She's not a chimpanzee in the zoo."

The ladies promptly ignored Bernadette and walked over one at a time to introduce themselves.

"It's good to meet you," the youngest of the three women said. "I'm Lauren Arnold. We've been exchanging cards for a long time. Mine is the one with four dogs on the front."

I pointed. "You always dress the dogs in costumes from nursery rhymes, but add a Christmas theme to it, right?"

The woman smiled proudly. "That's me. I'm a seamstress. I make custom costumes for kids for Halloween. Well, and now for pets too. People took a liking to my Christmas card and started asking if I'd make something for their pets. So now my business is almost fifty-fifty, human and animal costumes."

"I loved the Mad Hatter tea party scene you did last year."

After Lauren, I met Wanda and Rena and finally a lady named Hope. Hope was petite, had naturally white hair that suited her, and the most gorgeous green eyes. There was something familiar about her, so I thought perhaps we'd exchanged cards and hers had a photo.

"It's lovely to meet you, Josie." She patted my hand and held onto it. "Your father was a dear friend of mine. I was so sad to hear about his passing years ago."

"Thank you."

Bernadette Macon handed me a glass of wine and piped in. "Hope here is being polite, because unlike me, she's an actual lady. She and your father were more than friends. They used to suck face in the stairwell at school every chance they got."

Hope blushed. "Bernadette, you hush now. Josie doesn't want to hear about that. We were just kids. Her father was a happily married man."

"Actually, I'd love to hear about my dad when he was younger. He died when I was thirteen, so I never had the chance to ask about his teenage years, other than knowing how much he loved living here in Laurel Lake."

"The two of them were inseparable from seventh grade on," Bernadette said. "So anything you want to know about your daddy, this one would know. If not, ask his best friend, Tommy Miller. He's going to be here a little later."

"Really? You and my dad were a couple for that long?"

Hope smiled and nodded. "And when I look back, I have nothing but fond memories of my time with Henry. He was a big personality, but also a gentleman even as a young man." Her eyes lost focus for a few seconds and her smile widened. "He also told the worst jokes."

I laughed. "Absolutely nothing changed then."

Bernadette ushered the other ladies to the door. "We'll leave you two alone to do some catching up. Come find me when you're ready for more introductions, Josie."

"Okay, thank you."

Alone, Hope and I sat down at the kitchen table. I couldn't help but notice the differences between her and Dr. Melanie Preston. Mom was tall with dark hair and eyes. She had a stern face, a practiced smile, and wouldn't be caught dead in public without lipstick. Hope was petite with a welcoming demeanor. She wore her naturally white hair in a ponytail, and her pretty face was free of makeup.

"Did you and my dad meet in school?"

She nodded. "We did. He was in marching band, and I was in color guard, and we also had algebra together. We were friends, but we were both pretty shy. Math came very easy to me, but algebra was an advanced class, and some of the kids struggled. I'd started helping a few of the girls. Your dad came to me one day and said he'd failed the last test and needed some help. He asked if I'd be willing to tutor him. We spent a lot of time in the library together, and eventually he admitted he'd never failed a test and didn't need help. He wanted to spend some time with me."

"That's so funny. You know he wound up being a math professor, right?"

She smiled. "I heard that. Got a real kick out of it."

"So you two were together since seventh grade?"

"Eighth, actually. Valentine's Day, to be exact." Hope shook her head. "Your dad came to school in a suit and brought me flowers, then asked if I'd be his girlfriend. The other boys chided him something fierce over wearing that suit, but Henry didn't care."

"That's so sweet."

"Your father was a very sweet man. I'm sure your mom is something special, too."

I forced a smile. "Oh, my mom is something alright."

Hope and I spent the next twenty minutes talking. She told me a few more stories about my dad. It was clear she and my mom had more than physical differences. The two women couldn't be more polar opposites of each other. Hope felt like the type of woman who would've fit perfectly with my dad. Yet no matter how much I felt like my parents were a round peg and a square hole, there was no denying my father had been head over heels for my mother. I suppose opposites do attract sometimes. Which made me think of my grumpy neighbor. We hadn't spoken since yesterday when he'd helped me rip out the deck and we'd shared a nice lunch—only to have him shut me down for talking too much. The man was as confusing as he was handsome.

"Can I ask you a personal question, Hope?"

"Of course."

"Why did you and my dad break up?"

"He got into Yale, and I was staying here to go to community college. I thought it was best if Henry got to experience things, so I broke it off. You know...if you love someone, set them free and all." She smiled. "Turns out it was for the best. He found the love of his life away at college. A few years later, I met mine. My Joseph passed two years ago."

"I'm sorry for your loss."

"Thank you. I'll never get over it, but I'm working on keeping myself busy. I teach a knitting class and do some volunteer work now." She smiled. "I'm sure your mom had to adjust after your dad passed. It's not an easy task."

I nodded, keeping it to myself that my mom was *definitely* not knitting or volunteering. My mourning mother hadn't even taken off the day of my dad's wake. She'd done two surgeries before afternoon viewing hours began.

"How long are you in town?" Hope asked.

"I'm not sure. Probably another month or so. My dad inherited a house here in Laurel Lake many years ago. It was my aunt's. When he passed, I inherited it. It's been rented for a long time, but the renter recently moved out. I came down to fix up the place a bit, but it's in worse condition than I thought. It's keeping me busy. But I have to go back to work eventually."

"Is the house your aunt Tessa's? I think that was your dad's only sister, right? Over on Rosewood?"

I nodded. "That's the place."

Hope smiled. "One of my sons lives on that block. You should reach out if you need anything. He's very sweet. And he does construction, so he's got every tool under the sun, too." Opal walked into the kitchen from the yard. Hope smiled at her. "He's actually Opal's boss now."

"You're..." I blinked a few times. "You're Fox's mother?"

"I am. Have you two met already?"

"We, umm..." I wasn't about to tell this nice lady that her son alternated between being a jerk and taking over construction at my house. Rather, I smiled. "He actually lives right next door."

"Isn't that something? I knew Tessa had lived on the block, but couldn't remember which house it was. Well, I hope he's been neighborly."

If neighborly means watching me do yoga from the second floor...sure. Though I stuck with the positive. "He's helped me quite a bit already."

She beamed with a mother's pride. "Wonderful. My son can come off as a curmudgeon at first, but he has a good heart. He makes time to have lunch with me every Thursday since his father passed, and he lets me come over and decorate his house twice a year—hang new curtains and stuff—even though I know he couldn't care less about all that."

I smiled. "You said one of your sons. Do your other children live in town, too?"

Hope shook her head. "It's just Fox now. My other son, Ryder, passed away years ago. I don't think I'll ever remember to say 'my son' rather than 'my sons'."

"Of course not. I'm so sorry for your loss."

"Thank you."

Opal interrupted our conversation. "Can I steal our guest of honor away for a bit? I want to introduce her around."

"Of course," Hope said. "It was wonderful to meet you, Josie. You're as lovely as your father was."

"Thank you."

The next few hours were a whirlwind. Opal introduced me to dozens of people, and most had a story to share about my father. I learned more about his childhood in one afternoon than I had in a lifetime. Henry Preston loved fishing, playing the drums, and he and his friend Tommy Miller were apparently a pair of pranksters. He loved to paint, like I did—something I'd never known about him. And he'd volunteered at the animal shelter, walking dogs and cleaning up after them. Ginny something told me he'd gotten her through math class in elementary school. She loved singing and hated math, so Dad had made up funny songs to help her remember formulas. She'd wound up becoming the local music teacher and taught his songs to her students for fun.

It was a great day, but by the time I left, I felt a bit overloaded—like I needed to sit in a quiet, dark room, or do something mindless and repetitive like ride a stationary bike. My brain needed to simmer for a while on all the information it had taken in.

I pulled into my driveway and looked over at my neighbor's house. Fox was outside, pushing a wheelbarrow across the lawn with no shirt on. I licked my lips. Sex would really work to clear my head, too. Too bad *that body* was attached to such a jerk.

I'd poked that chest with my finger, and it was impossible to miss how the seams of his T-shirts stretched to their limits around hulking biceps, but seeing all that flesh bared at once was something else. The man was seriously stacked. Chiseled pecs, deeply etched lines contouring the peaks and valleys of abs, thick bulging muscles on his arms and legs. There wasn't an ounce of soft anywhere on him. He didn't wax like Noah, but his chest hair was trimmed neatly, and it suited him. Clean shaven would've seemed odd on a man like Fox, a man who was so...primal.

I sat in my car, enjoying the free show from a distance. Fox went back and forth, shoveling mulch from a pile on the driveway into the wheelbarrow, then rolling it over to the flower beds and spreading it around. Forget riding a stationary bike or sitting in a quiet, dark room. *This* allowed my brain to power down. I wasn't sure how long I sat gawking, but by the time I got out of the car, there wasn't much mulch left in the big pile.

Instead of going right into the house, I thought I'd share what I'd learned about my dad's high school sweetheart. Plus, a close-up view couldn't hurt...

"Hey." I smiled. "Guess who I met today?"

Fox looked over and kept pushing the wheelbarrow. "A contractor to take over fixing up that shitshow of a house you got, I hope."

"It's not a shitshow. It just needs a little TLC."

"Yeah," he scoffed. "Truck Loads of Cash."

I frowned. "Now I don't even feel like telling you my funny news."

"Oh no," he said flatly.

"Jerk."

Fox pulled off a work glove and used the back of his hand to wipe sweat from his brow. His eyes dropped to my torso, like he was noticing I had one for the first time. He swallowed before speaking. "What's your news?"

"I met my dad's high school girlfriend today."

He shrugged. "Okay. I'll bite. How did it go?"

"It went well. She was super sweet and had nothing but kind things to say about him. Actually, the entire day was pretty amazing. But that's not the funny part."

"You look like you're going to burst if you don't get it out, Josie."

I smiled. "My dad's girlfriend's name was Hope."

Fox's brows drew together. "Hope who?"

"Hope Cassidy!" I clapped with excitement. "Isn't that crazy? Your mom and my dad were a couple, apparently for a long time—all through high school."

"She never mentioned that."

"Did you ever have a conversation about who she dated before your dad? I never spoke to my dad about that, or my mom either."

"I guess not."

"Anyway... I managed not to laugh when she called you *sweet*. You're welcome."

He narrowed his eyes. "Any other *fun news* you want to share, or can I get back to work?"

Fox being Fox, he didn't wait for me to respond. Just grabbed the wheelbarrow handles and started walking again. I followed.

"Don't you even find it the least bit amusing that our parents used to date?"

"Nope. Because now I'm going to get my ear chewed off about you when I go see my mother. You're already the topic of conversation at work because of Opal."

Fox set the wheelbarrow down on the driveway and picked up a broom to sweep the remnants of mulch. He scooped a shovel into the pile and dumped the last of the chips into the nearby flowerbed. I thought he was done, but then I noticed cases of plants lined up on the front porch.

"Are you making a vegetable garden?"

"Already have one." He pointed in the opposite direction of my house. "It's on the side. Better sun exposure there."

"I always wanted a garden. We never had one growing up. I was thinking of doing window plants in my apartment, but there's not much room."

Fox shook his head. "I don't know how you can live somewhere with no yard or grass."

"It's funny. I don't think I noticed it was missing in my life the last few years."

"Shame."

I looked around and sighed. "Yeah."

Fox scooped up two tomato plants from the porch.

"Do you want some help planting them?" I asked.

"Is that your way of saying you want to help, but we're going to pretend it's me who needs the help rather than you who wants to give it?"

I smirked. "Pretty much."

After a pause, he lifted his chin toward the garage. "There's an extra set of gloves in the top drawer of the cabinet on the right."

"Okay! But I think I'm going to change first."

"Whatever." Fox shrugged. He clearly wasn't as excited as me.

I returned a few minutes later wearing cut-off shorts and a tank top. This time, Fox didn't take as long to notice I had a torso. Every time I'd caught him looking before, I'd given him a free pass, not calling him out. Well, except for when I'd mentioned seeing him watch me from the window. But today, I felt bold. When his eyes made their way back up to mine, I arched a brow.

He ignored the challenge and walked around the side of the house. "Plants go six inches down and eighteen inches apart." He gestured to some garden tools. "Small shovel is there."

Over the next hour, Fox and I planted more than three-dozen tomato plants. We didn't talk much, which was perfectly fine with me. By the time we were done, I didn't feel overwhelmed by the day anymore. Oddly, I felt very much at peace.

I pushed a lock of hair behind my ear. "I really enjoyed doing that. Who knew digging in the dirt could be so mentally relaxing?"

"Working outside is good for the body and mind."

I brushed dirt from my hands and knees. "Thank you for letting me help. Especially since I know you would've preferred to do it yourself."

Fox nodded.

I rolled my eyes. "You could at least *feign* that I'm wrong and you enjoyed my company."

His lips quirked. "Thank you for helping me plant, doc."

I did a mock curtsy. "You're very welcome."

Even though I didn't want to go back home yet, it felt like it was time. "Well, I guess I should get going..."

Fox nodded again.

I hesitated a few more seconds, thinking maybe he'd say I shouldn't run off so soon. But of course, this was Fox. "Okay, then. You have a good night, I guess."

After I took a few steps, he sighed. "Do you want a beer?"

I turned with a smile. "Do you really want me to join you, or are you being nice because I called you out about not wanting me to plant with you?"

He closed his eyes and shook his head. "Do you want a beer or not?"

I shrugged. *Screw it.* "Sure."

CHAPTER 14

Everything is Just Ducky
Josie

"So your mom is so tiny," I said. "And you probably have to duck and turn sideways to walk into some rooms. Were you a big baby?"

"Eight-and-a-half pounds. My brother was ten."

"Wow. Ten pounds. Is he bigger than you now?"

"He passed away years ago."

I shut my eyes. "I'm sorry. Your mom mentioned that she'd lost a son. I wasn't thinking."

"It's fine. It was a long time ago."

"I say the exact same thing when people offer condolences about my father's passing—that it was a long time ago. I guess I want them to feel better about bringing him up."

Fox looked into my eyes. "It also nips the conversation in the bud."

I smiled. "Got it. Moving on..." I sipped my beer. "Your mom called you sweet more than once. Don't take this the wrong way, but it's not a word I would've used to describe you."

"Mothers are prejudiced."

"Maybe. But I don't think that's it. I think deep down there is a sweet guy in there. You just don't want people to meet him, for some reason."

"Or you're making up another fantasy in your head, like the one you held on to all these years about this town being some mythical place where everyone walks around smiling."

"Today I went to a party thrown in my honor at the house of a woman who was a complete stranger a week ago. Everyone smiled and had a great time. I think you're the one who makes up things in his head. Why don't you want this place to be as great as it is?"

Fox raised his beer to his lips. "High expectations usually lead to disappointment."

"Jeez. You're a bag of positivity. Maybe you could print that slogan on the nametags kindergarteners wear on the first day of school. That would shut down all optimism from the get go."

His lip twitched. "Cute."

"I am, aren't I?"

He chuckled softly. "So what interesting characters did you meet at Bernadette Macon's today?"

"It might be quicker to ask what boring people I met. This town has a cast of characters. But let's see...I met Tommy Miller. He was my dad's best friend growing up. Do you know him?"

"Flaming red hair and a laugh that sounds like it's coming through a megaphone? He's kind of hard to miss."

"Yup. Then there was Ronnie Tremmel. He and my dad were in marching band together."

"The over-describer. He owns the paint shop in town. I hate going in there. I ask him for a few green paint samples, and he spends ten minutes telling me about the color of moss."

I laughed. "Oh my God. He does do that. He spent fifteen minutes describing the band uniform they used to wear—the colors, the lapel, even the shoes. And then he told me about a dish he makes, and he literally described the bubbles in the simmer. What about Georgina Mumford?"

"The waddle. She's going to end up being Georgina Zimmerman."

I couldn't stop laughing. "God, this really is a small town."

"What about your mom? Did you meet some of her friends?"

I shook my head. "No. Tommy Miller, my dad's best friend, met her once when she came down on a break from school with my dad. A couple of other people said they knew her younger brother. But I didn't get the feeling he was too popular. Their faces sort of changed when I said his name."

"What's your uncle's name?"

"Ray. Ray Langone."

Fox's face did the same thing everyone else's had done today. It was almost a wince, but people around here were too polite and covered it up. I pointed to his jaw. "That. That's what they did."

"Sorry."

"My mom never mentioned her family, but my dad let it slip once that Ray was a bad gambler. Apparently he called on occasion over the years to hit them up for money."

Fox nodded. "He's a gambler alright. Drinker and a con man, too. Did some time for taking money from people for down payments on car insurance policies."

"Did he not turn over the funds to the insurer?"

"Wasn't even an insurance agent. Just went door to door and got some older folks a few towns over to fall for his crap."

"Oh."

"As far as I know, he's kept out of trouble since he got out. Lives over on the north side."

"Wait...Ray Langone is alive?"

Fox's forehead wrinkled. "Was when I saw him a week ago. Something happen?"

"Well, my mom told me he was dead. A few years back, I'd been thinking about coming down to visit Laurel Lake. I asked my mother who lived here still from her side, and she said no one, that her brother had died from alcoholism."

"Saw him stumbling out of the Crow's Nest last weekend."

I sighed and shook my head. "Sadly, I'm not even that shocked my mother would say something like that when it's not true."

"How long did your mom live down here?"

"She didn't. Her family moved from Charlotte during her second year of college. Ray is ten years younger. They share the same mother but have different fathers. My mom was already living at Yale up in Connecticut when her mom and brother came to live in Laurel Lake. My parents actually met on a plane, flying home for Christmas break from school. They realized they went to the same school and were both going home to the same small town. The funny thing is, that was the last time my mom was ever in Laurel Lake. She didn't like it here. She didn't get along with her mother and hated that they'd moved again. Apparently, they struggled financially and got evicted a lot. They'd lived in a dozen places over the years. It's why we never made it back to visit before my dad died, even though he always wanted to. Something would always come up for my mom."

Fox sipped his beer, watching me over the bottle as he drank.

"Anyway," I sighed. "It was a nice party today. Bernadette was such a generous host, and your mom really was amazing. You two have the same eyes."

A fluttering sound turned both our heads toward the lake. A white duck sat on the water's edge, flapping its wings. It stood and attempted to walk but limped and crooked to one side.

"Is he hurt?"

"I don't know." Fox set down his beer and walked down toward the water. I followed. Close up, at first I thought the poor little guy only had one leg, but then I saw the other. It was bent up in a flamingo stance, except it looked like he was struggling to put it down.

"I think his leg's broken," I said.

"No. It's tangled in some damn fishing line." Fox scooped up the duck. It freaked out and flapped its wings. His orange bill opened and clamped down on Fox's hand. "Damn it! I'm trying to help you, you little fucker. Let go."

I walked close and stroked the terrified duck's back. He unclenched from Fox's hand, leaving a mark behind but the skin wasn't broken.

"Shh..." I said softly. "It's okay. Everything is going to be alright."

Fox shook out his hand and nodded toward the house. "I need a clipper to cut the line. I have one in the garage somewhere."

We walked around to the garage, and he set the duck down on top of a workbench as he rummaged through some drawers. Finding what he was looking for, he clipped at the clear fishing line.

"It's a catch-and-release fishing lake," he said. "Damn kids cut the line and throw the fish back in with the hook still set in their mouth because it's easier than removing the barb. The fish either die or they manage to work the hook out, but then the line catches the ducks when they swim by."

"Awww... This poor little guy." I stroked the animal's feathers, and he leaned his head on my shoulder and looked up at me.

"Sure," Fox said. "I pick you up and cut you loose, but you bite me and flirt with her."

It took about ten minutes, but Fox managed to remove all the tangled fishing line knotted around the duck. The line had cut into him and left a big gash on his leg. Fox set the bird down on the garage floor to see if it could walk. It limped a few steps toward the open door, but then came back and nuzzled against my leg.

"Oh my gosh. She's so sweet. We can't let her go back in the lake injured."

"He'll be fine."

"How do you know?" I petted the top of the duck's head. "Daisy might get an infection or her leg might not be strong enough for swimming."

Fox's forehead wrinkled. "Who?"

"Daisy Duck."

"How do you know it's a girl?"

"I can just tell. She's so sweet."

"*He* is also pretty big and has a curled feather at the end of his tail, so I hate to break it to you, but your Daisy Duck is more likely a Donald Duck."

"You're making that up."

Fox shrugged. "Believe whatever you want. But he's going back in the water."

Fox went to grab him, but Daisy snuggled her bill into my cleavage. He pulled his hands back and grumbled. "Definitely a boy."

"Let's bring her into the yard and see what she does. Maybe she's scared in the garage since she's used to being outside."

"Fine."

I carried Daisy to the backyard and set her down next to the deck. She seemed content until I sat down in the Adirondack chair. Then she limped her way over and parked herself between my feet. "See? She isn't ready to go back in the water yet."

"What are you going to do with it? Tuck it into bed next to you? Those things carry all kinds of bacteria and shit all over the place."

He had a point. But I couldn't let this cute little duck back into the wild if she wasn't ready. "She can stay in my garage."

Fox shook his head. "Ducks don't belong inside."

I scooped up my little buddy and set her on my lap. She seemed perfectly content. "I didn't know ducks were so friendly."

"They're not usually."

I grazed my nails lightly over Daisy's head. "I guess we got lucky then."

Fox was quiet for a few heartbeats. "Think he's the one who got lucky."

"Was that...a compliment? Because I'm still not recovered from the shock of the last one you gave me."

He squinted. "When was that?"

"You told me I looked *pretty good*. Obviously flattery isn't your strong point."

Fox lifted his beer to his lips, but his eyes dropped down and locked on my cleavage as he drank. After he emptied the bottle, he stood.

"You want another one?"

"Sure. Why not?"

He came back with two frosty Heinekens and passed me one.

"Where did you say my uncle lived again?"

"North side. Apartment complex over on Barnyard Avenue—at least last I knew."

"Maybe I'll reach out. I don't know much about my mother's family or her family's history."

"If you want. Though sometimes the past is better off left right where it is."

I don't know why, but I got the feeling he wasn't just giving me advice, but speaking from personal experience. A few minutes later, the automatic sprinklers on Fox's lawn went on. Every time a spray hit the bush behind me, poor Daisy jumped.

"I guess I should put the baby to bed," I said. "What do you think I should set up for her to sleep on?"

"How about grass or a lake."

"Ha ha. You know what I meant."

"I don't know. Hay?"

"I don't have any. Do you?"

"Nope."

"There's a bunch of old bedding in the garage. I was going to toss it, but I forgot when the dumpster was here."

"That'll work. Unless of course it's down. Might've been one of her friends."

I chuckled and stood. "Thank you again for letting me plant with you. And for the beer."

Fox stood. It wasn't the first time he'd done that—stood when I did. He had old-school manners, which I liked. "Good luck with Donald."

"It's Daisy."

"No, it's not."

I'd made it halfway across the grass to my house when Fox yelled. "Hey Doc?"

I turned. "Yeah?"

"You look more than pretty good."

My heart went pitter-patter like a schoolgirl's. "Thanks."

"Goodnight."

"Sweet dreams, Fox."

CHAPTER 15
Slippery When Wet
Fox

"Have you seen your neighbor around lately?" Porter asked.

I leaned against the pillar, fiddling with my phone, waiting for the building inspector to arrive. My employee was supposed to be inside laying tile in the last of the building's bathrooms. I wasn't sure what annoyed me more, the fact that he was slacking off at work or that he was sniffing around about Josie.

I didn't look up from typing into my cell. "I think Mr. Hanson goes up to visit his daughter for a few weeks in the summer."

"I meant your neighbor on the other side."

Of course I knew that. And I'd also seen Josie two days ago when she'd spent the afternoon testing my self-control—down on all fours in those cut-off denim shorts helping me plant. Yet I shrugged. "Not her keeper."

Porter lifted his baseball cap and spun it around backward. "I called her and asked if she wanted to have dinner this Friday night. She said she'd get back to me. Texted yesterday to check in but didn't get a response."

"Maybe you should take a hint."

Porter's forehead wrinkled. "You think she's not interested?"

The kid got rejected so infrequently that he wasn't even sure what it looked like. "You called her. She blew you off. You texted because you didn't take the hint the first time, and yet again she gave you the silent treatment. What part of that seems like she's interested?"

"I figured she was just busy or something."

"If a woman is interested, she's never too busy to respond."

"Ouch."

I went back to my phone. "It is what it is."

"Maybe I should send flowers."

I shook my head. "Damn, he still doesn't get it."

"I thought I felt something between us when we talked," Porter mused. "You know, like a spark."

This conversation was grating on my nerves. I lifted my chin toward the entrance to the building. "Don't you have tiling to do?"

"I finished everything I can. They shorted me on the border pieces, so I'm going to have to go over to Ludsville to pick some up."

"Ludsville? Didn't we get all the tile from Abbotts in town?"

"Yeah, but I called and Abbotts doesn't have the border tiles in stock. They'd have to order, and it would take a week to ten days. Tile Emporium has 'em now. It'll take me about an hour to get there and back, but I'll still be able to finish the bathroom today."

I scratched my chin. "I'll tell you what. I'll take the ride to Ludsville after Ernie from the building department comes and does his inspection. Why don't you get started installing the baseboard heating covers? They were delivered this morning."

Porter shrugged. "Sure. Whatever you want, boss." He reached into his pants pocket and pulled out a tile. "This is the border, so you can make sure it matches up."

"Thanks."

Ninety minutes later, I pulled into the parking lot of Tile Emporium. The store was dark. The sign on the front said they opened at ten, so I checked my phone. Nine forty-five. My cell also had a notification from my alarm company. Ninety percent of the time, it was a package being delivered or some random animal that set it off, but I had time to kill so I swiped to open and signed in to watch the video replay.

This time was no different than the usual, except the random animal the motion sensor picked up had a playmate today—and that playmate looked like a damn Playmate of the Month. Josie wore a white bikini, and she was running around my yard chasing a limping duck. I lifted the phone to my nose for a better look. What the hell was on the duck's head? I pinched the screen to zoom in. The video blurred as it got closer, but it wasn't so bad that I couldn't make out a blue-and-white polka-dot bow clipped to the feathers on the top of the duck's head.

I shook my head. They'd let that woman out of her *vacation* too soon. Josie chased the bird around my yard for a solid minute, running onto my deck, across the lawn, and eventually splashing into the lake before diving in head first. Sadly, that was the end of the bikini-show video. Though...my security system did have a live feature. And

I had the ability to control the camera remotely. When I clicked the LIVE button, my yard was still empty, so I panned the camera to the right.

Every time I thought this woman couldn't do anything more ridiculous, she surprised me. She'd set up a blue plastic baby pool in the middle of her yard, and a duck with a ribbon on its head was swimming around as Josie did the backstroke in the lake behind it. After a few minutes, she waded out of the water and parked her ass in the baby pool across from the duck, smiling. She splashed the duck. It stood upright, fluttered its wings, and splashed back. Josie's head bent back in laughter.

As idiotic as this was, I couldn't stop staring at my phone. Ten minutes went by as I sat in the parking lot of Tile Emporium. This damn woman had taken over my entire morning. Hell, it wasn't just today either. She'd starred in my dream last night, too. Eventually, a call coming in on my cell interrupted my spying. It was a client, so I reluctantly closed the security app and went back to business—though not before snapping a quick picture.

After I finished the call, I had the strongest urge to open the security app again, or at least pull up the photo I'd saved, but I had shit to do. So I leaned over to the passenger seat, opened the glove box, and tossed my cell inside. Out of sight. Out of mind.

Yeah, right.

Though I did manage to keep busy enough to only check the security camera twice more for the rest of the day. Unfortunately—or perhaps fortunately for my productivity—the yard was empty, hers and mine. Josie was probably inside watching a YouTube video on mastering duck calls or some shit.

On my way home, I stopped off at Laurel Lake Inn for my usual Tuesday-night bacon-wrapped pesto pork tenderloin, and by the time I pulled into my driveway, the sun was already starting to set.

It was a nice night, so after I dumped my laptop in the house and got changed, I went out to eat my dinner on the back deck. The plastic kiddy pool was no longer in the neighbor's yard, which was disappointing but definitely better for me in the long run. I opened the box with my meal and had just started to cut into the meat when I heard screaming from next door.

"*No, no, no! Damn it!*" Josie yelled.

A rickety metal door squeaked open and slammed shut, and the duck limped out to where Josie's rotted back deck used to be. She followed thirty seconds later.

"I can't believe you did that." She wagged her finger. "That was like...your cousin."

The duck quacked and nuzzled against her leg. If I didn't know better, I might've thought the thing was apologizing.

Josie bent and scratched its head. "Awww, It's okay. I'm sorry I yelled at you."

I shook my head and went back to cutting my meat, but before I could get the first bite into my mouth, the duck came running toward my deck.

Josie chased after it, stopping short when she saw me sitting there. She scooped the duck into her arms.

"Oh. Sorry. I didn't see you."

I gestured a circle with my fork. "Didn't want to interrupt your conversation with your friend."

She frowned. "Daisy stole my dinner off the table." Her nose scrunched up. "It was chicken."

I chuckled. "Maybe he's upset that you eat birds."

She pushed up on her toes to peer into my takeout tray. "Is that the roast pork from Laurel Lake Inn?"

"It is."

Josie ran her tongue across her bottom lip. "I tried it last week. It's delicious."

I'd skipped lunch today and probably could've eaten two servings of this meal, yet I wouldn't mind the company. "Would you like some?"

She waved me off. "No, that's your dinner. You enjoy it."

"There's enough here for two."

She gnawed that plump bottom lip of hers. "Are you sure?"

I stood. "I'll go get a plate."

"Actually..." She thumbed over her shoulder. "The stove is still on, and I already have a second glass of wine poured. Would you want to eat next door? I'll put Daisy to bed in the garage so she can't strike a second time."

I shrugged. "Whatever."

She rolled her eyes. "Don't sound so excited about it."

I lifted my food and shook my head. "Let's go—before I change my mind and the only thing you have to eat for dinner is that duck."

The inside of Josie's house looked a lot better than the last time I'd been here. The kitchen cabinets were all stripped of their hideous green paint, and the doors had been rehung straight. She'd installed new hardware, and the stainless-steel appliances that had been delivered last week gave the room a spruced-up feel. But it was the other side of the kitchen that caught my attention. Rows and rows of Christmas cards hung from strings on the wall.

Josie came in from putting Daisy to bed and noticed me staring. "They make me feel good."

136

"Wasn't judging. Just looking around. The place is really coming along."

She walked to the stove and turned the knob. "You weren't judging? Who are you kidding, Fox Cassidy? You think I'm weird. I see it in your face."

"Why would I think you're weird? Because you hang Christmas cards in the house in July and swim in a kiddie pool with a male duck you named Daisy?"

She squinted at me. "How did you know I bought Daisy a swimming pool?"

Uh-oh. I had no choice but to come clean. "I get notifications from my security system on my phone. You ran into my yard earlier today, and it sent me an alert."

She tilted her head. "And it shows you *my* entire yard too?"

At least come partially clean... "Most of it. Yep." Needing a change of subject, I pointed to a cabinet. "Those have plates in them? Food's getting cold."

She might've suspected I was full of shit, but at least she let it go. Josie took out a plate and utensils, then lifted a bottle of wine from the counter. "Do you like pinot noir?"

"I'll just have a little."

I split the takeout onto two plates, and Josie and I sat across from each other. "If you're ready to paint the living room"—I pointed in that direction—"I can throw a second coat of spackle on and sand."

"Thank you. But you've done enough. I'll find someone to do it. I was going to attempt it myself, but even YouTube said it wasn't an easy job."

"It is once you've done it a few times. Second coat is easier than the first. Won't take me long."

"Still." She shook her head. "It's okay. Plus, Porter offered to do it, so if I can't find someone, I can always call him."

I lowered my fork. "Porter wants in your pants."

Her nose wrinkled. "He did ask me out to dinner."

"Trust me. He's like a stray. You let him hang around once and he keeps coming back."

It didn't escape me that here I was again, too. Different day. Different scenario. But... My situation wasn't the same. I lived right next door. I wasn't trying to get into her pants. I was just being neighborly. Right? *The photo on my damn phone might say differently.*

"I ran into someone you know today." Josie forked a bit of her dinner.

"You're going to have to be a little more specific. It's a small town. I know a lot of people."

"Her name is Quinn. She owns the toy store in town. It's where I got the kiddie pool."

Shit. A lifetime ago, I'd made it a rule to not get involved with women who lived in Laurel Lake. Unfortunately, I made that rule *after* spending time with Quinn.

"Oh yeah?"

The twinkle in Josie's eye told me Quinn had shared more than advice on which toys ducks liked best. "She said you two were a couple in high school."

"I wouldn't exactly say that."

"No? What would you say?"

"We went out a few times."

"How come you broke up?"

I shrugged. "Just did."

Her smile looked like a cat that ate a canary. I put down my fork. "What did she tell you?"

"Nothing."

"You're a shit liar, Josie."

She laughed. "Okay, okay. She said you guys split up because you couldn't look her mom in the face anymore."

I closed my eyes. Why the hell did I still live in this town? That shit happened *sixteen years* ago. We were kids in high school, for Christ's sake. Guess Quinn ran out of locals to tell the stupid story to, so she had to start telling visitors.

"Did you really wave to her mom in the middle of oral sex?"

"I was *seventeen*. Her mom came home early from work. I was sitting on the bed, and Quinn was down on her knees. Her mother walked into the bedroom without any warning. I guess she didn't notice what was going on at first because she smiled and waved at me. Quinn still had no clue, so she kept going. I panicked and didn't know what to do, so I waved back." I shook my head. "The look on her mother's face when she realized what was going on a second later... She was horrified. I couldn't look at her ever again."

Josie laughed so hard, she held on to her stomach.

"Alright, alright," I said. "It's not that funny. And now you owe me an embarrassing high school sex story. Let's hear it."

"I can't. I didn't have sex in high school."

"You're shitting me?"

"Nope. I was a senior in college the first time."

"How come?"

"I don't know. I guess I didn't meet the right person until then."

"When did you start going out with the douchebag?"

"Noah?"

I nodded.

Josie bit her bottom lip, suddenly shy. "My senior year in college. But Noah wasn't my first. Though he was my second."

Damn. I had no idea how we'd gone from *a duck ate my dinner* to talking about blow jobs and Josie's lack of sexual partners. But this was definitely more interesting.

"So only two men...*ever?*"

She chugged the rest of her wine and stood. "I think I need more alcohol for this conversation. Do you want another glass?"

I put my hand over the rim. While she might need some liquid courage, I preferred to be sober for this. I wanted to remember it all. "I'm good."

Josie filled her glass with a heavy hand and sat back down with a sigh. "Yes, only two men. I wanted my first time to be with a boyfriend, so it would mean something. But after my dad died, I didn't let anyone get close to me. By the time I was twenty-one and a senior in college, I just wanted to get it over with. So I had sex with a guy I'd gone out with a few times. The funny thing is, I'd been afraid of getting close to someone and losing them, yet I dumped the guy less than a week after we did the deed. I met Noah a few months later, and, well, you know how that ended." She gulped her wine. "I guess that's my embarrassing story."

"Nothing embarrassing about not being promiscuous."

She shrugged. "I sometimes wonder if I've missed out. Then again, I'm a chronic overthinker, so I wonder about a lot of useless things."

"Didn't look like you were doing too much thinking while you were sitting in that kiddie pool today."

"I wasn't." She smiled. "It's easy to relax down here. I feel so different than I do in New York."

"That city is stuffed with too many damn people. I don't know how you live like that."

"It's funny. There are millions of people crammed into a twenty-two-square-mile strip of land. Yet I was lonely in a crowded room in Manhattan. Down here, I'm not lonely alone."

"Sounds like Laurel Lake is doing you good."

"I think so."

We finished our shared dinner, and Josie polished off another glass of wine. Her cheeks were pink and she giggled more than usual, so I thought she might be tipsy. I cleared the table and rinsed the dishes, and she stood next to me, loading them into the dishwasher. When we were done, she looked over like she wanted to say something.

"What?" I asked.

"Nothing."

"Seems like something's on your mind..."

She pushed off the counter and came to stand in front of me, toe to toe. "What were you thinking about when you were watching me today?"

"I wasn't watching you. I told you, I saw you in the yard because of an alarm notification."

She leaned into me. "Liar."

The best defense was always a good offense. "I think you've had too much to drink."

"I know you watched me."

"Maybe you're a little full of yourself, doc."

Josie pushed up on her toes and got in my face. I could smell the wine on her breath. Her eyes were bluer this close, and flecks of gold outlined her irises. My gaze stayed fixed until her lips started moving again.

"The camera moved and caught my attention. There was a *blue light*, Fox."

"So?"

"My mother has the same security system. When someone activates the live camera, a little blue light turns on at the top."

Oh fuck. "I hit the button by accident, so I watched for a minute. Figured I'd see what the hell you were doing chasing that duck."

The gold in her eyes glittered. "The blue light was on for at least *ten minutes.*"

I stared down my nose at her, debating how to play this. I could deny it, pretend I had no idea what she was talking about, or I could own it—take my lumps and admit I was a dog. My eyes jumped back and forth between hers, and I leaned down as much as she'd stretched up. Our noses were practically touching. "Fine. I watched you."

"And you watched me do yoga from the window too."

"You weren't exactly hiding it."

Josie reached behind me to the counter and grabbed her wine. Knocking it back over a six-second count, she leaned even closer, and her tits pushed up against my chest.

"What were you doing while you were watching me today?"

My nostrils flared. She wanted me to tell her I was jerking off. And right now, I would have, if it had been true. I would've described fisting my cock while staring at her in that little white bikini. But I'd been in my truck, in a busy parking lot on a main road.

I slipped the empty wine glass from her hand and set it down on the counter. "Nothing. Because this is a small town with a big mouth, and I know better than to get caught. Doesn't mean I didn't want to though." I moved my mouth to whisper in her ear. "But I'll tell you what. I'm going to go home now, because I'm a gentleman and you've had a few glasses of wine. And if you still want to know what I was doing while watching you tomorrow, just give me a call. Because you can be damn sure I'll be watching the replay as soon as I'm alone."

I stepped back to look at Josie's face. Her cockiness was gone, and she looked a little shell-shocked. I winked. "Sweet dreams, babe. I know I'll be having them."

CHAPTER 16

Besties

Josie

"Ugh." I held my hand up to block the sunlight streaming in through the kitchen window as I padded toward the coffeemaker and pushed start. "I'm never drinking again."

How many did I have?

Let's see... There was one while I was making dinner.

A second while I was eating dinner with Fox.

A third...

Shit. My brain backed up to Fox! I closed my eyes as the memories from last night flooded in. Why oh why did I have that third glass of wine? What had come out of my mouth was exactly the reason I always stopped at two.

Not only had I called Fox out for watching me over the security camera, I'd demanded to know *what he was doing* while he watched. I rubbed my temples with my eyes closed. Now I knew how Fox felt about his high-school girlfriend Quinn's mother. I was mortified. Packing up and leaving Laurel Lake today might be my only viable option.

The Keurig made a gargling sound, indicating it was done brewing. I gulped coffee from my mug like an addict mainlining heroin. Once I'd downed my fix, I went to the kitchen faucet and splashed water on my face. Then I made a second cup. While I impatiently waited for the drip to start, I looked out the front window—or more accurately, I looked to the right, to Fox's house. I'd slept pretty late, so I was surprised that his truck was still in the driveway. Leaning over to see more, I noticed the hood was up. And Fox was outside.

He walked around from the driver's side, looking at the engine while shoving a hand into his hair. The situation didn't look very promising. The last thing I wanted to do was see him after last night—or go out in the annoying sunshine, for that matter—but Fox had helped me so much. I really had no choice but to go over and see if I could return the favor. So I threw on shorts and a T-shirt and walked across the lawn with my mug in hand.

"Hey. Everything okay?"

Fox shook his head. "Truck won't start. I think it's the alternator."

His eyes dropped to my chest. I hadn't bothered with a bra, and my nipples were saluting their freedom.

Fox diverted his eyes back to the engine and cleared his throat. "I tried to jump it. Didn't turn at all."

"Do you need to get to work? You can take my car. Or I can drop you off, if you want."

"I texted Porter and told him I was going to be late. He said he'd come get me if I needed him to, but I have a meeting down at the building department in twenty minutes, and he's at least that far away on a jobsite."

"So take my car. Or I'll drive you."

"You sure you don't mind? I can get Porter to pick me up from the building department. But I could use a ride there. Ubers around here aren't too quick."

"Just give me two minutes to get my keys and put on some shoes."

He lowered the hood. "Thanks."

As we drove through town, Fox told me where to turn, but not much was said other than that. Once we got on the highway, though, it was just dead air. I got the urge to turn on the radio to fill the space. But instead, I decided to pull on my big-girl panties and own up to my big mouth last night.

"So..." I said. "About last night."

Fox's eyes slanted over. "I'm quiet because I'm thinking about all the shit I have to do today. Don't read into it. Last night was last night. Today is today."

I sighed. "Hello? Helpless overthinker here, remember? I can't stop myself."

"You're supposed to be working on that. Why don't you start now?"

"Well, my therapist said one of the things I should do is trust my instincts. So that's what I'm doing. My gut tells me we need to clear the air. I don't want it to be weird between us. You're like my best friend in town."

Fox's brows shot up. "*I'm* your best friend?"

"I take it from that response that I'm not yours?"

He chuckled. "We're good, Josie. I promise."

"I'm going to apologize anyway. If the shoe was on the other foot, and it was you who'd had a little too much to drink and pushed me to talk about sexual stuff, no one would find that okay. So it's not acceptable that I made unwelcome remarks."

"Fine. Apology accepted."

"Thank you. I'd make you my dad's cheesecake, but I left my recipe book at home."

"Cheesecake?"

"My dad made his own from scratch. For him, fresh cheesecake was the answer to any problem—if anyone ever got mad at him, he'd whip one up and bring it to them with an apology."

Fox smiled and pointed up ahead. "Make a right at the next corner."

The remaining few minutes of the drive was a series of turns, and then we reached the building department. I pulled to the curb and put the car in park.

"I'm around all day," I said. "If you need a ride, just give me a call."

"Thank you." Fox opened the car door. He set one foot onto the concrete, but stopped and turned back. "Just for clarification, your remarks last night weren't unwelcome. And my offer to tell you what I did when I got home while watching the security video playback still stands. Ball's in your court, sweetheart. Have a good day."

o o o

"Hello?" I answered the phone later that evening.

"Hey there, chickadee. It's Opal."

"Oh hi, Opal. How are you?"

"I'm good. Are you busy tonight?"

I looked down at my eight painted toenails. "No, not really."

"Could I bug you for a favor then?"

"Of course. What's up?"

"I'm supposed to pick up Fox tonight, but I'm stuck babysitting later than expected. My daughter is a nurse, and I watch her kids on Wednesday nights. She usually gets home at eight, but someone called in sick, and she can't leave until they find a replacement for her. I tried to call Porter, but he's not picking up, and Fox mentioned you'd given him a lift this morning."

Even though I'd obsessed over Fox all day, after what he'd said when he got out of the car this morning, he was the last person I wanted to see. Yet I couldn't say no to Opal any more than I could've ignored Fox's need for help this morning. They'd both been so generous. "Sure. No problem. Now?"

"Not until ten. Hope that's not too late?"

"No, it's fine. I didn't realize he worked that late."

"Oh, he's not at work. He's at the rink. He coaches a team on Wednesday nights. It's about a twenty-minute drive—hope that's okay. We had a rink in Laurel Lake, but the owner of the building sold the property to a developer last year. His practice is in Hollow Hills."

"Okay, no problem. Do you have the address? If not, I can look it up."

"I'll shoot it to your phone after we hang up."

"Great, thanks."

"You're a lifesaver, Josie. I owe you one."

"You don't owe me anything. Have a good night, Opal."

After I hung up, I finished painting my last two toes. Twisting the cap back onto the bottle, I had a heart-to-heart with Daisy, who was sitting comfortably next to me in a pink dog bed I'd picked up for her this afternoon.

"You've lived here longer. What do you think of our grumpy neighbor, Paul Bunyan?"

The duck tilted her head. It seemed like she wanted to hear more.

"I know. I know. He's grumpy and curt—not to mention arrogant, cynical, impossible to read, and judgy. Plus, he might have as much baggage as me. The one time his fiancée even came up, it was clear he had a lot to unpack." I sighed and stroked Daisy's head. "Yet there's something else there, too...something buried deep beneath the surface that he tries to hide, but it slips out every so often. People can never hide who they really are for long, not when it's part of the very core of their being. Fox is protective and thoughtful, honest and moral, with a real concern for the well-being of others."

Daisy stood and flapped her wings.

I nodded. "Oh yeah, there's that, too. He's pretty hot."

I'd never been particularly attracted to extra-large, burly-type men. Most of the guys I'd dated—not that there had been so many—had all looked the same: five ten, maybe five eleven, clean cut, nice lean build. Fox was a giant oak tree, with Atlas-like burden bearers for shoulders, and more testosterone in his pinky than any suit-wearing man living in Manhattan. Heck, the guy left the house clean shaven and sported a five o'clock shadow by midday.

Daisy had apparently decided she was done with our conversation. She jumped off her dog bed, wobbled to the kitchen, and pecked at the front door. I shook my head and opened it for her. She waddled toward the garage. "I'm even boring a duck with my overanalyzing."

After Daisy was safely tucked away for the night, I told myself I wasn't going to fix my hair or do anything special before going to pick up Fox. Yet I found myself with a mascara wand in front of the mirror anyway. Opal had said the rink was twenty minutes away, but I left almost forty minutes early, just in case there was traffic. The road was pretty empty, though, and I wound up pulling into the parking lot at nine forty. I parked right in front of the building so I could see the front door and turned on the radio, intending to sit and wait. But ten minutes later, all the water I'd consumed today to rehydrate and get rid of my hangover was suddenly pressing on my bladder.

I still had a little time until Fox finished up, plus the drive home would take another twenty minutes. So I needed to find a bathroom. There had to be one in the arena, so I went inside and looked around for a ladies' room. On my way out, I spotted people skating on the ice. It was easy to find Fox since he was so much larger than the others. He glided across the rink as if balancing on a thin metal blade was as easy as walking. When he got to the sideboard, he made a sharp turn and dug his skates in to stop. A heavy spray of shaved ice flew up and walloped the plastic barrier.

I didn't know much about hockey, but I was suddenly a giant fan. I walked closer to the rink for a better look. If I thought watching Fox skate did something to me, that was nothing compared to what happened when I got a look at the team he was coaching. I'd completely forgotten that Opal had told me he coached a team for players with special needs until I saw the faces of two men suited up in hockey equipment who were standing along the sidelines talking—both had Down syndrome. My heart squeezed. I was torn between wanting to hug the coach and jump him for how sexy he looked out there.

Everyone in the rink continued to go about their business, as if Fox Cassidy hadn't just skated into a phone booth and come out a superhero. But I couldn't take my eyes off the man. I watched in fascination as Fox stood in front of the net, and one by one, his team members skated to center ice and took shots. He yelled at one player to move his hands away from his body—something about giving his bottom hand more force. Another he instructed to dig his blade into the ice. I had no idea what any of it meant, but Fox grew sexier by the minute. At one point, he looked to the right side of the rink where I stood. His head had turned halfway back before he did a double take. He said something I couldn't hear to the next player in line to shoot the puck, and then skated over to the waist-high door nearest me.

"What are you doing here?"

"Opal called and asked if I could pick you up. Her daughter had to work late at the hospital."

"Shit. Okay." He nodded. "I'll wrap it up."

I shook my head. "No, it's fine. I'm not in a rush. Take your time. I only came in because I needed to use the bathroom."

"You sure?"

Up close, his green eyes were so much greener when contrasting with his red cheeks. "Yeah. I'm kind of enjoying watching."

I thought I might've caught a smirk, but couldn't be sure through the helmet. And of course, Fox being Fox, he skated off without another word. Though I didn't mind the abrupt departure this time, since the view from the back was equally as good as the front.

I took a seat on a nearby bench and watched my grumpy neighbor do his thing. He seemed like a good instructor; or at least there was a lot of head nodding from the players when he spoke. And I especially loved that he didn't appear to treat the team members any different than anyone else. He laid into them when they did something he didn't like and joked around in the typical way men busted chops. At the end of practice, Fox took off his helmet and gloves, and one by one the players slapped his hand as they exited the ice.

"I just need to grab my bag," he yelled over to me.

"Take your time."

With the rink now empty, and no Fox to heat up my blood, I realized how cold it was. I had on shorts and a T-shirt, and the air in here was cold enough to keep ice from melting. I was rubbing my arms when Fox returned.

"One of the parents wants to talk to me," he said. "Sorry. I'll only be a few minutes more."

"No problem."

He pulled a jacket out of his bag and wrapped it around my shoulders. "Be back."

"Okay."

Fox's jacket was heavy—the kind of weight you probably need when you spend hours in an ice arena. But that wasn't what warmed me. *It was the smell.* I couldn't help myself. I raised one shoulder to bring it closer to my nose for a sniff.

Mmmm...

Musky, with a hint of leather. Masculine, just like everything about the owner. It made me wonder if the scent was even a cologne. I smiled to myself. I wouldn't be surprised if Fox's pheromones alone smelled this good.

Of course, that was the moment Fox walked back. His eyes narrowed. "What are you grinning about?"

"Nothing." I hopped up from the bench. "You ready?"

"Yep."

On the drive here, I'd been worried the trip home would be even more awkward than the car ride with Fox this morning. But my experience in the arena had changed the vibe. I'd barely buckled in and started the car before my questions started.

"How long have you been coaching the team?"

"I guess about three years."

"You skate really well." My eyes were on the road as I pulled from the parking spot, but I heard the smirk in Fox's voice.

"That's sort of a prerequisite when you play professional hockey."

"You're allowed to skate with your bad knee? You said you blew it out and it ended your career."

"It holds well enough to skate around for coaching. But I can't play at the intensity level the league requires."

I nodded. "It must've been hard to have your career end so early."

Fox was quiet for a minute. "It was a rough time, yeah."

"Seems to have turned out well, though. Opal said you run a few jobs at a time these days."

"I got lucky. Some guys don't know anything but hockey."

I took a deep breath and nodded. "I get it. I've given a lot of thought to changing careers myself. But I have no idea what I would do. All I've ever wanted to do was work in research."

"Why would you change your career? Didn't you go to school for most of your life to get where you landed?"

"I did. But..."

Fox looked over at me. "Sometimes you don't get over what happens, Josie. You have to figure out how to walk around it instead. Otherwise you're stuck in the same place forever."

I sighed. "Yeah."

"Is that what you're really doing down here? Hiding from what happened?"

I shook my head and shrugged. "I don't know. Maybe..."

Fox looked out the window. "You can only run for so long. Eventually whatever's eatin' you catches up."

I forced a smile. "Yeah. Plus, I can't run to save my life. We used to have relay races in elementary school during gym class. I was always the last one picked."

Fox chuckled. He was quiet for a while, but this time it didn't feel weird or awkward.

"Thanks again for picking me up," he eventually said.

"Anytime."

"Probably be the last time. Two of the guys asked me if you were single on my way out."

"The players?"

He nodded with a laugh. "They're definitely the most cocky, confident bunch I've ever coached."

I smiled. "Their coach must be rubbing off on them."

Back on Rosewood Lane, I turned into my driveway. Whatever lack of awkwardness I'd appreciated on the trip home quickly disappeared when I turned off the engine. Neither of us got out right away. We sat in the dark, me looking straight ahead and Fox looking—I wouldn't know because I didn't dare glance over.

When I couldn't take the silence a second longer and thought I might burst, I turned and said, "Fox," at the same moment he turned and said, "Josie."

He lifted his chin. "You first."

I shook my head. "No, you. I didn't have anything important to say."

Fox nodded, yet he took a moment to look out the window before speaking again. "The last woman I went out with, I took out to dinner twice. I stayed at her place the second time, and I had to take her to Starbucks for coffee the next morning because I couldn't remember her name."

I scratched my head. "And you're telling me this because..."

"Another time, I was early to meet a date at a bar. Saw an ex-teammate and we got to talking. He asked me if I wanted to grab a bite at the restaurant next door. I said sure. It wasn't until I passed the woman I was there to meet that I remembered I was there to meet her."

"Are you trying to tell me you're forgetful?"

"No, Josie. I'm trying to tell you I'm a shit boyfriend. My ideal date is fuck first, eat some pasta, then go home and sleep in my own bed. I'm selfish, and I like my life the way I like my life. Simple. *You* are anything but simple."

I was still so confused about where the conversation was going. "Okay..."

"You also live in Manhattan. A place that is pretty much hell in my book. I'm not a people person. I like the quiet life."

I shook my head. "Fox, why are you telling me all this?"

"Because I want you to know what you're in for."

"I'm lost..."

He motioned between us. "You and me. There's something here."

My eyes widened. He wasn't wrong. Something had been brewing from the start. I just thought I was the only one who felt it. "You...have feelings for me?"

Fox smiled. "If having feelings includes me wanting to feel you up, then yeah."

"Oh my God." I laughed. "You just told me you might forget my name after I sleep with you, admitted you were selfish, probably wouldn't hang around for snuggling after sex, called me complicated, and told me you want to feel me up. Is this your way of asking me out?"

"Will you sleep with me without going to dinner first?"

I shook my head. "Probably not."

"Then I guess I'm asking you out."

"Is this the approach you use on all the women you date? Because if it is, I have to wonder why anyone would go out with you."

"You already had one douchebag let you down. I'm not going to make any promises I can't keep, Josie."

As crazy as it was, there was something endearing about his concern. I nodded. "Thank you for your honesty."

He searched my face, quiet for a few heartbeats. "So Friday night then?"

The anxiety in the pit of my belly morphed to a flutter. "How about if I make you dinner? You said you don't like to cook, and all I ever see you eat is takeout. You probably haven't had a home-cooked meal in a while."

Fox shook his head. "Not a good idea."

"Why? I'm a good cook."

"Got nothing to do with your cooking. Don't think I can be trusted with you alone anymore. Not unless you're up for eating spaghetti naked in bed after."

Naked spaghetti sounds pretty amazing at the moment.

Fox groaned. "Stop doing that."

"Doing what?"

"Thinking you can handle it my way. You'll drive yourself nuts overthinking whether it was a mistake when it's over. So let's do it your way. Plus, you deserve better."

My heart melted a little more. I smiled. "Okay."

"Be ready at seven on Friday."

"Alright."

Fox held out his hand. For a second, I thought we were going to shake on the deal. But when I put my hand in his, he yanked me to him. "Now come here and kiss me already."

The gruff sound of his voice shot those butterflies much lower than they'd been fluttering. Once I was close enough, Fox gripped my elbow and used it to lift me up and over the center console. He settled me on his lap, straddling his hips, and squeezed my neck to bring my lips to meet his.

I was momentarily thrown by how soft his lips were. They contrasted with the roughness of his hold and the hardness of his chest. It was a combination that set my body on fire. Fox's tongue dipped inside, and he used the hand at my neck to tilt my head and deepen the connection.

Oh God.

I could get lost in this man's kiss. It was just on the right side of aggressive, just like the man himself. His big hand wrapped around my back and pulled me flush against him. When he groaned through our joined mouths, I felt it travel from the tips of my toes to the top of my head. I was quickly running out of breath, but I didn't care. There was no way I was stopping to take a breath. I'd sooner die of lack of oxygen.

Fox's hand at my neck tangled into my hair, fisting a clump into a tight ball. He yanked to pull my head back, exposing my neck, and then drifted down to suck along my pulse line.

My eyes rolled into the back of my head when I felt a steely erection straining through his jeans. Everything between my legs swelled, and I couldn't help myself; I started to move back and forth.

"Fuck, Josie," Fox mumbled. "You better slow down or you're going to be eating spaghetti in ten minutes."

I smiled. It felt euphoric—enough to make my brain turn off and forget analyzing the million reasons this would likely end in a disaster. After a few more minutes of groping and grinding, it was Fox who pulled back. He gently nudged my body from his.

"Gotta stop now, sweetheart. Or I'm going to turn into a sixteen-year-old boy and embarrass myself."

I pouted, and Fox leaned in and took my protruding bottom lip between his teeth and gave it a firm tug. "Friday," he murmured.

I sighed. "You suck."

He chuckled and cupped my cheek. "I'll watch you walk in from here. I need a minute."

CHAPTER 17
The Talk of the Town
Fox

"Morning."

Opal's eyes lit up as big as her smile.

"Oh shit," I grumbled.

"You just walked in," she said. "What are you cussing for already?"

"There are only two reasons you smile like that. Either you're about to chew my ear off with some gossip I have zero interest in, or you...had a date. The latter means you're about to call one of your cronies and tell them all the details. The only thing I hate more than you droning on about people in this town I don't give two shits about, is hearing about your sex life."

Opal came out from behind her desk. While I dug into the file cabinet for some blueprints I needed, she perched her ass on the corner of my desk. I took a deep breath as I turned around. "You're fired if you talk about other people's business or your sex life." I looked her straight in the eyes. "You got that?"

She grinned like a damn Cheshire cat. "Not a problem, boss."

I dropped the stack of folded-up blueprints on my desk and made a *shoo* motion with my hand. "Park it somewhere else. I need the space to lay out the specs."

Opal stood, but didn't retreat to her own area. I pretended she wasn't standing there staring at me and went about unfolding the blueprints, hoping she would take the hint. But this was Opal, so no such luck. She made it about thirty seconds with her trap shut.

"So..." She clapped her hands in excitement. "You're going on a date with Josie!"

I looked up at the ceiling and took a few deep breaths. "I thought you just agreed not to talk about other people's business."

"I did." She smiled. "But this isn't *other* people's business. It's *yours*. So that's not included in what I agreed to."

Jesus freaking Christ. How the hell did she know anyway? Josie and I didn't get out of the car last night until almost ten thirty, and it was barely eight in the morning now. In the span of nine-and-a-half hours, Opal had already heard the news. I was about to tell her to mind her own business when the office door opened and Porter walked in. He saw me and flashed the same shit-eating grin as the town crier.

I threw my hands up in the air. "Seriously? Both of you?"

"If I'm gonna lose," Porter said. "I at least want it to be to a formidable opponent."

I shook my head. "How the hell did you two find out anyway?"

"I ran into Josie this morning at the Beanery," Porter said. "She was going to the home-improvement store.

Figured I'd take my shot, since the opportunity presented itself."

I gritted my teeth.

Porter noticed the look on my face and chuckled. "Don't worry. She shot me down. I invited her to dinner Friday night, and she said she already had plans. I asked who the lucky guy was, and she reluctantly spilled the beans." He came up next to me and put a hand on my shoulder. "Lucky dog."

I pointed a finger at him in warning. "*Watch it.*"

Porter raised both hands, showing me his palms. "Didn't mean any disrespect."

I went back to looking down at the plans and gestured toward the door. "Let's all get back to work."

The two of them backed off, but not before exchanging another goofy grin. Porter left to start laying a wood floor, and Opal had the week's payroll to run. I calculated what it would cost to make some last-minute changes on an upcoming job. At twelve, I headed to the little diner on the outskirts of town for my regular Thursday lunch. I got caught behind an accident on a one-lane road, so my mother was already seated at our regular booth when I arrived.

I bent and kissed her cheek before sliding into the seat across from her. "Hey, Ma. Sorry I'm late."

"No problem. I was catching up with Tricia Scalia." She leaned and whispered. "She's getting a divorce."

Even my mother couldn't help herself from time to time. I lifted the menu. "Wayne's a dick anyway."

My mother frowned. "Do you have to use that word?"

"Sorry."

She lowered her eyes to the menu. "So, anything *new*?"

I narrowed my eyes. "Why did you say it that way?"

Mom lifted her menu to cover her mouth. But the crinkles around her eyes gave away the smile she was trying to hide. "What way?"

My shoulders slumped. "You've got to be kidding me. Let me guess, you spoke to Opal today."

She hugged the menu to her chest. "I wasn't going to mention it, because I know how much you hate people digging into your business. But since you brought it up..."

"Uh-huh." I shook my head.

Mom reached out and touched my arm. "Oh, Fox. I'm happy for you. I'm glad you're getting back out there and dating. Josie is a lovely girl."

"I've dated."

"I don't mean mattress dancing. I mean *dating*. Getting to know a woman. But more importantly, letting her get to know *you*."

"I think you're getting a little ahead of yourself..."

"I don't think so. This is a big step after everything you've been through."

"It's really not a big deal."

She pursed her lips. "Does she...know?"

It was my turn to frown now. "We're not having this conversation."

"Oh, Fox." Mom worried her lip. "It's something a woman who means anything to you needs to know."

"Like I said..." I buried my face back in the menu. "Not having this discussion."

"Okay. Fine. But will you at least tell me where you're taking her?"

I sighed. "I don't know, Ma. I figured the Laurel Lake Inn."

The look on my mother's face told me I'd given the wrong answer.

"What's wrong with the Inn?" I asked. "The food's good."

"Nothing's wrong with the Inn...to take your mother."

"Let me get this straight. It's good enough for you but not a date?"

"Well, yeah. It's not romantic, Fox."

I rolled my eyes. It was on the tip of my tongue to say romance wasn't on my agenda, but finding out what was underneath the tight black yoga pants Josie wore all the time was. But I refrained and gave my mother an inch, because I knew she meant well. "Where would you suggest I take her?"

"Le Pavillion would be nice."

My brows shot to my forehead. "Seriously? The French place? It's more than a half hour away. And you have to wear a suit to that restaurant."

"Don't you think Josie will be dressed up? She's from Manhattan, honey."

I was sort of hoping for the yoga pants. Though... I'd gone out in New York City enough back in my hockey days. The ladies in the clubs *were* always pretty dressed up—slinky shit with no back and all. It was night and day from the way women looked when they went to the Inn, the nicest restaurant in this little town.

"Maybe I'll see if I can get a table at the steakhouse over in Chatrun."

Mom smiled. "That's a little better."

I nodded. Thankfully, Tricia came to take our orders, ending the conversation. She took out her little notepad and slipped the pencil from behind her ear.

"Hey, Fox. You want your usual?"

"I do. Thanks, Trish."

She turned to Mom. "We have the Greek salad you like as one of the specials today."

"Ooh. That sounds good." She held out her menu. "Thanks, Trish."

Mom and I caught up for a while. She told me about her knitting class, and I bitched about the delivery delays giving me a headache on one of the jobs I was trying to finish.

"I have a favor to ask, honey."

My mother never asked for anything. "What do you need?"

"Well, it's for my friend Greta. You remember her, right?"

I nodded. "Blue hair shaped like a helmet?"

Mom smiled. "Her hair is silver, not blue. But yes, that's Greta, and she's going to be losing that hair soon."

"Cancer?"

"I'm afraid so. She started treatment a few weeks ago. She's keeping it quiet."

"How can I help?"

"Her first treatment left her weak. She got up too fast and fell, broke her ankle in two places."

"Jesus. That sucks."

"It does. I went over to visit her yesterday. She lives in that big apartment complex on the north side, the one on Barnyard Avenue. She's on the first floor, but her unit is still up six steps. It's a struggle for her to go up and down because of the cast. She asked the property manager to install a small ramp, but they told her it would take a few months. By then, her cast will be off."

"Probably why they said it. They have to accommodate her under disability laws, but they can take their sweet-ass time to do it. You want me to make her a ramp?"

"If you have time. It would really help her out. I'll pay for the supplies."

"No problem. I got it. I'll do it this weekend."

"Thanks, sweetie."

Talking about the Barnyard Avenue apartments reminded me of something. "Do you know Ray Langone? He lives in the same complex as Greta."

Mom frowned. "I do. He's sort of elusive, isn't he?"

I smiled. My mother was too kind to use the word *shady*. "Yeah, he's elusive alright. He's also Josie's uncle."

"Oh gosh. That's right. She said her mother's maiden name was Langone. I didn't think of Ray. Is Josie close to him?"

"She thought he was dead until I told her he wasn't. That's what her mother told her. She sounds like a real peach." I shook my head. "You know if Ray still lives over there?"

"He does. I saw him when I was pulling in to visit Greta just yesterday. Why?"

"No reason. Just want to keep a tab on him."

Mom smiled. "You're already watching out for Josie. I might get grandchildren after all!"

"Jesus, Mom. Think you're jumping the gun a bit?"

"Maybe. But something tells me she could be the one."

CHAPTER 18
Monkey Suit
Fox

"This is ridiculous," I grumbled to myself while pulling the knot of my tie up in the mirror. The last time I'd put on a suit was a year ago, for a funeral. They definitely weren't my thing. Back in my playing days, the team had gotten dressed up for travel, and a lot of the guys liked it—wearing flashy name-brand shit that designers sent them, hamming it up for the camera as they strutted to the bus. But even back then, I wasn't into it. My teammates would bust my balls because I wore the same two suits every week, a navy and a gray. I was currently wearing the navy one and questioning whether my mother was wrong and Le Pavillion was too fancy for a first date. But the steakhouse and two other places I'd tried that were nicer than the Inn, yet didn't require a monkey suit, were all booked up.

I'd also gotten the truck washed and the inside vacuumed, and even stopped for flowers on my way home from work. I was starting to remember why I hadn't dated these last few years—it was a lot of damn work. Certainly more trouble than going to the bar a town over with a condom in my wallet and talking to the first pretty woman I met.

At seven, I left my truck in the driveway and walked across the grass. I could've driven and parked in Josie's driveway, but this town had enough to gossip about, so I figured discreet was best.

At the door, I wiped my palms on my pants—apparently it was warmer than I'd realized—and knocked. Josie answered with a smile. But when she got a load of me, it wilted. "Oh my gosh." She looked down and put her hand on her chest. "I'm underdressed."

I was going to *kill* my mother.

Josie looked gorgeous, wearing a pair of jeans and flirty white ruffled top. She smelled pretty damn good, too. But I felt like an idiot.

I shook my head and started to stomp back next door. "Sorry. I'll get changed."

"What? No!" She grabbed my arm. "It's my fault. I didn't realize we were going somewhere fancy. I'll change."

"It's fine. This was stupid…" I pulled from Josie's grip and went back to walking toward the house.

"Fox, wait…"

I kept walking. At least until her voice turned to a screech.

"Fox!"

I froze but didn't turn around.

"I'm going upstairs to get changed right this minute. So if you go next door and come back with jeans or whatever, you're going to make me look overdressed. Can you please just come in and not make this into a thing?"

I felt like a damn fool, but I took a deep breath and sucked it up.

Josie grinned when I got back to the door. "Wow. Whadda you know? He actually listened..."

"Go get your ass changed."

She looked down at the flowers I'd forgotten were in my hands. "Are those for me?"

"Yeah." I held them out. "Here."

She chuckled. "Come in. I doubt Mrs. Wollman left a vase, but you can look around for something to put them in while I get dressed."

"Fine."

Josie disappeared upstairs while I stood in the middle of the kitchen, wondering what the fuck I was doing. Meanwhile, the damn duck waddled across the living room, catching me off guard.

"Jesus," I mumbled. "You're still here."

It quacked at me and kept walking, settling into...was that a dog bed? There was a TV that looked shall we say *vintage* set up on the floor, playing cartoons. The duck made itself at home across from it in a pink orthopedic bed. I shook my head and looked around the kitchen. Three rows of festive Christmas cards hung along the wall. Underneath those, six different paint-sample squares had been taped up.

Between wearing this suit for a date and this place starting to feel normal, Josie wasn't the only one who needed counseling. But I was here, and I still had the stupid flowers in my hand, so I figured I might as well do what she'd asked and see if I could find something to put them in.

A search of the cabinets turned up nothing, but I found a green plastic watering can in the garage and filled it with water.

Josie came back down as I was not-so-delicately stuffing the stems inside. I reached for the collar of my dress shirt, as it suddenly felt too tight around my neck.

She bit her lip. "This is the only dressy thing I brought. I'm not even sure why I packed it. And with heels, it's a little on the short side."

I was going to have to stay close behind her, especially if she dropped something. And it wouldn't be easy to control the urge to punch every guy whose head turned, but spending the next few hours with her wearing *that* was totally worth the effort. The woman had enough leg to be six-foot tall, especially in those stilettos.

I might be thanking my mother instead of killing her after all... I swallowed. "You look gorgeous."

"Thank you." Josie smoothed the hem of her sparkly dress with a shy smile. "You look very handsome yourself. I'm sorry I was underdressed. There aren't too many fancy places in town so I just figured..."

"My fault."

She looked over at the flowers. "They're really pretty. Thank you."

I nodded.

Josie smirked. "I have to admit, I pegged you all wrong. I never would've guessed you'd show up for our date in a suit with flowers."

"How did you think I would show up?"

"In a pair of jeans, maybe a button up. To be honest, I was expecting more like us going to the diner and you mauling me in the car when we got there."

My face fell. "Wait. Hang on—is that an option?"

Josie laughed. She grabbed my arm and tugged me toward the door. "Come on. I don't know where we're going, but you look too handsome to be late."

Across the street, Yvonne Craddox was dragging her garbage pails out to the curb. She stopped when she saw me and Josie walking down the driveway. I ignored her and kept my head down, trying to minimize the damage, but she was still gawking when I opened the passenger door for Josie and chanced a look back. The phone lines in this town would undoubtedly be burning up in thirty seconds.

"So where are we going that's so fancy?" Josie asked as I backed out of the driveway.

"French place two towns over."

She nodded. "Are all your first dates so formal?"

I glanced over at her. "We don't have to go, if you don't want to."

"Oh no. I'm excited. I haven't had a reason to get dressed up in a long time." She shrugged. "I was just curious, I guess."

She waited for a response to her question. But it wasn't an easy thing to answer.

I kept my eyes on the road. "It's been a while since I had a date, so I don't really remember where I went last time."

Through my peripheral vision, I saw Josie's brows dip down. "How long is a while?"

"I don't know. Three years?"

Her eyes bulged. "You haven't had sex in three years?"

"Didn't say that. Said I haven't dated in that long."

"Oh."

She went quiet for a while.

"What's going on in that wacky head of yours?" I asked.

"You know, it's not polite to call my head wacky. Most people get offended when you make light of mental-health struggles."

I looked over at her. "Do you?"

"No, but that's not the point."

"Then I'm not sure what the point is. Because I'm not talking to most people. I'm talking to you."

"So...what? You just round up women and have sex then?"

I felt my brows knit, confused at the sudden topic change. I guess we were back to my dating history. "I usually only *round up* one."

Josie shifted in her seat to face me. "So is it a one-night thing then?"

"What are we discussing here?" I asked. "My dating history or us?"

"Well, both, I suppose. Were the women you've been with one-night stands?"

This was a dicey conversation. In my experience, when a woman brings up you having sex with another woman, it generally doesn't end well.

"Does it matter if it was once or four times?" I asked.

"Yes."

"Why?"

"Because I'd like to know what to expect. You're right next door. I'd rather things not be awkward between us."

"They won't be."

"How do you know that? Wasn't it ever awkward to run into a woman you've slept with once?"

"Yes."

"Okay, so that's what I'm trying to avoid here. If we set expectations now, there'll be less disappointment."

"It's not the same, Josie."

"Why not?"

We came to a red light, so I turned to look at her. "Because I don't want to just fuck you once."

"How do you know that? We haven't even done it yet."

My eyes dropped to her body, to that skimpy little dress and her shapely legs. "Trust me. I know."

"How?"

"Because I didn't come looking for you to help me work something out of my system. Just the opposite. I tried to steer clear of you, keep as much distance as I could."

"Why would you do that?"

My eyes locked with hers, and I tapped my chest. "Because I felt you in here, not in my dick."

Josie blinked a few times. When what I'd said seeped in, a goofy-ass smile spread across her face.

"What the hell are you grinning at?" I said.

"You like me."

I rolled my eyes. "Oh, Jesus. Let's not let it go to your head."

"And here I thought you just wanted to have sex with me."

"If we're setting expectations, let's get something straight, doc. I am going to fuck you. And I'm hoping that happens tonight—maybe as a reward for wearing this dumb suit. All I'm saying is that it's going to happen more than once."

"More than once tonight or more than once total?"

My lip twitched. "Both."

She smiled. "Okay."

"So we're good? No more dumb questions about dumb shit from my past?"

"Actually I have one more."

I lifted my chin toward the light. "That's been green for a long time. So make it quick."

"Do you have condoms? Because I don't have any."

"Bought a whole box at the drugstore next to the florist today."

172

Josie's eyes flared. "A whole box? How many times in one night can you..."

I leaned so we were nose to nose. "Until you're sore, baby. Until you're sore."

* * *

The thought of putting on a suit and driving two towns over to some pretentious restaurant had been balanced by the fact that one—Josie would more than likely wear a dress. I hadn't expected it to be as skimpy as the one she had on, so bonus points there... And two—it was unlikely I'd run into any of the local Laurel Lake motormouths this far from town. Apparently, I was only running fifty-fifty.

Opal's eyes widened bigger than the dinner plates when she caught sight of me and Josie at our table.

"Oh fuck," I grumbled and put my fork down.

"What? Is your steak not cooked right?"

I shook my head. "I wish. My life is about to go to hell at work."

"What are you talking about?"

I didn't have to answer. Opal swooped in to do that for me.

"I thought that was you two." Her eyes sparkled. "My, my, my, look at you, boss. All dressed up in a tie."

"Go away, Opal."

"Fox!" Josie's eyes narrowed. "Be nice..."

Opal waved her off. "Oh, honey, that *is* Fox's version of nice. Didn't you notice he didn't use a cuss word? He must be in a good mood."

Josie laughed. "It's nice to see you, Opal. *Isn't it,* Fox?"

I sulked. "No."

"*Fox...*"

"Whatever. Yeah, great."

I mostly zoned out while the two women made small talk—something about dresses and the restaurant, I think. But my attention snagged when I heard the name *Frannie*.

"You're here with Frannie Newton?" I asked.

Opal nodded. "It's her birthday. We treat each other to our favorite meal every year. Frannie likes the slugs in shells they serve here. Me, I never understood escargot."

Great, just damn great. The only mouth bigger than Opal's was Frannie Newton's. She worked at the post office, holding people captive while she sold them stamps and doled out other people's business. Her distribution network was equivalent to the daily mail. I had no doubt that by ten AM tomorrow, the only people who wouldn't know what I'd done tonight were the people away on vacation. And she'd fill them in when they came to pick up their held mail.

"Is this the first time you two have been here?" Opal asked.

I said *no* at the same time Josie said *yes*.

Opal looked between us, seeming amused.

Josie put her hand on her chest. "It's *my* first time here."

"Get the crème brûlée for dessert. It's orgasmic."

While I threw up a little in my mouth from hearing Opal say a word close to *orgasm*, Josie didn't seem freaked out at all.

She smiled. "Thanks. Maybe I will, if I'm not too full."

Opal leaned in and lowered her voice. "Did you hear that Sam from the home-improvement store put his house up for sale?"

"Oh? I hope everything's okay?" Josie said. "Sam is so sweet."

"He's dating Rena Arlo. She asked him to move in with her. They're looking at buying a condo in Florida and being snow birds with the money Sam gets from the sale."

"Good for them. I haven't met Rena, but Sam seems really nice."

"Sam's having a garage sale next weekend. His wife, God rest her soul, collected those Hummel figurines my sister who lives in Georgia collects. So I'm going to go early and scoop some up for her. I can pick you up on the way. I'm sure Rena will be working the sale with him."

"That sounds great. I love garage sales."

"You're welcome to come, too, Fox," Opal said.

"No thanks. Not a fan of looking through used shit people don't want. I got enough shit of my own I could get rid of."

"Then you should have a garage sale. I can come over and help you price things..."

I couldn't think of anything I wanted to do *less* than open the door for the entire town to come in. I held up a hand. "I'm good, thanks."

Opal ignored me like I wasn't there, continuing to yap at Josie. "Heard you ran into your uncle Ray?"

Josie squinted but then a look of understanding crossed her face and she nodded. "I was at Lowell's, earlier today. Sam pointed him out and introduced us. I expected my uncle to be different than he was. He was actually very soft-spoken and sweet."

Opal and I exchanged glances. Then our waiter came by with the second glass of wine Josie had ordered. Most people would take the interruption as a segue to say good-bye, but not Opal. She stood there, continuing to yap while my food got cold. I waited a few more minutes, but she still didn't stop. Frustrated, I picked my fork back up and waved it between my date and my employee.

"You think you could finish this conversation while shopping for used socks next week? Our food is getting cold."

Josie frowned. "You don't have to be rude."

Opal smiled and waved me off. "*Eh*. He doesn't bother me. But I should get back to Frannie anyway. You two enjoy your evening."

"You, too, Opal," Josie said.

I grunted and stuffed a piece of steak into my mouth.

But Josie didn't resume eating her meal. She sat back in her chair and folded her arms across her chest. "Why are you like that?"

"Like what?"

"Rude. You act like everyone in the world annoys you."

"Not acting."

"Opal is just being friendly."

"She was over here spreading gossip. And that's what she's going to be doing about us in thirty seconds, when she gets back to her table."

Josie shrugged. "So? What could she possibly say? That we ate dinner together?"

"I like my business kept my business."

Josie shook her head. "There's a guy who takes out my garbage cans and puts on a suit for a date under that grumpy exterior. If you'd let him out more, you might be happier."

"Who says I'm not happy?"

She searched my face like she was looking for something. "Were you always like this?"

"Hungry with a dislike for cold food? Yeah."

"You know what I mean. Were you always grumpy? Or did it change after..."

My eyes narrowed. "After what?"

"After you lost your fiancée."

"She's not lost. She's dead. And this is who I've always been." The legs of my chair skidded loudly against the tile floor as I pushed my chair back. Standing, I tossed my napkin on the table. "Excuse me. I need to use the men's room."

In the bathroom, I splashed some water on my face. Maybe this was a dumb idea after all. Josie wasn't a woman who would take what I could give and be happy. The fancy restaurant and flowers were only the beginning. Soon she'd be expecting me to pour my heart out. And go with her to dumb garage sales. Probably liked to spend hours talking after sex, too, instead of rolling over and getting a decent night's sleep. I looked in the mirror and shook my head. What the hell was I thinking?

Back at the table, our plates were gone. Josie gestured to the missing place settings.

"I asked them to heat up our food."

I took my seat across from her. "Listen, Josie, maybe this wasn't a good idea."

"What? A date?"

I nodded.

"Why?"

"Because it's going to set an expectation I can't live up to."

"What are you talking about? What expectation do you think I'm going to have after one date?"

I shrugged. "It's just not a good idea."

"Because I brought up your fiancée?"

My jaw clenched. "You want more than I can give."

"Seriously? I thought I was getting diner food and mauled, and I was okay with that."

"Maybe today, but..." I shook my head. "Down the road you'll—"

Josie put her hand up. "I'm going to stop you right there, even if interrupting someone while they're speaking is rude. You can't possibly have any idea what I'll want down the road. You know why?"

"Why?"

"Because *I* don't even know what I want. A few months ago I thought I wanted to be Mrs. Noah Townsend and cure cancer with miracle drugs. Now I'm happy planting flowers with the grumpy neighbor while staying in a town with a population smaller than the number of people in my building back in New York. I'm considering signing up for a *knitting class*, for God's sake. The only thing I know for sure about my future is that I'm going to make decisions based on what makes me happy instead of what the right thing to do is and what others expect of me."

I frowned. "Sorry."

The waiter came back with our plates, but Josie shook her head. "I apologize. But do you think you can wrap those up, so we can take it to go? Something's come up."

"Of course. Just give me a minute."

I felt bad for ruining the evening. "We don't have to leave."

Josie picked up her napkin from her lap and set it on the table. "Yes, we do. Because you're miserable wearing that tie, and honestly, this isn't what I want either."

I figured she meant going out with a grumpy asshole like me. It wasn't like I could argue she was wrong. So I nodded. "Okay."

She leaned over and lowered her voice. "Let's just eat the food on the back porch with a beer and go have sex."

All the breath left my body. "You want to have sex?"

She grinned. "See? You really have no clue what I want."

CHAPTER 19
Hungry
Josie

"I'm going to change." Fox thumbed toward next door with one hand and lifted the bag of takeout onto my kitchen counter with his other. "You want me to heat these up?"

The ride home had been quiet. I was pretty sure my date was still shocked by my declaration that I wanted to go have sex. Honestly, I hadn't expected to say it either. But now that it was out there, I felt liberated. Why not say what I wanted? I'd been attracted to the big grump since the first moment I'd laid eyes on him. And we had chemistry. I could feel it pulsing through my veins whenever he was near. Not to mention, I'd caught him watching me from the window and checking me out on multiple occasions when he thought I wasn't paying attention. So I knew I wasn't alone in my desires.

"I'm not really hungry anymore." I bit down on my lip. "For food anyway."

Fox's eyes darkened. "No? Tell me what you are hungry for."

"I think you know."

He stalked toward me. I'd been the one to poke the bear, but the determined look on his face had me taking steps back. When I hit the refrigerator, Fox closed the distance between us.

"I want you to tell me anyway."

"*You.* I want you."

He slid his fingers into the back of my hair and wound a fistful around his hand at the nape of my neck. "More specific."

"Sex," I breathed. "I want to have sex with you. I want you to make me forget my name."

He ducked his head and sucked his way up from my collarbone to my ear. "Hard or soft, baby?"

We'd barely touched, and yet my body was on fire and it was difficult to speak. It felt like the air was being pushed from my lungs, and my voice came out all breathy. "Hard."

Fox pulled his head back. His green eyes were so dark, they looked gray. "How about hard and fast first. Soft and slow the second time."

Ohhh. That sounded even better. I swallowed. "Whatever you're in the mood for."

He used the hand at my neck to pull me to him, and his mouth sealed over mine. Just like our first kiss in the car, he groaned through our joined lips, and I felt a jolt of electricity zip through my body. I didn't just forget my name; it wiped out all thoughts, all worries—everything but this kiss.

Fox slid a hand down to my ass and slipped it under my dress, palming a handful of cheek. He lifted until our hips were aligned, and my legs wrapped around his waist. Wide open, his thick erection pushed against my most sensitive spot, and a mewl tumbled from my lips as my eyes rolled back into my head. "Let's go upstairs."

Fox kept me wrapped around him as he tore through the living room and took the steps two at a time. He sat on the edge of the bed and set me on my feet.

"You have no idea how long I've been dying to find out if you have no panty lines on those tight little yoga pants because you're commando or wearing a thong."

I smiled. "Which would you prefer?"

"Right now, commando. Because it'll save time. But I'm happy to rip off whatever's in my way."

I reached for Fox's tie and yanked at the knot. He stopped me, his hand covering mine. "Step back and take off your dress. I'll take care of this."

I'd been bold since the restaurant, yet as I took two steps back, I suddenly felt shy. Fox worked his tie, but his eyes never left me.

"You need to take it off. It looks like too nice of a dress to wind up shredded if I do it."

I took a deep breath before slipping the thin straps from my shoulders. My dress pooled in a pile of silver around my ankles, leaving me standing in a lace thong since I hadn't worn a bra. Fox made it to the third button on his shirt before he froze.

"Jesus Christ. You're even sexier than I imagined with my eyes closed—every damn time I took a shower."

I tilted my head, feeling less shy after his praise. "Are you saying you pleasured yourself to thoughts of me in the shower, Fox Cassidy?"

"Every fucking day. And I hated myself for it."

He hooked his arm around my waist and hauled me against him. With him sitting and me standing, my breasts lined up perfectly with his face. Fox wasted no time taking advantage of the position. He gathered both my wrists in one of his hands, holding them captive behind my back as he sucked one nipple into his mouth.

"And now I feel the urge to make you pay for what you did to me," he said. His teeth clamped down on my swollen bud. Before the pain fully registered, he soothed it with his tongue and pushed his hand between my legs.

"Open wider," he murmured against my skin.

I felt vulnerable standing practically naked, arms clamped behind my back. Yet I was panting and shamelessly did what he asked. Fox pushed my thong to one side, parted me with his fingers, and slipped one into my warmth. It felt so good as he pumped in and out; I closed my eyes and gave in to the moment. When my head fell back, he pulled all the way out and pushed two fingers back in.

Fox was no different now than the man I'd come to know outside the bedroom. He unapologetically took charge, knew exactly what he was doing, and paid attention. Before long, my knees started to buckle, and he scooped me off my feet and tossed me on my back to the bed. Noah had been in shape, but Paul Bunyan flinging me around like I weighed nothing was a whole different experience.

Fox stood to finish unbuttoning his dress shirt. He only had a few left when he lost patience and yanked it open. Buttons pinged across the room in different directions.

I laughed and pushed up to my elbows. "I would've helped you."

"No time." He slipped his fingers under the material of my thong and yanked hard. My expensive, lacy underwear snapped in his hand.

"Oh my God. You're crazy."

Fox was already unbuckling his belt. "Up on all fours, sweetheart."

My eyes bulged. "You mean hands and knees?"

He stepped out of his pants. "You know another way to get up on all fours?"

"You're not even going to pretend to be romantic? You know, look into my eyes while you make love to me at least?"

He hooked his thumbs into the waistband of his black boxers. "Hard to see your eyes when you're ass up, babe."

"But—"

I froze when his boxer briefs came down.

Oh.

My.

God.

Fox looked up, likely to see why I hadn't finished my sentence, only to find my mouth hanging open.

The man was huge. I'm talking Paul Bunyan-sized *everywhere.* His dick stood at full attention, pressed against his stomach, reaching almost to his belly button.

I pointed at it. "Holy crap."

Fox flashed a cocky smile.

I sat all the way up for a closer look. Nibbling on my fingernail as I stared, there was no doubt it was the biggest I'd ever seen. "Can I touch it?"

"That's kind of the point." Fox stepped forward.

It wasn't just long and thick, it was also oddly nice looking—smooth and a warm light-brown color—not red or purple or overly veiny. Even the crown was symmetrical and lovely. I ran the pad of my pointer finger along the length of it, and Fox's breath hissed out between his teeth.

"It's so big and...pretty."

"*Pretty* isn't a word a guy wants to hear to describe his dick, babe."

"What would you like to hear?"

He smirked. "The sound of you gurgling. Maybe a little choking."

I covered my smile with my hand. "I think we're going to have to build up to that. It's pretty intimidating."

I spent another thirty seconds swirling my finger around the glistening head. When a big drop of precum leaked over and dripped down the side, Fox growled. "Alright. Show and tell is over. Give me your mouth back or something else is going in it."

The playful moment quickly elevated to heated. Our hands explored while our tongues tangled in a frenzied kiss. I couldn't decide what part of him felt better beneath my fingers—the hard ridges of his chiseled abs, sculpted biceps, or the long, firm dick my hand struggled to wrap around. When I gave it a squeeze, Fox groaned and reached for my waist. He flipped me over in one swoop, then hoisted me up on all fours. I didn't want to think about why he was so good at that.

A few seconds later, I heard the distinct crinkle of the foil wrapper of a condom. I craned my neck to look over my shoulder and gasped at what I saw. Fox was a vision of splendor. Up on his knees, his muscles strained as his chest heaved up and down. He rolled the condom over his length and fisted his cock at the base before lining himself up at my opening.

Our eyes locked as he pushed inside. He eased in and out a few times as I watched, but when he plunged deep, I lost the strength to keep my head up. Fox buried himself to the hilt, his front flush to my ass, then stilled. One of us was shaking, I just couldn't be sure which.

"Relax a little. You're gripping me so tight, I won't be able to last."

I closed my eyes and focused on loosening my muscles, but it was his size more than my clamping down. "I'm trying."

"You ready?"

"For what?"

"To get started."

My eyes widened, and I craned my neck to look back at him once again. *"We haven't even started yet?"*

Fox grinned. "You might want to hold on to the headboard."

He might've smiled, but he hadn't been joking. Fox started moving, and I reached up to hold on. His thrusts were fast and deep. My skin was on fire, slicked from sweat dripping down my back. My orgasm brewed like a hurricane forming, swirling and threatening to demolish everything in its path. The sound of our wet bodies—his front to my rear—smacking against each other had me in a preorgasmic haze. It was the most erotic thing I'd ever heard.

Fox cursed as his pummeling intensified. I wanted him to struggle, to feel as on the edge as I was. So I pushed back, meeting his ferocious thrusts one by one.

"Fuck, Josie!" He sounded like he was about to lose it, and it became my personal challenge to get him to come before me. I thought I might win, too—at least until he reached around and pressed on my clit. Without warning, my entire body burst into a symphony of fireworks—pulsing and shaking. I don't know how long it went on, but it was enough to wipe me out. Behind me, Fox shuddered with a roar and then stilled.

I guess I didn't win that challenge.

I collapsed to the bed under the weight of my own body. Fox was careful not to follow and crush me. Instead, he slid his mouth up my back and to my shoulder, finding his way to my neck. It was soothing, in direct contrast to what had just transpired.

He rolled onto the bed next to me and kissed my forehead. "You good?"

"Are my legs still attached, because I don't feel them yet."

He smiled and brushed a lock of hair from my face. "I'll take that as a yes."

I yawned. "I feel so sleepy."

His thumb stroked my cheek. "Rest. I want you with me for slow and sweet, not drifting off somewhere else."

"I'm just going to close my eyes for a few minutes."

He grinned. "Sure you are."

CHAPTER 20
Life's a Gamble
Fox

"Get rid of the smile."

I didn't have to look at Opal to know she was sporting a shit-eating grin when I walked into the office on Monday morning. Hell, she probably got here at the ass crack of dawn to prepare the interrogation questions she'd been formulating since seeing Josie and me Friday night.

"It's not a crime to smile," she said.

"It is in my place of business. You don't like it, don't let the door hit you on the ass on the way out."

Undeterred, Opal crossed the office and parked herself on the corner of my desk.

"So..." She couldn't contain it. A smile spread from ear to ear. "How was your weekend?"

I wasn't about to let on that I'd spent three nights in a row in Josie's bed. I wouldn't even have come up for air this morning if we weren't on deadline for this job. "Fine. What time is the electrical inspector getting here? And the alarm company too."

"Nine and ten." She checked out the paint job on her too-long claws. "Did you do anything special?"

I sat down at my desk and pulled open the top drawer without looking up. "You're going to have to get your gossip somewhere else. I have shit to do, and my business is my business."

"Maryanne Foley's son is twenty now, you know. He's in college, but he makes deliveries on the weekend."

"And I need to know this why?"

She grinned. Apparently I'd just taken her bait. "If you really want people not to know your business, you should try changing up your restaurant orders once in a while."

"What in the hell are you talking about?"

"Half of Laurel Lake knows you go to the Inn for the pork and mashed potatoes. So when not one, but *two* meals are delivered to Josie's house, and one of them is your signature dish, word gets around."

"You're telling me Maryanne's kid delivers Uber Eats, and he went home and reported Josie's order to his mother, who picked up the phone and called you?"

"He mentioned to his mother that the woman who answered the door in the old Wollman place was hot. I saw Maryanne at church yesterday, and she asked me if Mrs. Wollman had died. We got to talking."

I shook my head. "I gotta get the hell out of this town."

"Where would you go?" Opal grinned. "*Manhattan?*"

I jabbed my finger into the air, pointing to her desk on the other side of the room. "Go."

She hadn't even made it back to her area when Porter walked in. His smile was also too big, too wide.

"Morning, boss." He shoved his hands into his pants pockets and rocked back and forth on the balls of his feet. "Heard you had a *banging* weekend."

I pointed to the door. "Out! Get the hell out of my office before I physically remove you."

"Boy, someone's cranky. After a weekend like you had, I'm usually in a good mood. Aren't you, Opal?"

She cackled. "I can't remember back that far."

"So are you guys a couple now?" Porter asked. He held up his hands, surrender style. "I'm not asking because I'm hoping to make a move on Josie. But if you are, I figured I'd let you know the winery over in Woodbridge is having a festival next weekend. I took Meryl, the nurse I was dating, last year. They had music, wine tasting, and all kinds of games and vendors. We stayed at a bed and breakfast down the road. It was a nice time. Romantic. Might be cool to take your new girlfriend somewhere outside of Laurel Lake, especially since you like your privacy and all."

I took a deep breath. "Run over to the school jobsite and pick up the scissor lift. You need to install hurricane brackets on all the gabled ceilings today before we close it up tomorrow."

Porter tapped two fingers to his forehead in a salute. "You got it, boss."

At least he went away. If only Opal was that simple. Maybe I should cut this office into two small ones so I wouldn't have to deal with her daily tongue wagging? While I mulled over that thought, I made the mistake of glancing over. Opal's eyes were still on me, still glittering gossip. Luckily, her phone rang, and she got busy putting in a rush order for supplies we needed delivered to a jobsite.

I gathered the revised plans I needed for my morning meeting and headed out to run some overdue errands. I would have to stop back at the office at some point later, but hopefully the gossip train would have moved to the next station by then and what I did this weekend would be forgotten.

Just as I arrived at the school to meet the electrical contractor, my phone chimed. I got a little too happy for my liking when I saw the name that popped up.

Josie: Morning! I didn't hear you sneak out this morning. I just woke up a few minutes ago. Can't believe how late I slept.

Feeling the need to play it cool, I decided to wait five minutes to answer. I made it two.

Fox: Must've been all the exercise you had this weekend... How you feeling?

I watched the dots bounce around feeling like a damn schoolgirl waiting for her crush to respond.

Josie: A little sore. You know...down there. But I'll be fine.

I'd lost track of how many times I'd been inside her over the last few days. Other than stepping out yesterday morning to get some supplies and build a ramp for my mom's friend, we'd spent the entire weekend in bed. But I'd thought she winced when I pushed in last night. I asked her if she was okay, and she said she was fine. I didn't believe her, so I tried to pull out, but she wasn't having it. She climbed on top and rode me so good, I almost believed I'd imagined the wince. Though after she fell asleep, I looked up how to treat soreness from too much fucking. Just in case, this morning I'd stopped by the drugstore and picked up supplies.

Fox: I left a bag in the mailbox that might help. Would've brought it in, but I wasn't thinking and locked the door on my way out.

Josie: What is it?

Fox: Epsom salt and an ice pack. Throw the salts in a warm bath. Then ice pack ten minutes on, ten minutes off, for a half hour.

Josie: Oh my God.

Fox: What?

Josie: Is this a regular parting gift you leave your hookups?

I frowned at my phone. Didn't like her thinking that.

Fox: I looked it up after you winced last night. Even though you denied that it hurt.

Josie: Oh.

Bill Merryman, the owner of the electrical company I was coming to bitch at for shoddy work, pulled into the parking spot next to me. He looked over and waved. I lifted my chin and went back to my phone.

Fox: Gotta run. Just got to the jobsite. Let me know if you need anything else. I can pick it up on my way home tonight.

Josie: Thanks. But I should be good. It was thoughtful of you to grab that stuff though.

Fox: Don't spread the word I did something thoughtful. It'll ruin my reputation in this town.

Josie: LOL! I won't. Though I could do some pretty fast damage today. I don't think I mentioned it, but I'm meeting my uncle at Rita's Beanery. That place is a prime stop on the gossip trail.

Fox: How'd that come about?

Josie: We exchanged numbers when we met at the home-improvement store. He called and said he wants to get to know me better.

I frowned. Ray Langone was trouble. I didn't trust him as far as I could throw him. But he was her family, and I'd already given my thoughts on the subject. So I bit my tongue.

Fox: Have a good one.

Josie: You, too.

The day got away from me after that. By the time I got back to the office, it was after four o'clock. Opal was on the phone with one of her cronies. From the sound of it, she wasn't gossiping about me, this time at least. Though she probably only clammed up on that topic when she heard me come in. After a few minutes of her *tsk*ing alternated with some "*Lord have mercy*," she hung up.

"Trying to change the old timers in this town is as useful as attempting to bend steel with your bare hands," she said.

I had shit to finish up, so I wasn't taking the bait this time. I sat at my desk with my head down to work on the lumber order I needed to place before the yard closed at five.

Not surprisingly, Opal didn't take the hint. "I never understood gambling. I work too hard to hand my money over and risk it all on a horse."

I didn't engage. Still didn't stop her...

She shook her head, talking *at* me instead of *with* me. "Don't know how two people can be cut from the same cloth and be so different, either."

I opened my laptop and shuffled some papers while it booted up to keep busy.

"How does Josie feel about her uncle Ray?"

Now she had my attention. I mentally flipped back through what she'd already said to play catch up. "Ray's gambling again?"

"Rachael Minton told Bridget Hagerty who told Georgina Mumford that she saw Ray at the Crow's Nest bar today. He was bragging how he had a *sure thing* for some dog race and was putting big money on it so he could pay off all his debt and take a sweet trip this winter."

"Where would Ray get big money?"

Opal shrugged. "Who knows."

I tended to think the worst of people, so I hoped I was wrong. But I dug my phone out to check in with Josie anyway.

Fox: Hey. Have a good lunch with your uncle?

She texted back a minute later.

Josie: Yeah. He's very sweet. But I found out he's sick. No insurance either.

I shut my eyes and swore under my breath. "Opal, can you set up a lumber order I need placed before five? I'll text you what to get."

"Of course."

I grabbed my keys and stalked toward the door.

Opal called after me. "Where you running off to in such a hurry?"

"To put a stop to old habits."

○ ○ ○

I hadn't kept tabs on Ray Langone like I'd planned to, but I had a hunch where to find him. My first stop was the Crow's Nest, but the place was empty except for the two retired lo-

VI KEELAND

cal cops who owned it. The dog track two towns over was my next stop. They started racing at five, so I stepped on the gas to get there before the betting window opened.

My stomach turned as I walked inside. It could have been the place or the reason I was looking for Ray. I wasn't certain, but it made my foul mood even worse, which didn't bode well for the man if what I thought had happened today turned out to be right.

I did a lap around the track. There weren't too many people, but they all seemed to resemble Ray—same age range, leathered skin, drinker's noses, and looks of disappointment on their faces. As I turned the last curve, I'd started to think I'd wasted my time, but then I looked down at the field and spotted a guy talking with his hands and sporting a big smile. No doubt Ray was spewing about his *sure thing*.

I knew my size. Hadn't often used it to my advantage since my hockey days, but sometimes actions spoke louder than words. Squaring my shoulders, I came up behind Ray and looked down at his five-foot-six frame. My shadow announced my arrival.

Ray lifted his chin high as he turned, probably ready to tell whoever had stepped into his personal space to back off. Until he saw me.

"Fox Cassidy." He flashed a hesitant smile. "Long time no see, buddy."

"Not your buddy."

The guy he'd been talking to couldn't wait to scurry away. "I'll talk to you later, Ray. Thanks for the tip."

I folded my arms across my chest. "Where'd you get the money to bet today?"

His face wrinkled. "Why do you care?"

"Answer the question, Ray."

"I had it."

"Bullshit. You lost your job working construction with Pat Egmont last month because you couldn't show up on time. You'd have to drive an hour to find someone who didn't know someone who fired your ass, and you can't do that when you spend most of your days getting loaded at the Crow's Nest."

"What the fuck, man? Are you my mother?"

I held out my hand. "Give me the money your niece gave you today."

I'd been hedging, of course, but the look on Ray's face told me I'd hit a bullseye. "How do you know about that?"

"I didn't. You just told me. Now cough it up. Or I'm going to grab your ankles, turn you upside down, and shake until everything falls out of your pockets."

His face turned red. "You can't do that."

"Look around, Ray. Who's going to stop me?"

"Since when do you shake down people for a living? I thought you were a do-gooder who volunteered his free time because your pockets were lined from your days in the big leagues."

"Don't shake people down. Just retrieve things for people who were scammed."

"What are you talking about? My niece gave me the money. We're family. She's helping me out."

I stepped closer so he had to look up to see me. "What did she give you the money for?"

"That's my business."

"Not when you're taking advantage of Josie, it's not."

A look of understanding crossed Ray's face. "*Ohhh.* Now it makes sense. You always liked the pretty ones. Like that Evie girl." He grinned. "How's she doing these days? Maybe you should keep away from my niece so nothing bad happens to her like that other piece of ass."

I snapped. Grabbing the asshole by his shirt and maybe some skin underneath, I lifted him off his feet and into the air. *"What the fuck did you just say?"*

At least the guy had enough brains to look scared. "I was teasing. I was teasing."

Still dangling him in the air, I used him for a bicep curl, bringing his face nice and close to mine, and motioned to the track below. "Are you giving me back Josie's money, or am I tossing you over this railing?"

"I don't even have it all! I had to pay my bookie."

"I'll take whatever's left."

"But I got a sure thing!"

"Trust me, the only sure thing you have is me breaking a few bones if that cash isn't in my hands in the next ten seconds. I'm not fucking around, Ray. You got me?"

I waited until he nodded before setting him back on his feet. He dug into his dingy pants pocket and pulled out a wad of cash. When he handed it over, he huffed and turned to leave, but I put a hand on his shoulder, stopping him. "Not so fast. Give me what's in the other pocket."

"I don't have anything in the other pocket."

"Then inside-out it and show me lint. Otherwise, I'm going to do it for you, and getting that close to your junk is only going to piss me off."

Ray mumbled something I couldn't make out, but he reached into his other pocket and pulled out a second, smaller wad of cash.

I took it and gave him a little push. "Now go the fuck home. And if I find out you ever ask Josie for so much as a ride, we won't be having a gentleman's conversation like we just did. You'll be swallowing all your teeth before you even get a look at who did the punching."

CHAPTER 21

Therapy
Josie

I hit the Join button at 5:59. It might've been the first time I'd looked forward to my therapy session. My head had been spinning all day, after the amazing weekend I'd spent with Fox, and I thought it might be nice to talk through what I was feeling with someone.

Cynthia joined right on time with a smile. "Hi, Josie."

I adjusted my laptop screen so she could see my whole face over Zoom. "Hi. How are you?"

"I'm good."

"Your hair looks nice. Did you do something different?"

"No, I just blew it out for a change."

"Are you going somewhere special tonight?"

I didn't have any plans, but a certain grumpy neighbor had texted and asked if he could stop by later. "Not really. Well, umm...I guess someone's coming over."

Even fourteen-hundred miles away and talking over the Internet, my therapist could read me. She smiled. "Do you want to talk about whoever is coming over?"

I let out an anxious breath. "I actually do."

"I'm going to guess it's a male guest?"

I nodded. "My neighbor Fox."

"Oh. You've mentioned him before. When you first got down there, I think. He's the one who gave you a hard time about doing the construction yourself, right?"

I nibbled on my bottom lip. I'd forgotten I'd brought him up during one of my previous sessions. "Yes. He did give me a hard time. But he's also helped me a lot. That's sort of Fox's MO, a giant contradiction. But the house wouldn't be in half as good a shape without everything he's done."

"That's great. Helpful neighbors are worth their weight in gold." She paused. "Is there anything else you want to tell me about him?"

My mind immediately fired off lots of things...

He's great in bed.

His dick is scary huge.

We didn't get out of bed the entire weekend.

But instead I went with something more conservative.

"We've been spending time together. Intimate time, I mean."

Cynthia kept her face neutral. "Okay. And how do you feel about that? Do you think you're ready for a relationship?"

I shook my head. "Oh, it's not a relationship. It's just... sex."

"That type of relationship definitely has its perks. Of course, it also has its pitfalls."

"I've only experienced the perks so far." I couldn't help but crack a smile. "*Lots* of perks, actually."

My therapist smiled. "I'm glad to hear that. But tell me why it's a sex-only arrangement and not the beginning of something more. Is that your doing?"

"I'm not even sure, to be honest. I think we both have a lot of baggage and want to keep it simple. He took me on a date to a fancy restaurant because he thought that's what I would expect. Then when I mentioned his dead fiancée during dinner, he disappeared to the bathroom. When he came back, he tried to tell me our going out was a bad idea because he couldn't give me what I needed. That's when I suggested we take the food home and just have sex."

"Oh my. His fiancée died?"

I nodded. "I'm not even sure how. The only thing I know is her first name was Evie. He definitely shuts down at the mention of her, even casually."

"And this arrangement is what you really want? Sometimes relationships like this can get sticky. Even when two people go into it with the same mindset, things can change. Despite the best of intentions, one of you could develop feelings while the other doesn't."

"That wouldn't be a good idea for so many reasons— the biggest being I live in New York, and he lives here."

"That's an obstacle not a barrier. People can move."

I laughed. "Not Fox. The man doesn't like change. He's a creature of habit. He eats the same thing for dinner on the same night every week. If you look up the word *immovable* in the dictionary, I'm pretty certain there's a picture of Fox Cassidy. And of course, my work and apartment are in New York."

"I see." Cynthia paused and wrote some notes. "Aside from this new arrangement with the neighbor, how have you been feeling? How has your sleeping been?"

I'd slept better than I had in years after sex with Fox. The man was like a sleeping pill. "Really good, actually."

"What about your energy level? Have you been spending time in bed when you're not sleeping?"

"Well, this weekend I spent *a lot* of time in bed not sleeping."

Cynthia smiled again. "Right. I guess I walked into that one. Appetite okay?"

"Are we still talking about the time I spent in bed the last few days?"

She laughed. "I was referring to your hunger for food. But I think it's great that your sexual appetite is strong."

"I've been eating pretty well, too. Honestly, I feel like the old me again—the one before the meltdown, I mean."

Cynthia and I spent another forty minutes talking. For a change, when our session ended, I didn't have the urge to climb into bed and curl into a ball.

This afternoon, when I'd gotten back from lunch with my uncle, I'd made meatballs and sauce while I tiled the backsplash in the kitchen. The pot had been cooking all day, so I lowered the temperature to simmer. Not long after, Fox knocked. My heart rate picked up, which caused an internal war.

This is just sex, Josie. Don't get excited to see the man.

Why can't I be excited to see him? Maybe I'm excited about the prospect of having sex with him again and not about his company.

No, you're not.

Yes, I am!

I wiped my sweaty palms on my pants and opened the screen door with a smile. "Hey. Come on in."

Fox stepped inside. An awkward few seconds ticked by. We'd been making out for days, so it seemed odd not to kiss hello. Unnatural almost. His eyes immediately zoned in on my mouth, so I thought he might be feeling the same way, though neither of us made a move.

Fox cleared his throat and looked away. "You cooking? Smells good in here."

"I am. I made meatballs and sauce. Are you hungry? I can make you a plate. Though I have to warn you, the meatballs are heart-healthy. Made with mostly turkey. Only a little beef for flavor. I'm not sure you'd approve. You seem like a real meat-and-potatoes guy—with the meat being the unhealthy kind."

Fox's lip twitched. "I like healthy foods."

I thumbed behind me. "You want some?"

"No thanks. I ate already. I need to head to the rink. We had to shift practice to Monday this week because the rink is getting some work done on Wednesday, and I told one of the guys we'd run a few miles together beforehand. He wants some extra training."

"Oh. Well, have fun."

He nodded and took an envelope out of his back pocket. "I just stopped over to give you this."

"What is it?"

"Your two-thousand dollars. The part Ray didn't spend already, anyway."

I took the envelope and peeked inside. "I don't understand. Why do you have it? I gave it to my uncle for his medical bills."

"There are no medical bills, Josie."

"What do you mean?"

"I got wind that Ray was shooting his mouth off about a sure thing he was going to lay heavy cash on. Found him at the dog track before the betting window opened."

"So he lied to me and was going to gamble the money?"

Fox put his hands on his hips. "I hate to break it to you, but your uncle is a piece of crap. He lies, cheats, and steals. I know you look for the good in everyone and want to think he's changed. But he hasn't. I understand if you want to get to know him, though I don't think he's worth your time. But please don't give the asshole any more money. I might wind up in jail getting it back next time."

I looked down at the ground, feeling like an idiot. "Okay."

Fox put two fingers under my chin and tilted my head up so our eyes met. "That's on him. Not on you. You feel me?"

"I really thought he'd changed. He was so sympathetic and believable."

"That's what makes him a good con man, sweetheart."

"But *you* knew it..."

"That's because I'm cynical as fuck. You're optimistic and all things good."

I sighed. "Thank you for getting it back."

He nodded. "No problem. How you feeling? Did the Epsom salt help?"

"It did."

"Good. I got a busy week. School job should've been done by now, but instead they're still giving me pages of revisions to the plans. And we start a new job tomorrow, too." He looked at his watch and nodded toward the door. "I gotta get to the rink. Probably won't be around much this week. But if you need anything, call me."

I was disappointed, yet forced a smile. "Okay. Thanks, Fox."

He was halfway out the door when he turned around and walked back in. "Forgot something," he said.

"What?"

He responded by hooking an arm around my waist and hauling me close. His lips crashed down on mine. "This."

After he was done kissing the shit out of me, he pulled back, his eyes dark. "You got plans next weekend?"

I hadn't yet found my voice, so I shook my head.

"Good. There's a wine festival not too far out of town. Thought maybe we could spend the weekend. Maybe stay at a nearby B&B."

"Oh." I blinked. "Yeah. That sounds great."

"Alright then. I'll talk to you soon."

And just like that, my sex-only stud walked out the door, as if it wasn't a big deal that he'd just moved whatever was going on between us into new territory.

o o o

The following day, I drove to a flooring store a half hour away to get new carpet. I also found some tile that looked like wood flooring that I thought I might install downstairs. It wasn't cheap, so I wanted to do my homework before I decided for sure. On the way home, I passed the Crow's Nest bar. My uncle's beat-up car was parked outside, so I decided to stop.

Inside was dark. The lights were on, but with dingy wood paneling and a worn brown bar, there wasn't too much for them to bounce off of. There were only three people in the entire place, so it wasn't difficult to find Uncle Ray. He was sitting at the far end, staring down into a glass of amber liquid. He didn't look up until I was next to him. Then he frowned.

"I don't want no more trouble," he said. "That Cassidy threatened my life."

I took that statement with a grain of salt and sat down on the stool next to him. "Why did you lie to me?"

"Would you have given me the money if I'd told you what it was for?"

I shook my head.

He shrugged and lifted his glass to his lips. "Well, there's your answer."

I sighed. "You know there are gambling-addiction groups and counselors if you have a problem."

"Only problem I got is you at the moment. You sitting here looking down your nose at me."

The bartender walked over and placed a napkin in front of me. "What can I get you?"

I waved my hand. "Nothing for me. Thank you."

Ray tossed back the rest of whatever was in his glass and held it up. "I'll take another."

"You gotta pay up front, Ray. You know that. Cash before I pour."

It sounded like Fox wasn't the only one who had my uncle's number.

"I gave you my last damn ten dollars already. Just spot me one."

The bartender shook his head and pointed to the register. "There's a list of people we can't extend credit to or take checks from. The owner wrote your name in red and underlined it twice. Sorry."

I knew I shouldn't do it, but I thought he might be more amenable to talking if I covered his drink. I pulled out a twenty and placed it on top of the bar.

"I'll pay for his."

Ray smiled at the bartender. "My order was a double then."

The bartender shook his head and looked to me, asking if it was okay. I nodded.

We sat side by side in silence until there was a half-full glass of amber liquid in front of my uncle again.

"Can I ask you something?"

"As long as you're buying..."

"Why did my mother tell me you were dead?"

Ray scoffed. "Figures."

"Did you two have a fight or something?"

He took a big swig of his drink and set it down with a clank. "Your mother was always too hurdy-turdy for me. Too hurdy-turdy for everyone and everywhere, including this town."

"What was your mom like?"

"Boy, she didn't tell you about your grandmother either?"

"Not too much."

"If you ask most, they'll tell you she was a nice woman. She kept to herself, not a lot of friends and such. Rose Langone was all about appearances. So the curtains were drawn while Ma drank her four martinis a day. And from what I understand, your mother's pop was kind enough to only have one girlfriend at a time. Eventually he took off with one who didn't have two mouths to feed. And my father moved in a month later. He liked to beat on us, and your grandmother pretended it didn't happen." He shrugged. "Just your normal, run-of-the-mill happy family."

I guess I knew why my mother was the way she was. She cared what people thought and had a general disdain for men. Her not wanting to visit Laurel Lake made more sense now, too. Maybe it was better that I grew up not knowing much.

"Any other questions?" my uncle asked.

I shook my head.

"Good. Tell that boyfriend of yours he owes me a new hat."

I stood. "Fox isn't my boyfriend."

Ray picked up his glass once again. "That's good. Wouldn't want my only niece to turn out like that man's last girlfriend."

CHAPTER 22
A Lifetime Ago
Fox

Four-and-a-half years ago

"What the hell?" If I didn't know better, I would've thought I'd walked into the wrong backyard. There were people milling around all over, and I had no idea who any of them were.

A skinny brunette wearing only the bottom of a bathing suit stumbled over to me. She threw her arms around my neck. "You're cute. Who are you?"

I peeled her arms off. "I think the better question is who the hell are you and where's your top?"

She pouted. "You don't sound very fun."

I ducked around the woman and dumped my equipment bag onto the back deck, scanning the yard for Evie. I found her in the lake with a red cup in her hand, so I walked down to the edge. Guess my plan to come home early, curl up on the couch, and watch a movie with my girl was out.

"Evie? What's going on?"

She squinted. When she realized it was me, she smiled and waved. "Come in! It's so warm."

"Why are you in there with all your clothes on?"

"I felt like it."

I motioned to the twenty or so people in the yard. "Who are all these people?"

"Some old friends from Coopsville."

Lately, there had been two Evies—depressed and in bed sleeping, or partying like she didn't have a care in the world. It was one extreme or the other. I'd been encouraging her to get out more, spend time with her old friends or make some new ones, maybe find something to occupy her time. But this wasn't exactly what I'd been thinking. "Why don't you come out of the lake?"

"Why don't you come in?"

"Because I'm dressed, and I just got home from two days on the road."

"So?" She leaned back and laid on top of the water, floating on her back. "It's so warm."

I looked around the yard. To my left there was a woman straddling a guy while they made out. Behind me there were a couple of guys smoking a joint. "How about we tell people it's time to go?"

Evie lifted her head out of the water and sulked. "Party pooper."

"I'm going to go take a shower and get changed. I'll show people the way out if they're still here when I'm done."

I didn't wait for a response before turning around and going inside. There were a few women in the kitchen playing a high-school drinking game. In the living room, a guy was slouched on the couch with one hand down the waistband of his pants and his dirty sneakers up on my coffee table. I kicked his feet off. He startled and jumped up like he was going to have a problem with it, but then stumbled and had to grab the arm of the couch to avoid falling over.

When he got a look at me, he swallowed. "What's up, man?"

"Party's over. Get your shit and get out."

"Who are you?" He tilted his head. "You look familiar."

"The guy who owns the house." I thumbed toward the stairs. "I'm going to change. Be gone by the time I get back. And take your friends with you."

I didn't wait for him to respond before lifting my bag again and taking the steps two at a time. In the shower, I let the water rain down longer than normal, hoping it would ease some of the tension in my neck. But even after fifteen minutes, I still wasn't in the mood for a party full of drunken strangers. I wanted Evie to have friends and make a life for herself, but her drinking had me concerned. After I dried off and got dressed, I looked out the window to the yard. Evie was saying goodbye to people, so I stayed upstairs until the last stragglers disappeared. I eventually found her sitting on the steps of the back deck, alone.

She looked up when she heard the screen door open and close. "Are you mad?"

"This is your home, too. So I'm not going to say you can't have friends over. But walking in to find random drunk guys sleeping on my couch doesn't feel good, Evie."

She sniffled. "I didn't get the job at the rink."

I sat down next to her on the step. "How come? I thought the interview went well."

"They hired someone with more experience skating teaching. I mean skating teaching." She shook her head. "No, I mean...whatever."

"I'm sorry."

"I don't know what to do with myself for the rest of my life."

"I wish I had an answer. Only you can figure that out. But I know the answer is not drinking like this."

"It helps me forget for a while." She leaned over and rested her head on her soaked jeans. "I just want to go back to when I still had a shot. Even if it was a long shot, there was hope. Now I feel...hopeless."

"Maybe you should talk to someone? Go see a doctor?"

She frowned. "I just need a plan. Something to do with my life." A few seconds later, she abruptly stood and stumbled over to the nearest flowerbed, dry heaving at first. I stood behind her and held her hair back as she vomited. When she was done, she wiped her mouth with the back of her hand. "I don't think the tequila agreed with the lake water I swallowed."

"Yeah, probably not."

She started to cry. "I'm sorry I'm such a fuck up."

"You're having a rough patch. You'll get through it."

"I don't want to turn out like my mother."

"So let's nip this in the bud. Quit the drinking."

"I drink before noon."

I'd suspected that to be the case on more than one occasion. But when I asked, she'd said she was hung over. Not that that was much better.

"You want me to take you somewhere? To a detox or rehab?"

"Do you think I need to?"

"I think I want you to get better. So if you're up for it, let's give it a shot. It can't hurt, right?"

"I guess not."

"I'll make some calls."

"Can it wait until tomorrow?"

"Sure."

"I'm going to get better for you."

I shook my head. "No, Evie. You need to get better for *you*."

CHAPTER 23

Pack the Epsom

Fox

"What are you up to this weekend, boss?"

I didn't need Porter knowing I'd taken his suggestion to take Josie to the winery, so I stared straight at the road as we drove back from the jobsite in my truck on Friday afternoon. "Not much."

I caught him smirking in my peripheral vision. "Uh-huh."

I wasn't sure if that meant he knew something or suspected, but I left it at that. Porter went back to playing some game with annoying cartoon sounds on his phone.

But a few miles later, he couldn't help himself. "I'm not usually a wine drinker, especially reds. I went for the ambiance and because it made the girl I was seeing happy. But they make this wine that tastes almost like black cherries. I think it was called petit verdot."

My eyes flashed to him and back to the road. "Who told you?"

Porter snickered. "Miss Hope called the office. She told Opal you were going out of town for the weekend."

I shook my head. "My own mother."

"Now don't get upset with her. She didn't spill the beans intentionally. The other day, you sent me over to the home-improvement store to pick up a spool of electrical wire. While I was there, Sam happened to be working up an estimate for some flooring. I saw Josie's name on top, so when he asked if I needed any help, I told him to finish up what he was working on. Figured I was on the clock and you wouldn't mind. Anyway, Sam said it wasn't a rush because the customer had come in yesterday to get an estimate, but she was going away for the weekend. I put two and two together after Opal hung up with Miss Hope and asked if I knew you were going out of town this weekend. Don't worry, I didn't mention the connection I made to Opal."

"Good. Let's keep it that way."

Porter smiled. "Glad you took my recommendation, though."

I'd been hoping to get away without acknowledging that. But I felt like a dick now that I'd been caught. "Thanks for the idea."

He smiled bigger than if I'd just given him a raise. "You're welcome."

○ ○ ○

"Alright, now I know you're probably as nervous as I am about my weekend. But I think it's time."

I walked out on my back deck and found Josie kneeling on the grass at the water's edge, having a conversation with the duck. The scene was too entertaining to interrupt.

She stroked his feathers and pointed behind her. "You have a nice new house. Well, it's not *new new*. I got it at the garage sale I went to with Opal. But it's clean and new to us. So if you decide you're not ready to go back with your friends yet, your bed is fluffed up and waiting."

Jesus Christ, I hadn't even noticed the new addition to the yard. The woman had bought a wild duck a *dog house*. I suppose that was fitting, seeing as he slept on an orthopedic bed.

She leaned forward and nuzzled the duck. When she stood, the thing flapped its wings and started to walk into the water. Josie smiled and covered her heart with her hand. "Come back and visit soon, Daisy! I left food in your new house in case you get hungry!"

I leaned a hip against the deck railing, watching Josie watch the duck swim off. Fifty feet into the lake, a gang of similar-looking ducks swam over, and Josie's little friend joined their group.

I cupped my hands around my mouth and yelled, "I'm glad you put him back where he belongs. I was concerned you might try to stash him in your bag and bring him this weekend."

Josie jumped before turning around. "You scared the crap out of me! How long have you been standing there?"

"Long enough to know you're nervous about this weekend."

A hint of pink flushed across her cheeks. "I was just trying to make Daisy feel better, like she wasn't alone."

"*Uh-huh.*"

Josie rolled her eyes. "I'm not nervous to spend time with you."

"Maybe you should be."

"Why is that?"

I looked her up and down, drinking in how good she looked in yet another pair of yoga pants—this time blue—

and a matching cropped top. "Because I'm going to do very bad things to you."

Her jaw went slack. I liked it when she got that look, like she was visualizing me pleasing her. Yet she kept up the charade, folding her arms across her chest. "Is that so?"

I pushed off the railing and stalked over. Josie lifted her chin and stood her ground, which turned me on even more. When we were toe to toe, I looked down my nose at her and tugged at a piece of her hair. "It is. Got a problem with that?"

"What if I say I do?"

"Then you'd be missing out. I was planning on fingering you in the driveway before we even left so you'd be relaxed for the trip. Mrs. Craddox would probably be disappointed too. I'm sure she can't remember the last time she saw an orgasm face."

Josie play-smacked my stomach, laughing. "You're so crass."

I cupped my ear. "What's that? Did you say you want it in the ass? That can be arranged..."

Her cheeks reddened, but I could tell she enjoyed my teasing. Well, I was *mostly* teasing. Wrapping an arm around her waist, I pulled her to me. "So is this how it's going to be? When I see you, I'm going to have to take a kiss because you're not going to offer me one?"

"Am I supposed to do that? I wasn't sure of the protocol. I've never been in a sex-only relationship."

That last statement should've set off a band of warning bells—there was a reason some women only ever did relationships. They couldn't separate the physical from the emotional. Yet instead of making me think twice, I was ecstatic to know hookups weren't her thing. It was a ridiculous double standard, of course, considering those were the only thing I'd done for the last couple of years. But it was what it was.

I ducked my head down and planted my lips on hers. It took all of three seconds before my jeans grew snug, so I knew I needed to pace myself. But the week had been long, and Josie had been my first thought when I woke up every day and my last thought when I fell asleep at night. So it wasn't easy. I wanted her stripped naked and calling my name the way she did as soon as possible.

Begrudgingly, I pulled back from the kiss and rubbed my hands up and down her shoulders. "You ready to go?"

"Pretty much. I just need to throw a sweater or a sweatshirt in my bag in case it gets chilly."

"Why don't you do that? And I'll grab my stuff and pull around into your driveway."

"Okay." She smiled.

One good thing about whatever was going on between us, I no longer had to pretend I wasn't watching her. When she got to the back door, she turned. My eyes took their time lifting to find hers, so it was clear what I'd been doing.

"Still checking me out, huh?" She smiled smugly.

"Damn straight. By the way, doc, you might want to pack the Epsom salt. And the ice pack."

◦ ◦ ◦

"Heard you were thinking about putting in new flooring."

Josie looked over at me. We were an hour into the drive and about a half hour from the B&B I'd booked. "How did you know that?"

"How does everyone know anything around here?"

She shook her head. "It's really bizarre how fast things travel. My flooring isn't even scandalous. But yeah,

I'm thinking about doing the first-floor kitchen with new tile, the kind that looks like wood. The existing stuff is so outdated."

"Well, let me know when you decide. I'll place the order for you. I get a contractor's discount."

"Oh wow. Thanks. Will they still install it for me, though, if you order it?"

"I'll install it for you."

"I can't ask you to do that."

"You didn't ask."

"Still...you've done so much already."

I wiggled my brows. "I plan to do much more. You just wait."

Josie laughed. "Maybe you can show me how to install the floor and we can do it together?"

"If you want. But I can knock it out in a few hours by myself."

"I've actually discovered that I enjoy learning and doing the work. When I decided to come down here, I thought fixing up the house would keep me busy. But it's turned into more than that." She looked out the window for a moment. "When I was little, after I realized I couldn't dance for crap and ballerina was not likely happening, I wanted to be a painter. Not the artsy kind, but the kind who uses a roller on the walls."

"Really?"

She nodded. "We had this painter my mom always used. His name was Roland, and he always had a smile on his face. He would paint the living room while humming to the songs playing in his headphones or singing along. He let me help him do the roller whenever my mom wasn't home."

My brows dipped together. "Only when your mom wasn't around?"

"Melanie Preston would never allow me to hang out with someone doing work on the house. She treats people who work for her like they're hired help, two steps below her. Plus, she wouldn't want me to get any ideas about career choices. She'd already decided I was going to medical school. It was disappointing enough that I went for my PhD and did research and not *real medical school*."

"Why would what you do be disappointing? Aren't they both doctors who heal people?"

"It's more about the prestige for my mom than the actual work. She wanted me to be a surgeon like her. Research also doesn't pay as well as medical doctors, and she measures success by things and awards. That's probably why she and Noah got along so well." She paused and grinned. "My mother would probably hate you."

"Because I do construction?"

"And because you were a hockey player. My father used to have to watch football in the basement because she found contact sports barbaric."

The thought of her mother disliking me might've amused Josie, but it made my jaw tic with tension. It shouldn't have mattered. Meeting the parents wasn't on my agenda, yet it hit a nerve for some reason. "Your mother sounds like she should use her surgical skills to get the stick out of her ass. Hope you don't mind me saying so."

Josie chuckled. "Not only don't I mind, but it's one of the reasons I like you so much."

Her adding *so much* at the end of that sentence soothed my bent feelings a bit. I reached over and rested my hand on her thigh, and our eyes met briefly for a silent smile before returning to the road.

"My dad would've liked you, though," she said.

"Oh yeah?"

She nodded. "He liked honest people who didn't put up pretenses."

"How did he wind up with your mom, then?"

"I've always wondered the same thing. But he loved her. I'd often see him watching her from a distance with a smile on his face. Like, she'd be in the kitchen pouring a cup of coffee or whatever, and I'd find him leaning against the doorframe watching her when she wasn't looking."

I thought back to the way I'd watched Josie today, enjoying the moment. And how I'd watched her in the yard from the second floor, or stolen a few moments of her toiling in the kitchen through the front bay window on more than one occasion. But that was different, wasn't it? At least that's what I told myself.

"Anyway..." Josie shifted in her seat to face me. "I feel like I'm always talking about me. Tell me about you."

"What do you want to know?"

"I don't know. What was it like playing professional hockey? Did women wear your jerseys and ask for your autograph?"

"I loved playing, and women did."

"But did you have groupies? Like women who wanted to be with you because you were a player?"

This was a line of questioning that a man played chess with. One answer could lead us down a path she might not want to go. So I moved a piece that kept my king from being checked. "Feels like a lifetime ago."

She grinned. "So that's a yes. Did you have a girlfriend the entire time you were playing?"

I shook my head. "Not until the last year."

"What about in college?"

"I went out with someone for most of freshman year."

"What happened with that?"

"She was three years older. She graduated and moved back home, and I got drafted into the league."

"You went into the pros that early?"

"It's not early for hockey. Most guys are in by nineteen."

"I didn't realize that."

"Do you follow hockey?"

"I've never actually watched a game."

I chuckled. "Average retirement age is twenty-nine. So if you're not in early, you're significantly cutting down your chance at seeing ice time. There are outliers. Gordie Howie and Chris Chelios played twenty-six seasons. But for every one of them, there are ten guys who don't make it two years."

"Retirement at twenty-nine. Wow. That's so young."

"It's a physically demanding game. There's a reason players are shifted in and out every minute or so."

"They change players every *minute*?"

I laughed. "You weren't kidding around. You've never watched a hockey game, huh?"

"No. Never. A minute seems so short."

"Not when you're playing the game. I think the average shift is about forty-seven seconds. Top players can stay in for a minute or better; lower-level guys sometimes are out in forty seconds. All depends on stamina."

"How long were your shifts?"

I wasn't cocky about too many things in hockey. I was never the best, never the worst. But I was proud of my play time during my heyday. "A little over a minute."

"Jeez. No wonder I needed the Epsom salt."

She gazed out the window after that. I wondered what she was thinking, even considered asking—something I would normally never do. But she beat me to the punch.

"Did you have a good time when we...you know?"

She couldn't possibly be questioning whether I liked fucking her. "You know...what?"

"When we fooled around. Had sex."

"Why in the world would you ask me that?"

"I don't know. I guess because we did it so many times. When we were in the moment, I thought it was because we couldn't get enough of a good thing. But after...I don't know. I guess I have doubt because of Noah cheating on me. If he was satisfied, why would he have cheated?"

I shook my head. That asshole ex of hers had done a number on her, even more than I'd realized. "Sweetheart, when a man cheats, it usually has nothing to do with his sex life or the woman he's with. They cheat because they have *self* problems. They're self-absorbed and have low self-esteem. How hard would it have been to break things off with you before deciding to fuck around? Not hard at all. But he wanted to have his cake and eat it, too. Don't let that asshole put his issues on you. Got me?"

She didn't look convinced. So I put my blinker on and got off at the next exit, even though we still had a half dozen to go before we got to the one for the place we were staying. Once we were off the highway, I pulled into an empty parking lot.

"What are you doing?"

I parked and made sure I had her full attention. "Fucking you was phenomenal. I missed my exit driving to the lumberyard the other day—a place I could get to with my eyes closed—because I was picturing what my dick looked like going in and out of you, the way you milked me like a tight fist, only better. Every day this week, I woke up thinking about you underneath me, and I went to bed jerking off, remembering the sound you make when you come.

So whatever dumb-ass doubt that moron you were with planted in your brain, get rid of it. Because I didn't have a good time, Josie. I had *the best* time."

Her eyes watered. "Oh my God. I needed to hear that."

"Didn't tell you because you needed to hear it. Told you because it's the truth."

She unbuckled her seatbelt and crawled over the center console onto my lap. Pressing her mouth to mine, she mumbled, "I want you."

"Here?"

She nodded and reached down for the button of my jeans. "Please."

The only thing better than this woman taking charge was her saying *please*. I wanted to hear that word from her lips every damn day. Which was a problem...but one I'd think about when I wasn't about to have Josie Preston sink balls-deep onto my cock.

CHAPTER 24
Slap a Label On It
Fox

Josie watched the dance floor while I watched her. That comment she'd made in the car yesterday—how she knew how much her father loved her mother because she'd often caught him staring at her—crept to the forefront of my mind. But I pushed it back and looked away, sucking back my last wine sample.

"You know, you're supposed to *taste* the wine," Josie commented. "Let it roll around your tongue to savor the taste and figure out the flavors you recognize. Not knock it back like a shot of tequila."

"You have your way, and I have mine," I said.

She smiled and looked back at the crowd swaying to the music under the tent. I hated dancing. Vertically anyway, but she'd given me what I wanted—and then some—last night and again this morning, so I figured it wouldn't kill me this once. I stood and held out my hand.

"Really?" Josie seemed as shocked as I was that I was initiating this shit. "I didn't even ask because I figured there was no way in the world Fox Cassidy would dance."

I was starting to realize there wasn't much this woman couldn't get me to do. Here I was, not at home or work on a Saturday—but at a winery, of all places. And last night I'd slept in a room with floral wallpaper and frilly curtains, followed by a morning where we joined strangers who thought it was fun to get to know the other guests at breakfast. But the moment I held Josie up against me on the dance floor, I forgot all about what I did or didn't normally do.

She rested her head against my chest as we swayed to the music. After once around the dance floor, she looked up at me with a smile. "This place is really nice. Do you come here often?"

I shook my head. "First time."

"Oh." She seemed to think about my response before her eyes met mine again. "Is there a different winery you usually go to?"

"Nope."

"Have you been to the B&B we're staying at before?"

"Never stepped foot in a bed and breakfast until last night—unless you count the Hilton Garden Inn since they technically give you a bed, along with a free breakfast in the lobby the next morning."

Again, she considered my answer. "What made you bring me here then?"

I shrugged. "Seemed like something you'd like."

"It is." She smiled. "Thank you."

We went back to gliding around the dance floor in silence. But Josie had the type of brain that didn't turn off so easily. Not even with the help of a little wine. She looked up at me. "Fox?"

"Yeah?"

"Are we...more than just sex now?"

"I don't know, Jos. Do we need to put a label on it?"

She sighed. "No, I guess not. I guess I just like to compartmentalize things."

I hated the look of disappointment on her face. "What comes after sex?" I asked.

"Sleep?"

I chuckled. "I meant in your compartments. You've got sex and just having fun at one end and married at the other, right? What comes in between?"

"Oh. A relationship is somewhere in the middle, I guess."

"What comes before that?"

"I don't know. Dating, maybe?"

"How about we call it that? Dating."

"Okay." She smiled. "I never really thought about all the different stages. But I would think dating is somewhere between hooking up and an exclusive relationship."

My eyes narrowed. "So dating means you can see other people?"

"I would think so. If we're keeping it casual."

The thought of her with someone else made me feel like chewing up an imaginary guy's teeth and spitting them out. "Then we're adding a new compartment. Exclusive dating."

"Really? You don't want to see other people?"

"Are you good with that?"

She nodded. "I'm not really someone who can date more than one person at a time anyway. Besides, then maybe we can forego the condoms. I think they contributed to my soreness last weekend. If you're good with that, I mean. I had a checkup after I found out Noah was cheating, so I know I'm clean."

I stopped in my tracks. "Are you on the pill?"

"No, but I have an IUD."

I bent down and wedged my shoulder into her belly. When I stood, Josie flopped over my shoulder. She screeched while laughing. "What are you doing?"

"Getting the hell out of here."

"What about my tasting flight?"

I bent as we passed the table we'd been sitting at and scooped up the wooden mini-glass holder along with her purse.

Josie wiggled in my arms, but I didn't let her down—not even as people stared while I walked through the winery, and not even as the security guard standing at the front door told me I couldn't leave with the glasses in my hand. I kept moving—long, purposeful strides until I got to the truck and dumped her inside. Jogging around to the passenger side, I passed her the wine samples. "You should probably keep these low, open container-in-the-car laws and all."

"I cannot believe you just carried me out of the winery."

"You told me you want me bare. You're lucky we're not in the bathroom right now."

Her eyes sparkled. "Anxious much?"

"You have *no fucking idea*."

I drove double the speed limit to get back to the B&B. Inside, the host tried to strike up a chat about some snacks they'd be putting out later. But the only thing I'd be eating was the woman I was practically dragging up the stairs to our room.

Once the door was shut, I got scolded. "You're so rude. That nice old lady was looking for someone to talk to."

I started to unbutton her blouse. "I know. That's why I nipped that shit in the bud."

She shook her head, but I could see she wasn't really upset. I finished the last button and went for her jeans. "Tell me how you want it, babe."

"You always ask me that."

"That's because I want to make sure it's what you're in the mood for."

"What about what *you're* in the mood for?"

"That's easy. You."

She laughed. "No, really. I think it's your turn. Tell me what you want." Josie put her palms to my chest and walked me backward. "You sit and think about it. And I'll get undressed."

I tried—I really did. But as I watched her shed her clothes, my mind raced through a million things I wanted to do to her, not how she could give to me. When she wiggled out of her jeans, I thought about tapping that beautiful ass. When she sucked the flesh of her pouty mouth in, I thought about slipping my cock between those luscious lips. But when she unclasped her lacy pink bra and her tits spilled out so close to my face, my mind settled on one track.

Josie took a step back and caressed her tits. "So, have you decided what you're in the mood for?"

I licked my lips. "It can be anything?"

"Anything."

"I can't wait to come inside you bare, but if I go in without a release first, I'm not going to last thirty seconds."

"Okay. So what would you like to do?"

"You're really up for anything?"

"Why not?"

I stared at her gorgeous, natural breasts. "Then I want to titty-fuck you and come all over your neck."

She blinked, but after the initial shock wore off, she smiled. "How do you want me?"

Fuck yeah. I felt like a kid with free rein in the candy store. "On your back, on the bed."

Josie climbed up and settled in the middle of the mattress. I didn't take my eyes off of her while I got undressed. When she squeezed her breasts together, my sock tore from my foot.

"You tear a lot of clothes," she laughed.

"You try a lot of patience." I lifted a knee to the bed. "You sure you're okay with this?"

"I'm excited for it."

My head fell back for a quick thank you to the man upstairs before I leaned and licked a line up her breastbone. Then I straddled her ribcage and also licked my hand before spreading the lubricant all over my cock.

Josie watched me rub up and down the shaft. "I like when you do that," she said. "Touch yourself, I mean."

"Oh yeah? Then you'll be seeing me do it more often."

I licked my hand once more and pumped a few times. I wanted to be inside her in the worst way, but I wanted the first time without a barrier between us to be good for her. Squeezing my cock between her tits would likely get me off just as fast. But I'd get her off while my body recharged, so we could both enjoy it without feeling frenzied.

Sufficiently lubed, I took a deep breath, attempting to calm myself before getting started. My cock was rigid straight, so I had to lean over her and help it down to reach her cleavage. Josie sandwiched me in the middle, holding me almost as tight as her pussy did.

I thrust once and cursed. "Fuck. Every part of you feels like heaven."

She leaned up on her elbows and was greeted by the head of my cock peeking out between her mounds of flesh.

"Oh my God." She gasped. "That is so hot. Keep going."

Happy to oblige, I pumped my hips back and forth. This was only the prequel to the main act—getting to fuck her bare, and yet it was better than anything I'd felt in a long time. Josie's hooded eyes locked on my cock. Watching how turned on she was might've been better than the physical part of what I was doing.

I didn't want to bruise her skin by rubbing too hard or too long, so when my release started to barrel down, I didn't fight it. My eyes dropped to her neck, to the delicate hollow at the center of her collarbone that had been driving me nuts since the first time I laid eyes on her. This damn woman made me feel like a caveman. I wanted her to submit the most vulnerable part of her body for me to shoot my load all over. I'd never had the urge to conquer a woman like this before. It should've scared the living shit out of me. But in the moment, nothing else was important. I gave zero fucks about anything other than decorating her neck with some pearls.

I growled as I spurted hot cum onto her creamy throat. My heart raced, and I felt a little lightheaded. It wasn't like me to collapse after a release. Then again, this whole weekend wasn't like me. So screw reading into it. I might freaking snuggle, too. Though I needed to clean her up first.

Josie was still breathing deep when I returned from the bathroom with a damp towel and gently wiped her neck. Her smile was big and goofy, as if she'd been the one who just shot a piece of her brain through a pinhole.

"I had no idea that would be such a turn-on," she said.

"Was that your first time?"

She nodded.

Forget caveman, I felt like a freaking astronaut planting the first flag on the moon.

"What else haven't you done?"

"I'm not sure. If you'd asked me that question a little while ago, I probably wouldn't have thought to put that on the list. I'm thinking my sex life might've been a little boring. Noah didn't ever ask me how I wanted it. We usually did it the missionary way. He didn't even like it when I was on top."

"Do *you* like it on top?"

She flashed a shy smile. "I love it."

"Well, then that's what you'll get." I tossed the towel over my shoulder and scooped her off the bed. "*After* you ride my face."

● ● ●

I woke to a thin beam of sunlight streaking across my eyes. Those girly curtains weren't only ugly, they didn't do shit to keep out the light. Yet I didn't move, because Josie and I were a tangle of limbs—another thing I didn't normally do. I liked my space when I slept. At least with other women I did.

Josie's head was on my chest. I'd thought she was sleeping until I felt eyelashes tickle my skin.

"You awake?" I whispered.

She tilted her neck back to look up at me. "I am. My phone woke me. My boss texted, and I couldn't fall back asleep. Did you just wake up?"

"Yeah. How long have you been up?"

She shrugged. "Maybe an hour."

"What time is it?"

"Almost ten. We slept late." Josie ran her fingers through my chest hair. "Noah shaved his chest."

I had opinions on men who did that, but that's not what had me clenching my jaw. "Don't know if I like being compared to your ex."

She caught my eyes. "Your dick is twice the size."

A cocky smile inched up my cheeks. "Maybe I like comparisons after all."

She giggled, then sighed.

"It's Sunday. Everything alright at work? Why was your boss texting you?"

"Yeah. He wants to know when I'm coming back. When I left, I put in for twelve weeks—the max you can take under the Family Medical Leave Act. But I told him I might return sooner, if I felt up to it."

I studied her. "You're leaving?"

She shook her head. "Not right away. I'm going to tell him I'm not coming back early."

I felt relief, for a couple of seconds anyway. "When is your twelve weeks up?"

"Four weeks from tomorrow. But I should probably go back earlier to settle in. I'm sure whatever I left in the refrigerator looks like a science experiment by now."

I'd always known Laurel Lake wasn't Josie's home. But it was starting to feel like she was mine... I cleared the morning grog from my throat. "I'll help you finish up the house so you can take off whenever you're ready. Maybe you can make me a list of what else needs to be done."

She frowned. "What will happen when I leave?"

Realistically? She'd go back to New York and forget all about me. Get busy with her job, probably meet another doctor, or maybe a professor or lawyer. And I'd go back to burying myself in work and eventually to mindless fucking with no strings attached. Though I couldn't imagine jumping right back into that after this.

I skirted the question I knew she was asking. "You'll get another renter, and I'll try to keep my eye out to make sure newspapers and VHS tapes show up in the garbage from time to time."

"I meant between us."

"It's kind of hard to date from fourteen-hundred miles away." As soon as I said it, I felt like a shit. But what was I supposed to say? That we'd take turns visiting and spend countless hours texting? My fingers were too damn big for the little keypad on a cell phone. A long text from me was a sentence, and I wasn't even good at local relationships. Plus, she just got out of an engagement where the guy had let her down. I wasn't about to do the same.

Josie looked away. "Yeah, of course." She pulled the covers off and climbed out of bed. "I'm going to take a shower."

"You want company?"

She smiled sadly. "Maybe another time."

I nodded. She obviously wasn't happy with my response to what would happen between us when she left. But Josie deserved better than me, even if part of me didn't want to let her go.

CHAPTER 25

A Lifetime Ago

Fox

Four years ago

"Fox?"

I didn't recognize the number, but I knew it was a local one.

"Who's this?"

"It's Lieutenant Druker."

I froze. Evie hadn't been home when I got home tonight.

"What's happened?"

"I got your girl down at the station, son. Picked her up on a drunk and disorderly call."

"Is she okay?"

"We removed her from the ice rink. She'd had too much to drink. Rink guard told her she had to get off the ice because she was endangering the other patrons—kids and parents mostly, during an open-skating session. She tried to knock him over and then started doing dangerous jumps and stuff while inebriated. Fell at least once while we were trying to grab her. I would imagine she's going to be sore tomorrow, and probably have a wallop of a headache, but she should be fine."

I raked a hand through my hair. I'd just sat down to ice my own bruised hip after four days of games on the road. Going down to the police station and dealing with a drunk Evie was not what I felt like doing. I sighed. "Is she going to be released?"

"She'll have to appear in court next week, but you can come get her when you're ready."

"Thanks, Lieutenant. I'll be right there."

It took both hands to push myself up off the couch, I was so banged up from last night's game. Lately, I was starting to appreciate why the average player retired before thirty in this sport. I took my time driving down to the police station, and limped my way up to the front desk.

Joe Redmond was behind it. We'd gone to high school together.

"Hey, Cassidy." He extended a hand. "Good to see you. Tough loss the other night."

Considering my team had lost six out of our last seven games, I wasn't sure which night he was talking about. But it didn't much matter. I nodded. "Yep."

"I think they should've ejected Hartman for that slashing crap he pulled."

"Me too. If they had, my hip wouldn't be screaming from the fight that came after he got out of the box." I lifted my chin toward the door I knew led to the holding cells. "I'm here to pick up Evie Dwyer."

"Give me a minute. I'll grab her from the drunk tank." He started to walk back, but stopped. "I should warn you, she puked all over herself. Might want to throw a blanket down in the car. It's hard to get that smell out once it gets into the seats."

"Great," I mumbled.

A few minutes later, Evie ambled out from the back. Mascara stains streaked her cheeks, and her shirt was still damp with what I assumed was vomit. She looked at me and her big hazel eyes welled up. "I'm sorry."

I ignored her and spoke to Joe. "She need to fill out paperwork or anything?"

"Nope. She's good to go. She's got the citation with her court appearance date folded in her purse."

"Thanks, Joe."

"Good luck."

I wasn't sure if he was referring to the rest of the season or Evie, but I could use all the help I could get with both.

Outside, I opened the truck door and made sure Evie was inside before shutting it. I still hadn't said a word to her. I slipped my key into the ignition, but stopped shy of turning it. "What the fuck, Evie?"

She started to cry. Normally I was a sucker for a woman and tears, but I was all out of sympathy these days.

"I'm sorry. I don't know why I do what I do."

That was a cop out and pissed me off even more. "Well, maybe I can clue you in on why the hell you're acting the way you are. Because you *left rehab after five days when they wanted you to stay for thirty*."

Six months ago, after I'd come home to Evie swimming in the lake and vomiting in the flowerbeds, she'd agreed to go to rehab. None of the decent facilities had any beds available, so she'd had to wait two days to check in, and I was going to be away for a game the afternoon she was due to show up. She'd promised to go, but she never did. Instead, I came home to a clean house and a sober Evie—a combination I hadn't seen in months. I don't think

I even realized how bad things had gotten until that day, when coming home to what should've felt normal wasn't even familiar anymore. Ever since she'd moved in, she'd gotten herself into a vicious cycle of binging for three or four days while I was traveling, and then sleeping it off for a day or two when I got home. So either she was a mess, or she was crashed in bed.

She stayed sober for two weeks that time, and I'd actually seen a glimpse of the woman I'd met at the ice rink almost a year earlier. But then she'd slipped up, and things went back to the same old shitshow real fast. After another month-long binge, I sat her down and gave her a choice: me or the tequila. The following day I drove her to rehab. But after a five-day detox, she signed out against the doctor's advice while I was on the road again. She'd said she felt like she could do the rest on her own. She'd hated being there because the older women all reminded her of her mother. I didn't agree with the decisions, but she was good for almost two months after that. Until she wasn't.

I shook my head. "I can't live like this anymore, Evie."

"What are you saying?"

I wanted to end things. We'd had maybe three good months in total since she'd moved in with me. But I was afraid of what it might do to her. She didn't have anyone in her life to take care of her, and I didn't want to be the cause of a tailspin, because I cared about her. So I felt trapped.

I looked over at her. Fear was palpable in her eyes.

"I'll do anything. Take me to rehab right now. Just give me another chance. I can't lose you, Fox."

"You need to want to get better for *you* in order for it to work. Not for me."

"I do want to get better for me. For us."

I was wary, but what was I going to do? Dumping her back at her mother's would be a disaster, and taking her home again, even if she stayed clean for a few days, would just be doing the same thing over and over and expecting a different outcome. So really, what choice did I have?

"Let's go home. You can take a shower while I call and see if we can get you a bed in rehab again."

o o o

"God, I missed you." Evie threw her arms around my neck. There was a counselor waiting outside the room, so I gave her a quick peck and pulled back.

"You look good," I said.

She smiled. "I feel really good."

Evie had been at South Maple Recovery Center for nineteen days now. I'd visited whenever I was home and allowed, but today was more than just a visit. It was a *loved one counseling session*. Not really my cup of tea, but I had to show her support. Especially since she'd invited her mother to come last week, and she hadn't shown up. Not a shocker—not to me anyway.

Knock. Knock.

The woman who'd introduced herself as Eleanor walked in and smiled. "You two ready to get started?"

Evie took a deep breath and nodded.

"Mr. Cassidy, why don't you go around to the other side of the table so you two are sitting across from each other, and I'll sit over here on this end?"

"It's Fox, please." I pulled out Evie's chair before walking around to sit opposite her. As soon as my ass hit the seat, she reached across the table and took my hand. Clearly, she was nervous.

"So..." Eleanor began. "Group therapy is about opening up the lines of communication and starting to rebuild relationships. The goal is to share each other's concerns, while trying to avoid conflict and confrontation." She looked to me. "How does that sound, Fox?"

I shrugged. "Good."

"Great. Evie and I have been working together in one-on-one sessions the last few weeks, and she's discovered some things about herself that she'd like to share with you. So why don't we start there?"

"Okay."

Eleanor and I both turned to give our attention to Evie. She chewed on her bottom lip before squeezing my hand and taking another big breath. "I had my first drink when I was nine."

My jaw fell open. It took a lot to shock me, but she'd thrown me for a loop.

"I know." She smiled sadly. "It's a lot to wrap your head around—even for me, looking back now, and I lived it. But I've been drinking ever since."

"I don't understand. You didn't drink when we first met."

"No, I just didn't let you see it. I don't let most people see it. I never did until recently."

"We've spent full weeks together in my off season, those times I traveled with you to competitions."

"Yep. And I always had a bottle in my bag, hidden. I'd drink in the bathroom when I had to. That's why I always had a candy in my mouth."

"You told me you had low blood sugar."

Evie shook her head and looked down.

"It's never been easy to talk to anyone about why I did it, but I think you might understand the pressures of being an athlete as much as I do. By the time I was seven, the rink had become my second home. At first, I loved it. People would stand on the sidelines and watch me practice, and I felt like I was on top of the world. I was nine when I entered my first big competition. I'd been a superstar at my local rink, practiced twenty hours of skating and ten hours of dancing every week." She paused, and her eyes went out of focus, like she was visualizing what came next. "I remember walking into that first competition and thinking I was the best and going to win." She shook her head. "I didn't even make the podium. It was devastating, a real eye opener. That night I struggled to sleep, feeling like all my hopes and dreams of someday making it to the Olympics were a joke. I'd watched my mom get pissed off or upset about things for years. Her way of dealing was to have a few drinks. So the next night, when I was still feeling awful, I waited until she was passed out and snuck a few sips from her bottle. It allowed me to forget that I'd lost the competition long enough to sleep. At first, I only drank when I lost. But eventually I used it to console myself after a bad practice, a guy blowing me off, or..." She shrugged. "Anything really."

"Jesus, Evie. I had no damn clue. I thought this was something new, that you were struggling because you didn't make the Olympic team."

"Well, I was, but it's not new."

"Does your mother know?"

She shrugged. "If she does, she's never said anything. But my father knows. He could pick out a drunk a mile away after living with my mother for a dozen years. He tried to help years ago, but I would never admit the truth. It's why I cut off our relationship. I didn't want to deal with it."

"He didn't stop talking to you when he got remarried and started a new family like you said?"

Evie looked down. "No."

Eleanor interrupted. "How does Evie sharing this revelation make you feel, Fox?"

I shook my head, still in shock. "I don't know. Stupid for not seeing it. Sad that she's been going through it alone for so long. Anger—toward her mother for not seeing that her nine-year-old was drinking." I looked up and met Evie's eyes. "Scared that it's much worse than I thought, and you might not be able to stay sober..."

Tears streamed down Evie's face. "I'm sorry. I'm sorry I'm such a mess."

Over the next hour, Evie did a lot of talking. Some of it really hurt, like when she admitted that she'd gone from feeling inadequate in skating to feeling like she wasn't enough for me. It wasn't true, but as she spoke about her lack of self-confidence, I realized she'd often sought reassurance from me, and I'd brushed it off as dumb. I didn't get that she truly had low self-confidence and felt like a failure and needed more from me. And I felt like a failure myself for not being able to see that the woman I lived with—the woman I was planning to marry—was an alcoholic.

When we finally came to a lull in Evie's confessions, Eleanor jumped in.

"I think this was a lot for one day—both for Evie to say and for you, Fox, to hear. I'm sure you need some time to absorb everything."

I nodded. "Yeah, definitely."

"Do you have questions for Evie? Or for me before we wrap things up for today?"

"Is she getting everything she needs here? It seems dumb to say it now, but I thought she was just coming in for alcohol addiction. It sounds like she has a lot of other stuff she needs to work through."

Eleanor smiled. "She has a whole team. I'm a psychologist, so I talk to Evie the most, but she also has an addiction counselor, a primary-care physician, and a psychiatrist on her team. Of course, there are various nurses and support staff, too. Everyone has a different role, but we work together."

"What's the difference between what a psychiatrist and a psychologist do?"

"That's a good question. People often confuse the roles, but the psychiatrist mainly treats by prescribing medications and a psychologist treats with behavioral and talk therapy."

I felt my brows pull tight. I looked to Evie. "So you're taking medication?"

She nodded. "Dr. Cudahy diagnosed me with clinical depression. She's prescribed antidepressants."

"So you come in for one addiction and the answer is to give you pills?"

Eleanor interrupted. "I understand how that can seem counterproductive. But often the reason people drink is because they're trying to self-medicate to calm an underlying mental-health issue that has gone untreated. One of our goals here is to get to the root cause of the drinking and treat that so the patient doesn't have to self-medicate in an abusive form."

That sounded like trading one vice for another to me. Or worse, the treatment for the underlying mental health issue failed, and the patient was now addicted to *two* vices. But I didn't know much about this shit. So I nodded. "Alright. I guess you know what you're doing."

CHAPTER 26
The Elephant in the Room
Josie

"Hey, sweetheart. What's shaking?"

I tucked my cell between my shoulder and my ear and leaned forward for one last brushstroke. "Hi, Opal. Not much. Just painting the inside of the kitchen cabinets. Nothing too exciting."

"Well, good. Then there's no reason you can't join us. I'm meeting some of the girls for dinner tonight. Elsie Wren is in town. She moved down to Florida to be near her daughter, but she comes up once or twice a year, and we try to get together. She lived a few houses down from your dad growing up. They were pretty good friends. Thought you might like to meet her."

Fox had texted a little while ago and asked if I had plans tonight, but I hadn't responded yet. Things had been off ever since our conversation Sunday morning, yet neither of us had spoken of the reason why. I'd felt like something was missing the last four days, not speaking to him or seeing him. It made me realize how deep I was already in, and I was terrified of falling any more when there wasn't a future for us. If four days felt like a lifetime, what would four months without seeing him feel like?

So it was good that Opal had called. She would give me the distraction I needed. "I'd love to join you. Thank you for thinking of me."

"Great. Seven at the Laurel Lake Inn. Gotta run before the boss gets back and finds me on the phone again. He was particularly grumpy after hearing me talk to my mother about menopause this morning."

I laughed. "I'll see you then."

After I hung up, I finished painting and washed the brushes. Then I shot off a quick response to Fox.

Josie: Sorry, I have plans tonight.

A response chimed before I could set my phone back down.

Fox: Are you upset with me?

Josie: Why would I be upset?

Fox: Because I fucked up Sunday.

I sighed.

Josie: You were only being honest. It is what it is.

Fox: Can I stop over later when you get home?

I needed to protect myself, even if I didn't want to.

Josie: I think I'll be too tired. Maybe another time.

Feeling glum, I tossed my cell on the table and decided to go out back and get some fresh air. The lake always brought me a sense of peace, and I really wanted to look for Daisy again. I'd checked every day since Sunday, and there had been no sign of her. This morning a cluster of ducks swam by, and I thought it might've been the group she'd joined, but I couldn't be sure. I only knew Daisy's markings.

After a while, with no sign of her again today, I gave up and went inside to get ready for dinner.

As I was about to leave, my cell phone rang. My pulse quickened, thinking it might be Fox. But it wasn't. Noah's name flashed on the screen. I ignored it, but after a minute it started ringing again. So I swiped to answer on speakerphone while starting the car.

"Hello?"

"Oh hey. I was expecting to go to voicemail again. I called a few minutes ago but you didn't pick up."

"Is something wrong?"

"No. I didn't leave a message the first time because I figured it would give me an excuse to call back. But then I realized that was stupid and you would probably never answer when you saw my name, so I called back to leave a voicemail." He paused. "It's good to hear your voice, Josie."

"What do you want, Noah?"

"Can I ask how you're doing first? I'm guessing once I've said what I called to say you're going to rush me off the phone."

He was right. I regretted picking up the phone and having to talk to him this much already. "I'm fine. What's up?"

Noah sighed. "I got an email reminder about the vacation we have booked next month—to Aruba."

I'd forgotten all about that trip. "What about it?"

"It's non-refundable."

Other than being glad he'd been the one to put down the deposit, I wasn't sure what he expected of me. "Okay..."

"I was hoping maybe we could still go. As friends. It would give us a chance to talk things through. We have a suite with a living room, so I could sleep on the couch, if you wanted."

Is he serious? "There's nothing to talk about, Noah."

"We've never even had a civilized conversation about what happened."

"You cheated on me. I caught you with your dick in a woman's mouth. There's nothing more to discuss."

"I made a mistake. A big one. I miss you, Jos. Can't we talk about it? I'll do whatever you want to get you to forgive me."

"It's not about forgiveness, Noah. It's about trust."

"We can rebuild it."

"No. We can't. Trust is fragile, like a mirror. Once it's broken, it's shattered. Even if you put all the pieces back together, you always see the cracks. It's never the same. Besides, I've learned a lot about myself over the last few months. And I don't think we were as good of a fit as I made myself believe."

"That's not true. We were perfect together."

It made sense that Noah thought that. I'd never given him any indication that I wasn't happy before that night in the hospital parking lot. And truthfully, I'd thought I was happy too. But being in therapy and spending time with a man who asked me what I wanted had made me realize I was selling myself short. In a weird way, I was grateful Noah had cheated. Otherwise, I might have settled.

"I have to run. You should use the trip. Go by yourself and do some reflecting."

"I'm not going without you. I'd be miserable. You can go alone, if you want. I still have your passport. You left it here when I was booking everything."

I shook my head. "I'm not going to go either, Noah. But I do need my passport."

"I'll mail it to you, with the itinerary for the trip, in case you change your mind."

"I'm not home."

"I know. You still share your location with me on your iPhone. You don't know how many times I've been tempted to get in the car and drive down to Forty-Six Rosewood Lane to talk to you."

Oh gosh. I'd obviously given him that access during better times. Now I felt almost violated. I knew what I'd be doing the minute I hung up. "I gotta run, Noah."

"Can I call you again?"

"I'm sorry. I'd rather you didn't."

Not surprising, Noah hung up without saying goodbye after that. He was never tolerant when he didn't get his way. It was probably only a matter of time before he started to angry spew, so it was for the best. Plus, I needed to get on the road or I'd be late. Though it would have to wait another minute or two—until I figured out how to stop Noah from seeing my location.

◦ ◦ ◦

"There she is!" Opal engulfed me in a hug the minute the hostess brought me to the table. It was only one minute after seven, but I was the last to arrive. "Let me make the introductions. You already met Bettina at her twin sister Bernadette's house party. And Frannie here works at the post office, so you know her."

I nodded to both of them. "Hi. It's good to see you."

Opal motioned to the last person at the table—the only face I didn't recognize. "And this here is Elsie Wren."

The woman stood and extended her hand. "Lovely to meet you. Your father was a dear friend of mine. I was very sad to hear about his passing."

247

"Thank you."

As soon as we sat, the waiter brought over a bottle of wine. Opal looked to me. "We ordered a merlot. Is that okay with you? If not, they have others by the glass."

"Merlot is great. Thank you."

Opal leaned over and whispered, "Heard you had some wine this weekend?"

I was pretty shocked that Fox would share that we went away together. When she saw my face, she cackled.

"No, the big galoot didn't tell me. Porter started dating a schoolteacher recently. Rita—as in Rita's Beanery and Bettina here's little sister—happens to live next door to the woman. Porter told the teacher who told Rita who told Bernadette who told Bettina who told me." She shook her head. "I can't believe Porter kept it a secret from me. But anywho..." She patted my hand. "I'm happy for you. Fox is a pain in my ass, but he's a good, loyal man. I love the grumpy butthead. But don't you go telling him that."

I laughed. "I won't."

Bettina grabbed a breadstick from the middle of the table and waved it at me. "Did your father ever stop pulling his pants down? I forgot all about him and Tommy Miller's shenanigans until Elsie just reminded me."

"Stop...pulling his pants down?" I said.

Elsie chuckled. "When they were about ten, your father and Tommy made a contest out of mooning each other when the other least expected it. Tommy would knock on Henry's door, and Henry would answer by pressing his butt cheeks up against the storm door. Or Henry would be riding his bicycle behind Tommy, and Tommy would drop his shorts and flash him where the sun don't shine. It went on for years."

"I definitely never heard about any mooning before."

"This one time, half the girls in our grade saw your daddy's backside. Henry was in the marching band. When it rained, they would practice in the auditorium on the stage. Tommy didn't play an instrument, but those boys were connected at the hip. So Tommy did the stage lighting and worked the curtains and stuff. One afternoon, Henry thought it would be funny if he was bent over on the stage when Tommy opened the curtains to get ready for practice. He hadn't anticipated that the girls' soccer team would walk into the room right before Tommy drew the curtains. *With* their coach."

Everyone laughed, and it set the mood for the next hour. Elsie had a million funny stories to share, but the others all interjected little bits and pieces along the way. It made me envious of how they'd gotten to grow up. Sure, people were in each other's business, but the upside of that was the community felt like one big family. It was the polar opposite of how I'd been raised—going to private school where people were too busy with things like cello lessons and fencing competitions to get to know each other. My sterile house where only the nanny was ever home lacked the warmth the people of Laurel Lake exuded when talking about their childhood. It made me question how I'd want to raise my own kids someday, something I'd never given any real thought.

We were in the middle of ordering dessert when Opal elbowed me. She lifted her chin toward the hostess stand. "Look what the cat dragged in. And it's not even Tuesday..."

I looked across the room, and my heart skipped a beat. All eyes at our table joined me in looking at the man talking to the hostess.

Fox glanced up, probably feeling ten eyes burning into him. He locked gazes with me and smiled. But the corners of his lips quickly fell when he took in the other people at my table. He shook his head and closed his eyes.

"You better not be trying to pretend you don't see us!" Opal yelled across the restaurant.

For a second, I thought Fox might make a run for it. But after he finished talking to the hostess, he walked over. The look on his face was something I might expect when a man walked to take his place in front of a firing squad. He did *not* look thrilled.

"What are you doing here?" Opal asked. "Last time I looked, it was Thursday. Pork tenderloin is your Tuesday meal."

Fox's eyes slid to me. "Came to get a piece of cheesecake, since I can't bake one for shit."

"You don't eat sweets."

I smiled, touched that he'd remembered what I'd told him about my dad using his homemade cheesecake as a peace offering. I wiggled my fingers. "Hi."

We shared a wordless smile, and a minute later the hostess walked over with a brown paper bag.

"Here you go, Fox."

"Thanks, Syl."

Fox didn't seem to know how to handle himself in front of the crew I was seated with. He was uncharacteristically awkward, which I found endearing. He nodded toward the door. "Can I talk to you for a minute?"

"Sure." I put my napkin on the table and looked to four beaming women. "Excuse me. I'll be right back."

Fox and I walked into the empty lobby. Once we were out of sight, I pointed my eyes to the bag in his hand. "Hankering?"

He shoved his empty hand into his pocket and looked down. "I was hoping to bring it over when you got home later, if it's not too late. I owe you an apology."

I wanted nothing more than to spend some time with him. A few days had felt like forever. But I also recognized that a quick fix now would only make breaking the addiction harder in the long run.

I smiled sadly. "Fox, you don't have anything to be sorry about. You didn't do anything wrong. You've been clear since the first time we met that you weren't looking for more than what we had. And quite honestly, it was the absolute last thing I was looking for, too."

Fox's eyes seared into mine. "Sometimes what you're looking for comes when you're not looking at all."

It was like someone took a bicycle pump to my deflated heart and pumped it back up again. Hope bloomed inside my chest. Though there was still fear there, plenty of it, and I needed what he meant spelled out. "What are you saying?"

Fox reached for my hand and lifted it to his lips for a kiss. "Text me when you get in. Let's talk without an audience."

I hadn't thought we had one, but Fox lifted his chin causing me to turn. All four of my dinner companions were out of their chairs, leaning to one side of the table to spy into the lobby. One head on top of another, they looked like a totem pole. Seeing us turn and catch them, they all scurried back to their seats. I couldn't help but laugh.

"I shouldn't be too much longer. We're finished with dinner."

Fox nodded. "Safe drive."

CHAPTER 27

You Are My Sunshine

Fox

I was sitting on Josie's front porch when she pulled into the driveway.

Almost an hour had passed since I got back from the Laurel Lake Inn, and I'd grown impatient sitting at home. I also wanted to make sure she didn't change her mind and blow me off.

I stood as she got out of the car and lifted the bottle of wine in my hand. "Brought something to wash down the cheesecake with."

She smiled, and the miserable mood I'd been in for the last few days was forgotten. When I wasn't around her, it felt like every day was gray and cloudy. She made the sky blue and the sun shine, and I didn't want to think about what that meant anymore. I just wanted to bask in the warmth.

Josie opened the door and tossed her keys on the counter as I followed her in. All of the cabinets were open, and the kitchen smelled like paint.

"You do that yourself?"

She nodded. "The wood was all chipped inside, and there were stains on the shelves."

I glanced around. "It looks good. The place has come a long way. Your flooring should be in next week."

"Oh great. Thank you."

The wine and cheesecake were still in my hands. Josie pointed her eyes to the bag. "I skipped dessert at the restaurant to save room for that. Are you going to share it? Because it looks like you might not want to."

"Grab two forks, wiseass."

I opened the wine while she took down glasses and kicked off her shoes. I'd told her I brought wine to wash down the cheesecake, but I needed it to settle my nerves. I rarely drank more than a glass of wine or beer, but tonight I might make an exception. It was time to come clean with her on some shit I hadn't talked about in a long time.

Josie set the dessert between us and scooped a spoonful between her sexy lips. When she shut her eyes to savor the taste, I had to conjure up a picture of my grandmother to keep myself in check.

"Mmm... Try some," she said. "It's delicious."

"I will. In a minute." I took a long pull from my wine glass. "Listen, Jos. I had a great time this weekend. I didn't mean to ruin it with what I said about our future."

Josie set down her fork. "Can we even have one? I got upset with you for not considering it was possible. But realistically, what would that look like for us? I know you have no desire to ever leave Laurel Lake."

"That's not the problem. We could figure that shit out."

"It's not?"

I shook my head.

"Then what is?"

I took a deep breath. Vulnerability didn't come easy to me. Josie must've sensed it.

She reached across the table and took my hand. "Talk to me. What is it?"

My other hand squeezed the wine glass. I had to make a conscious effort to relax or I'd be heading to the ER for stitches in my palm. But I had so much suppressed anger and guilt. Instead, I finished off the wine and refilled.

Josie squeezed my hand. "Whatever it is, I'm sure it's not as bad as you think."

I looked her in the eyes. "I've lost two people that I loved."

"Your brother and your fiancée?"

I nodded.

"I pulled back from people after my father died," she said. "I understand it's scary to get close after losing loved ones."

I swallowed. "It's more than that."

She shook her head. "What is it then?"

"Both were my fault. If I'd been a better brother, a better boyfriend..."

Josie touched her chest, and her eyes filled with tears. "No. You can't do that, Fox. You can't carry the responsibility of someone's death. Trust me, I did it, and I wound up in a very bad place. Do you know how many times I beat myself up? Why aren't I a better scientist? Why didn't I check for negative reactions against old vaccines? The one thing I learned from therapy is that guilt can either hold you back or teach you a lesson. It's a choice only you can make. It's not healthy to carry it with you. Guilt is like nourishment to a storm. The more you feed it, the stronger and more destructive it grows. Please don't let it hold you back. Don't let it keep you from being happy. Even if that's not with me, Fox."

"You're the first thing that's made me happy in a long time."

Tears spilled over and tracked down Josie's cheeks. I wiped them away. I wasn't sure if it was seeing Josie upset or telling her why I'd shut down, but it felt like I'd torn a hole in my chest and bent back my ribs, leaving my heart beating under a giant open wound.

Josie got up from her chair and sat on my lap. She cupped my cheeks between her hands. "Take a chance. Take a chance with me."

I shook my head. "I don't deserve another chance. I don't deserve you."

"Oh, Fox. Don't say that. You're a beautiful man, inside as much as outside. You make me happy. I want to do the same for you. You said you like simple. Well, it's as simple as this: Let me. And we'll see if we can work."

I swallowed and tasted salt. Deserving or not, this woman was all I wanted. "I don't know what tomorrow looks like, Jos."

"Who does? For the first time in my life, I want to do what feels right, what I want—not what I'm supposed to do or what might please someone else. Laurel Lake gave me that clarity. *You* gave me that clarity. I have no idea what the future looks like, but it feels like you're worth taking a chance and figuring it out."

I closed my eyes and nodded. When I opened them, the guilt didn't disappear, but it seemed a little lighter. I'd also done enough talking for one night. With my mouth, that is. Well, unless my mouth was on this woman. "Can you forgive me for being an asshole?"

"*Clearly.* Since you're an asshole most of the time."

Cradling Josie in my arms, I stood. She yelped, but the smile was back on her face.

"What are you doing?"

"Gonna finish my apology...inside of you."

CHAPTER 28
More Apologies, Please
Josie

The man knew how to apologize, that was for sure.

Fox slid down my body, draping my legs over his shoulders. His hands slipped under my ass, and he lifted as he lowered his head. He didn't start with a gentle flutter or tease, he dove in with his full face.

Oh God.

He sucked and licked, the scruff on his cheeks and chin scraping against my sensitive flesh turning me on more than I ever thought something like that would. He alternated between long strokes with a flattened tongue and tunneling into me. It was *nothing* like I'd ever felt before. I'd had men go down on me, but this...this was *eating me out*. I usually found the term kind of cringy, but I clearly hadn't understood how it differed from *plain old oral sex* until now.

My back arched from the bed. Fox reached up and held me down. I was on the edge already, and we'd barely started. His tongue lapped at my arousal as my fingers threaded into his thick hair. When he sucked hard on my clit, I couldn't control how roughly I yanked the strands.

"*Fox!*" My breath shook.

"That's it, baby. Come on my tongue. You taste so good..."

My body started to vibrate from the inside out. I moaned his name, and Fox responded by slipping two fingers inside me. He pumped in and out once...twice... On the third time he sucked my clit into his mouth and did some magical swirl, and I exploded. My orgasm packed a punch so hard that I saw nothing but stars as it washed over me.

By the time I could see again, Fox was on the move. He hovered over me, one arm on either side of my head, bearing his weight.

"You good?"

I hadn't caught my breath yet, so I nodded.

"Need you. Now."

He aligned his swollen head with my opening and leaned down to gently kiss my lips.

"I want to watch your face while I sink inside of you. That okay?"

"Yes."

I braced myself for what would come next, expecting the ferociousness to continue, but Fox once again surprised me. He took his time, slowly entering me. This felt different from the other times we'd been together, even from five minutes ago. It was more intimate, more loving. The way he looked at me made me feel like we were the only two people in the world. There was a reason for that— Fox and I had never done it missionary style. As he gazed into my eyes, I realized he was making love to me for the first time. It made my eyes well up.

He glided in and out slowly, moving with purpose and rhythm. His eyes brimmed with the emotions I felt, deep inside my chest. We stayed that way for a long time, connected mind, body, and soul, as our orgasms built. I never wanted the euphoric moment to end. But eventually, Fox's face grew strained, and his thrusts grew harder and faster. The sounds of our wet bodies slapping against each other echoed around the room. All of my senses were filled with this man, consumed by this man, as my orgasm rushed over me.

"Fox..."

He kept going, his jaw rigid as he strained to hold on. "So fucking beautiful."

Somehow he managed to maintain as my body convulsed around him. Only when the last wave of my ecstasy started to ebb, did Fox let go. Feeling the heat of him seep inside me had my body trembling with aftershock.

He continued to glide in and out of me leisurely.

I grinned up at him. "Wow. Fox Cassidy does slow and sweet."

He smiled. "Don't spread the word around town."

"Your secret's safe with me." I stroked his cheek. "Thank you for opening up to me tonight."

Fox nodded and kissed my lips. "It's been a while. Have patience with me."

"I will."

His eyes searched my face.

"What?" I asked.

He smiled. "Wondering how I got so lucky."

Hope bloomed wild in my chest. Maybe, just maybe, my luck would be better this time, too.

◦ ◦ ◦

The following morning, my phone rang a little while after Fox had left for work. I was sitting on the grass in the yard, looking for Daisy, and I smiled seeing Nilda's name on the screen.

"Hi," I answered. "I've been meaning to call you."

"How are you, sweetheart?"

I sighed. "Really good, actually."

"That's wonderful to hear. Laurel Lake might've been just the medicine you needed."

I couldn't agree more. "It's a pretty amazing place."

"That sounds like you might not be coming back?"

My eyes drifted to the house next door. Could I live here? I loved the feel of being in a small town, where you stop in for coffee or at the home-improvement store and people know you by name. Sure, there was a downside to that—like everyone in your business—but that didn't bother me as much as it did Fox. Because none of it was done with malice. Plus, I doubted there was a pharmaceutical company for hundreds of miles, maybe more. Though since everything happened at work, I'd been kicking around moving into academia. I'd been a TA in college and grad school and had really enjoyed teaching classes. In fact, once I'd mentioned maybe doing that instead of research. But my mother had been appalled. *"Universities don't pay professors like big pharma does,"* she'd said. *"You'll be living in that one-bedroom apartment forever."*

"I don't know what I'm doing," I said. "But...I've met someone."

"Oh? Tell me more."

I laid back on the grass and shut my eyes. "Well, he's grumpy, hotheaded, hates change, and is probably the last person I would've ever thought I'd be a good match with."

"I'm hoping there's more to this description, honey..."

I laughed. "There is. While he's all those things, he's also thoughtful, protective, generous, respectful, and fiercely loyal."

"Those qualities sound a lot better."

"He's also tall, broad, and devastatingly handsome."

"Now you're talking. You should have led with those. I like tall. Keep going..."

I chuckled. "Fox is really hard to explain. He used to be a professional hockey player, and now he owns a construction company. He's exactly what you would picture when I say that—rugged and tough. Neither of us was looking for someone. I think it's pretty safe to say Fox was *fighting* finding someone."

"Do you think you'll stay down there?"

"I don't know. Things are so new. I haven't had time to give it any serious consideration. But I have to be back at work in three weeks. Kolax and Hahm are growing impatient, and I've maxed out my leave."

"Would this Fox ever consider moving to New York?"

I laughed out loud. "Definitely not. He'd be miserable."

"You have a lot to think about, then. But you sound happy. How has your sleep been?"

"I can't remember the last time I slept so well."

"Probably all that fresh air."

Or the orgasms. So much better than Ambien. "Maybe. But tell me about you. How are you feeling?"

Nilda and I talked for another ten minutes. After we caught up, she broached the subject she always did. "Have you spoken to your mother?"

"Not recently. How is she?"

"She's doing well. You should give her a call. Maybe tell her about this new guy you're seeing."

That would definitely not be happening. "She would hate the thought of me spending time down here and dating a guy who does construction instead of neurosurgery. I think I'll pass on that."

"She misses you."

Nilda meant well, so I didn't argue.

"Before we hang up," she said. "I need to talk to you about something. I've been putting it off, hoping to talk to you in person when you get back, but I'm afraid that's not going to work out."

That sounded ominous. "What's going on?"

"I'm moving, honey."

"Moving? You mean you aren't going to live with Mom anymore?"

"No, sweetheart. I mean I'm moving to South Carolina. My sister Bessy doesn't walk so well anymore, and I want to be closer to help out. Plus, the weather's nicer, and I'm getting old."

I sat up, feeling my chest grow tight. Nilda was in her late sixties now, but I was selfish when it came to her. "Oh my God, Nilda. You've been with me since I was a baby."

"I know, sweetheart. But you don't need to be taken care of anymore, and it's time."

"When are you leaving?"

"In a few weeks."

The skin on my chest felt hot and itchy. No doubt I'd have a rash soon. I rubbed it. "I don't know what to say. I can't imagine my life without you."

"Your life will never be without me, not as long as I'm breathing. You'll come visit me, and I'll come visit you. Charleston is only a few hours from Laurel Lake. If you wind up moving down there, we'll be closer than if I was here with your mom."

I sighed. "Does Mom already know?"

"She does. I gave her a few months' notice. It just never seemed like the right time to tell you."

"I'm sorry I don't sound happy. I promise I will be. Just give me a little time to digest it. You're my everything, Nilda."

"And you're mine, too, sweetheart. None of that is going to change. This is going to be good. For both of us."

It sure as hell didn't feel good at the moment, but I knew she was right. If my mom called and told me she was moving to Australia, I wouldn't have been this upset. Nilda was the one person in the world who was always there for me. She was my rock.

"I'll call you in a day or two. Okay?" I told her.

"I look forward to it."

I sat on the lawn, staring out at the lake for the better part of an hour after we hung up, remembering all the good times I'd had with Nilda. After my little pity party was over, I texted her.

Josie: I'm sorry about how I acted. I'm happy for you. Really, I am.

As usual, she took hours to respond. Nilda only checked her phone a few times a day. She kept it turned off in her purse, because she didn't want the battery to die.

Nilda: Thank you. Family is in your heart, so you'll never be far from me, no matter where we are.

I smiled, feeling genuinely happy for her now.

Josie: I love you, Nilda.

Nilda: I love you, too. Maybe we'll both be moving on soon. New beginnings don't always have to come from painful endings.

CHAPTER 29
The Lake
Josie

Professor job openings near Laurel Lake.

Nine days later, I found myself on Google, typing in words I couldn't believe I was typing on an early Sunday morning. But after the incredible week Fox and I'd had, I was starting to think about the possibilities. What was keeping me tied to New York now anyway? Six months ago, I would have said my fiancé, Nilda, and my career. But with Noah out of my life and Nilda moving, the only real tether I had was my job. And even that I was no longer certain was right for me. I had a few good friends, but they either worked a lot like me or were starting a family. Even my best friend, Chloe, who still lived near my mom's house in New Jersey, I didn't see more than once or twice a year. Sometimes I went out for happy hour with colleagues from work, or a friend from my building, but none of those people kept me anchored to New York.

I sipped my coffee and scrolled through the search results. Halfway down the first page, after an absurd amount of ads for online colleges, was a link to Rehnquist University. They had a pharmacology program, so I clicked and maneuvered to the school's job openings page. I scrolled to almost the end, stopping when I found an interesting post: *Adjunct Professor of Pharmacological Sciences (Tenure Track)*. Reading the description, the position required candidates to have an MD or PhD, along with three years of research experience. It started in the fall, and there was still almost two weeks until the deadline to apply.

I stared at the screen for a long time. But when I heard footsteps coming down the stairs, I promptly shut my laptop. Fox had been in the shower.

He walked over and kissed the top of my head before motioning to my Mac. "Something you don't want me to see?"

"Uh, no. I was just looking at a job posting."

Fox walked to the coffeemaker and opened the cabinet above it. He looked over at the mug in my hands. "You need a refill?"

"No, I'm good."

He went about fixing his coffee, then sat down across from me at the table and raised his mug to his lips. "You're changing jobs?"

I shrugged. "I'm not sure. It's something I've been thinking about."

"Because of what happened?"

"No. Well, not entirely, I guess. I'm good at what I do, and I make a great salary, but I think there are other careers that might be more fulfilling. Ones with less stress, too."

"Is there something specific you think you'd like better?"

"I've always toyed with the idea of teaching, being a professor. I was a TA for organic chemistry in college. It's a subject most students really struggle with, so they resort to memorization rather than actually learning the subject. I loved when I was able to get students to dive in with me and fall in love with science."

Fox smirked.

"What?"

"I would've tried to fuck you in college, if you were my TA."

I chuckled. "Anyway, it's just something I'm thinking about."

"Where was the position you were looking at?"

Shit. Fox and I had definitely moved into relationship territory, but I wasn't sure how he'd react to me looking at jobs down here. So I told a little white lie. "I'm not sure. I was mostly looking at the requirements."

Fox looked at me over his mug as he sipped. From the way his eyes squinted, I got the feeling maybe he'd seen the website. But if he had, he didn't say so.

A few minutes later, he set his mug in the sink. "I'm going to take a ride over to Lowell's to pick up some new base moldings. The old ones are shit and don't go with the new floor."

Fox had spent his entire Saturday installing new flooring in my kitchen and living room. Well, technically not the entire day since we'd wound up having sex when he was halfway through. But I didn't want him to spend Sunday working, too. He needed a break.

"You've done enough. You need at least one day of rest."

"Won't take long. Two or three hours, at most."

"Alright, but I'm helping, and I'll take the ride with you."

"You wanted to take a walk around the lake to look for Daisy. Why don't you do that while I'm gone getting supplies? It's gonna be hot today, so you're better off doing that early."

I had wanted to look for her. I'd picked up a pair of binoculars earlier in the week and thought she might be near the state park, across the lake, but I wasn't sure. Opal had told me about a trail on the other side that ran along the water. "You don't mind?"

"Not at all."

"Alright then." I pointed out the back windows, to the lake beyond. "Do you know where the trail starts on the other side?"

He nodded. "It's on my way. I'll drop you."

Twenty minutes later, I hopped down from Fox's truck. I had my hand on the door to close it when he stopped me.

"Hey. Hang on a second."

"Yeah?"

"Rehnquist is a good school, about a twenty-five-minute drive." We locked eyes, and he smiled. "Knowing you, you'll be doing some deep thinking while you're walking on that trail. I think you'd like it down here. I know I'd like you down here."

My heart went pitter-patter as I smiled back. "Okay."

○ ○ ○

That evening, Fox walked up behind me while I stood at the lake's edge. After my walk, I'd spent a few hours painting outside, using the supplies Porter had dropped off weeks ago. My half-finished handiwork was drying in the sun. He wrapped his hands around my waist, locking them in front.

"Wow. You're good."

"Not really. But I forgot how much I enjoy painting nature. I haven't done it since college. My mom's house is on a beautiful piece of property. I used to like to sit outside and paint the trees and stuff. I find it peaceful. Lets my brain unwind."

He kissed the top of my head. "You should do it more often."

I turned in his arms and clasped my hands around his neck. "I think I will. I don't know what it is about this place, but I feel like it's reminding me of who I used to be."

"Maybe you should stick around."

I pushed up on my tippy-toes and planted a kiss on his lips. "Maybe I will."

A duck quacked behind us, so I twisted around to look at the lake. But it wasn't my little buddy. I frowned. "I'm worried something happened to Daisy."

"Like what?"

"I don't know. What if her wound opened up again and she got an infection, or she was attacked by a bear?"

"I've never seen a bear around here. Maybe a coyote, though."

My eyes widened. "You think a coyote ate her? They sense when another animal is injured and easy prey."

"Didn't say that. Was just telling you who the natural threats to ducks are locally. I'm sure he's fine."

"I think I'm going to go out on the lake and look for her. Earlier I saw ducks hanging out on that island in the middle. Maybe she's there and she's injured. Would you come with me on your kayak?"

"I don't think that's a good idea."

"Why not?"

Fox looked over at his yard, to the water's edge. His face was serious. "It's dangerous."

My brows shot to my hairline. "To kayak? I can swim, you know."

When he didn't respond, something dawned on me. "Oh my God. Do you not swim? Is that why you never go in the lake?"

"I can swim."

"Are you nervous because it's going to get dark soon?"

"Just...I'll go take a look at the island and see if the duck is there. Alright?"

"Is it only a one-person kayak?"

"No."

"Then come on..." I walked toward Fox's yard. "The island isn't far. We'll be back in twenty minutes."

At the water's edge, I turned to ask where the paddles were kept and realized Fox hadn't moved. I laughed. "Are you coming or not?"

He didn't look too happy about it, but eventually he walked over. He wiped away a few cobwebs and lifted the kayak off the wooden stand.

"Paddles are under the back deck," he grumbled.

"Okay! I'll get them while you put that in the water."

I jogged to the deck and ducked under, grabbing the paddles off the top of a pile of water stuff I hadn't realized was under here. "You have a floating mat and paddleboards?" I said, walking back. "Why don't you ever use that stuff? I've never tried a stand-up paddleboard. I bet it's great exercise."

Fox took a paddle from my hand. "Get in, and I'll push us off."

I took off my socks and shoes and left them on the dock. "Alright, thanks."

Once I was seated, Fox climbed in. The narrow boat rocked back and forth a few times, which I thought was funny. Fox, not so much. He had such a serious look on his face as he started to paddle. We'd made it about thirty feet from shore when I realized my feet were getting wet.

"Was there water in here when you put the kayak in?"

Fox looked down. "What the fuck?"

Water was coming in from somewhere, and my end seemed to be floating lower. Not to mention, my feet were almost covered now. I leaned up to look at the floor behind me. "Oh shit. There's a hole under this seat cushion!"

Fox started to paddle fast, attempting to turn the kayak around and head back to shore. But the hunk of plastic wasn't going anywhere but down. The lake quickly filled up the hole we were seated on, and my side tilted down.

I stood, wobbling. "I think we need to abandon ship."

Fox wrapped an arm around me, and we jumped from the sinking kayak together. He didn't let go as he swam toward the shore.

"Fox, I'm fine! I can swim on my own."

But he kept going, like he was a lifeguard and I was a drowning swimmer. The entire scene was pretty comical. He didn't even let go a few strokes later, when I told him I could feel the bottom under my feet. After a few minutes more, we were back at the shore, and Fox finally released the death grip he'd had on me. Our clothes were soaked as we climbed to our feet, and I couldn't help but laugh because—hell, it was funny.

"I'm going to call you Mitch from *Baywatch*," I said.

"It's not funny."

"Seriously?" I bunched up the hem of my shirt and twisted, wringing it out. "It *so* is."

Fox looked me up and down. "You okay?"

"I'm fine." I laughed. "Maybe a fractured rib from your death-grip rescue, but otherwise I'm all good."

"Sorry." He frowned. "I'm going to change." He didn't wait for me to respond before turning toward his house.

I yelled after him, still laughing. "I was joking. My ribs are fine. Come over when you're done. I'll put dinner in the oven."

I figured Fox's grumpy mood would be cured once I put the food I'd made earlier today in front of him. When I was at the Laurel Lake Inn with Opal last week, I'd mentioned that I'd love the recipe for the pork Fox loved so much. Not long after, she'd disappeared for a few minutes and came back with a sticky note and winked. Apparently, her sister's best friend's husband worked in the kitchen, so all she had to do was ask.

I put the roast into the oven and hopped in the shower. But when an hour passed and Fox still hadn't come over, I texted him.

Josie: Hey. Dinner will be ready in about forty-five minutes.

I waited a few minutes, but no return text came in. In fact, my message didn't even show as read. When the alarm I'd set for the roast went off forty-five minutes later, I took it out of the oven and picked up the phone to call Fox. Could he have fallen asleep? Or shoot—maybe his phone had been in his pocket when we jumped into the lake and now it was dead. His phone rang and rang, eventually going to voicemail.

I bet it was in his pocket. That must be it.

So I slipped on my shoes and walked out the front door. But I stopped short when I realized Fox's pickup truck wasn't in his driveway anymore.

Where the heck did he disappear to?

CHAPTER 30

Drunk on Love
Josie

"Hello?" I answered on the first ring.

"Hi, honey. It's Opal. Any chance you know where the boss is?"

My shoulders slumped. "No. I was actually hoping you were him. I don't think he came home last night."

"Where'd he go?"

I shook my head. "I have no idea. He didn't say. I've texted him a few times, but he hasn't answered. I think his phone might have broken."

"He was supposed to meet the fire chief this morning for a final inspection at the school. It's not like him to blow off something like that."

I'd grown more and more worried every hour since the first text I'd sent Fox had gone unanswered. But now I was really freaking out. "I'm nervous something might've happened to him."

"When did you last see him?"

"About seven. He was kind of grumpy when he left, but he knew I'd made dinner."

"Did you two have a fight?"

"Not really. He was kind of annoyed with me. I wanted to go look for a duck that we found injured on the lake a few weeks back, and he didn't. But I wouldn't say we had a fight." I shrugged. "At least I didn't think we did. But you know how Fox is; he doesn't say too much. Maybe he was more pissed than I thought."

"The man does have a temper. He probably just needed to blow off some steam."

"Maybe…" Though I didn't feel like that was it.

"I'll make some calls. I'm sure he'll turn up soon. Don't you worry, honey."

"Will you call me back if you find out anything?"

"Sure thing."

I'd barely slept all night, waiting for him to come home. Around two, I'd gone upstairs to bed, but I'd left the window open so I could hear if his truck came back. I'd doze for a few minutes, then worry I'd missed the sound of him pulling in and have to get up and look out the window.

There was no way I could sit around here waiting any longer. I needed to *do* something. So I grabbed my purse and decided to drive around. Laurel Lake wasn't that large, and his big truck was easy enough to spot.

I started in town, slowly driving by the Beanery, the bank, and all of the little stores on the three-block-long Main Street. There was a municipal lot a block off Main, so I checked there, too. Then I hit the home-improvement store, the tile showroom, and a few restaurants on the outskirts of town before driving to the ice rink. But I came up empty everywhere. I knew he'd picked up some supplies recently about a half hour away at a place called Wolfson's, so I googled where that was and got on the highway. I drove around for at least two hours before my cell rang.

"Hey, honey. It's Opal. We found him."

I let out a shaky breath. "Oh thank God. Is he okay?"

"He's fine. Probably gonna have one hell of a headache and need to sleep most of today, but he'll be fine."

"What happened?"

"He tied one on pretty good and got into a fight. Well, if you can call it that. When a tree trunk of a man like Fox Cassidy hits you, there is no fight. You go down for the count. But that's what happened. Someone called an ambulance, and the police came. The other guy was fine, but they arrested Fox for assault. Sheriff said he tossed him in the drunk tank to sleep it off. Porter just went to bail his ass out, since I got the fire chief to come back and meet me for the inspection that still needs to be done."

"I can't believe that. Fox barely drinks."

"Probably what made it so easy to tie one on."

I sighed. "Is there anything I can do?"

"No, it's all good. Depending on whether Fox is sober enough to drive, Porter will either drop him at his car or give him a lift home when he's out."

"Alright. Thank you for calling, Opal."

"No problem. You have a good rest of your day."

I wasn't sure that was going to happen. Obviously Fox was more pissed at me than I'd thought. But I didn't understand why. I drove back to the house, trying to figure out what would've made him so upset that he would blow me off and go out drinking without a word. It didn't seem like something Fox would do.

Did the kayak have sentimental value to him, and he was pissed that it sank to the bottom of the lake?

Did he really think he'd needed to save me and was upset that I hadn't taken the whole thing more seriously?

Could he have been pissed that I'd forced him to go with me and then he'd wound up soaked and swimming back to shore?

I supposed any of those could've been the reason, yet none of them felt right. To me, the strangest part of the entire thing was Fox disappearing. He was the type of man who dealt with things head-on, rather than taking off and avoiding an argument. While I was relieved he was okay—I'd been thinking the worst there for a while—an uneasy feeling sat in the pit of my stomach for the next several hours.

Around noon, I went to use the bathroom. When I came back, Porter's truck was next door in the driveway. He walked out of Fox's house just as I made it to the front door.

Porter pulled the door shut behind him and headed my way. "Had to pull over twice on the drive home from the courthouse so he could puke his guts up. He's going to feel like shit today. Maybe tomorrow, too. But he'll be fine."

"What the heck happened?"

"Sheriff said he got called to the Crow's Nest at two AM. Bartender had cut Fox off at twelve thirty. Fox got pissed and tried to reach over the bar and take a swing at him, but he lost his balance and fell off the stool. A couple of locals helped him up and over to a booth. Fox conked out for a little while. They woke him up when it was almost closing time, figuring they would put him in a cab home. But when he got up, he started a fight with Ray Langone."

"My uncle?"

"Bartender said Ray didn't say a word to him. Fox just stumbled over from the booth, and when he saw Ray, he clocked him."

"Is Ray okay?"

Porter nodded. "Sheriff said he'll have a good shiner, but drunks never seem to get hurt too bad."

I shook my head. "I can't believe it. I don't even know what set him off."

"You two have a fight or something?"

"Not really. At least I didn't think we did. We had a really great weekend. About seven last night, I wanted to go look for a duck that got injured a while back. I thought she might be on the little island in the middle of the lake. Anyway, Fox definitely didn't want to go with me, but he did. We went out on his kayak, and about thirty feet out, it started to take on water. The kayak sank, and we swam back. I thought it was funny, but Fox seemed upset by the whole thing. We were never at risk for drowning or anything, so I don't know why he would be so shaken."

"Oh shit." Porter nodded. "Well, it makes sense now."

"What makes sense?"

"Fox hasn't gone in that lake for years."

"I noticed that, but why not?"

"You don't know?"

"Know what?"

"How his fiancée died?"

"I thought she died in an accident?"

"She did." He pointed toward the yard. "On that lake."

CHAPTER 31
A Lifetime Ago
Fox

Three-and-a-half years ago

I'd missed my early-morning flight on purpose.

I'd been in Minnesota for two days for an off-season appearance with a bunch of my teammates at a charity event, one of the things I was normally anxious to get back home from. Though not this time, not after talking to a slurring Evie last night.

I rolled over in bed and grabbed my buzzing phone from the nightstand without opening my eyes. I knew it was safe to swipe without checking the screen because there was no way in hell Evie would be out of bed before late this afternoon.

A ray of sun slashed across my face. I threw an arm across my eyes to block it and brought my cell to my ear.

"Hello?"

"Cassidy? It's Will."

My agent. I sat up and cleared my throat. Will Koker was as much of a conversationalist as I was, which was one of the things I liked about him. He got to the point. But that also meant when he called, he had a point to make.

"What's going on?" I asked.

"You skipped out last night before we got to talk. What time is your flight today?"

"Was supposed to be a half hour ago. Overslept."

"Got time for some lunch then?"

Why not? It wasn't like I wanted to rush home anyway. "Sure."

"Twelve in the hotel restaurant?"

"Sounds good."

I stayed in bed another hour before showering and packing my shit. The team travel agent rebooked me on a five o'clock flight, so I figured I'd check out of the room and head to the airport after lunch.

Will was already seated at the table, on his cell phone as usual, when I walked into the restaurant. He waved me over.

"Alright, let me talk to my client," he said. "But if he agrees, we're going to need approval of the final copy for the script and an acting coach to work with him on his lines. And of course, first-class accommodations." He gestured for me to sit and laughed into the phone. "No, thanks. I don't need any."

He swiped the phone off and set it down on the table. "Freaking Viagra-type commercial offer for one of my retired clients. I'm presenting the offer over the phone, because there's a distinct possibility he might punch me when I tell him about it." Will shook his head. "Why can't these advertising companies want tennis players or baseball wimps? Nope. They gotta have the biggest, burliest, toughest hockey guys to promote their shit."

I laughed. "Just putting this out there now. You can decline if they ever come for me. Don't care how broke I am. Not peddling dick pills."

Will's phone vibrated on the table. He checked the screen, but then hit the button at the top. "Sorry about that. Things have been hairy lately."

"Uh-oh," I said. "You never turn that thing off. Should I be scared of what this lunch is about?"

"I turn it off."

"No, you don't. I saw you answer it at Vince Farone's funeral."

"That was an important call. I was negotiating the longest contract extension the league's ever seen."

"So is today just a friendly lunch, then? You felt like shooting the shit?"

"Not exactly..."

The waitress came over and asked to take our drink orders. Will ordered a scotch on the rocks. I wasn't normally a day drinker—or much of a night one, for that matter—but I thought I might need it today. For multiple reasons.

"I'll take a vodka 7UP."

"Coming right up."

Will leaned back in his chair. "Talk to me. What's going on with you?"

"What do you mean?"

"Your game is off. You're even less friendly than usual. And when I called Doug Allen to open up discussions about another contract extension the other day, he said your coach had mentioned he thought maybe you were looking to retire. He said he usually sees a change in his players right before they hang up their skates. Thought he might be seeing that in you."

Oh fuck. I scrubbed my hands over my face. "I'm definitely not ready to retire."

"Something going on? You nursing an injury you don't want to tell anyone about because you're afraid you'll get benched and some whippersnapper will steal your spot?"

"No. It's not that."

"Then talk to me. What is going on with you?"

I hesitated.

Will sighed. "Give me a penny."

"What for?"

He held out his hand. "Just give me a damn penny."

I reached into my pocket and pulled out the change I had. "I don't have a penny."

"Then give me that quarter. It'll do."

I picked the coin out of my palm and tossed it over to the other side of the table.

Will caught it. "Thanks. I'm on retainer now."

"Retainer for what?"

"I might not practice anymore, but I'm still an attorney. Now I'm yours. We have privilege, so tell me what's going on. You kill someone? Drug problems? A diagnosis you don't want anyone to know about?"

I rubbed the back of my neck. "It's not me. It's Evie."

"The skater? You two still together?"

I nodded.

"Haven't seen her around in a while. The other guys brought their wives to the fundraiser last night. Why didn't you bring her?"

Because I can't trust her not to disappear into the bathroom stall like Clark Kent and come out Superdrunk. "Evie's got some issues."

"Health?"

I met Will's eyes. "Mental health. She's also got a drinking problem."

Will frowned. "Oh, man. I'm sorry to hear that. Has she tried rehab?"

"Three times. A five-day detox and two thirty-day stints."

"My old man was a drunk. It's not easy."

"Was? Is he sober now?"

Will nodded. "I think he's been clean about ten years."

"What made him stop drinking?"

"I'm not sure I know the answer to that question. It was after my mom left him with us, but not right away. Probably two years after. He was on and off the wagon from the time they got married until I was twelve. He'd lose his job, we'd go stay at my grandmother's with my mom for a while, and then he'd show up clean shaven and sober and convince her to come back and give him another chance. But it would never last." Will shrugged. "Took more than losing everything for him to get better. All those years he tried for my mom. I think he really did love her. But it never stuck until he did it for himself."

My face fell.

Will noticed and smiled sadly. "Hits home?"

"Right on the damn nose."

The waitress brought over our drinks. Will held his glass out to me. We clinked and both took healthy swigs. After my agent set his glass down, he folded his hands on the table and leaned forward. "I'm sorry to hear what you're going through. I really am. But I'm going to give it to you straight. You need to get your head back in the game, or you're not going to be happy with your renewal. Management doesn't know what's going on, so they're thinking the worst—that you're on your way down. I can hold off pushing the contract talks any further until the season starts up again so you can show 'em they're wrong. But you need to find a way to get your shit together."

I blew out two cheeks of air and nodded. "Got it."

"If you want to talk, I'm here. The quarter gets you a lot of hours."

"Thanks. I appreciate it."

"A few months after we left my dad, I asked my mother if we were going back, like we always did. She said no, so I asked why not? I'll never forget the answer she gave me. She said, '*Because I finally figured out that you can't love an alcoholic into sobriety, but you can love yourself enough to let go.*'"

o o o

I laid back on the paddleboard, set the paddle across my waist, and inhaled the smell of the morning lake. This house...this lake had always been my solace. But the only way I could get any peace lately was to come out here and float.

I'd been back for three days now. Normally when I came home to a shitshow like I had the first night—a dented car, six stitches in Evie's finger, and a recycle bin that weighed more than the garbage one—Evie would sleep for a day and then cry and apologize. Not this time. She just kept drinking. And I was miserable in my own home. Last night, while we were arguing, I'd thought about going to a hotel. But instead I came out here and laid down on the board to think. By the time I went back inside, she was passed out.

Our relationship wasn't fun anymore—not that any relationship had to be fun all the time, but there needed to be a balance. This was a seesaw that hadn't teetered up in a very long time. If Evie were any other woman, I would've ended things by now. But she wasn't. She'd dedicated twenty years to a sport rather than create friends and a life. And the only real person she'd ever been close to was her mother, and that woman would only drag her the rest of the way down. So what was I supposed to do, kick her to the curb? I cared about her, loved her even if I didn't like her very much. Though what Will had said the other day at lunch kept rattling around in my head. *"You can't love an alcoholic into sobriety, but you can love yourself enough to let go."*

I stayed out on the lake, soaking up the sun for the better part of two hours, trying to figure a way out of this mess. The only conclusion I came to was walking away. I think I'd known for a while that was the only choice. But I wouldn't leave her high and dry. I'd find her a house and rent it for her so she had a place to go. And I'd be there for her as much as I could, just not as her fiancé and not living in the same house. I'd reach out to her father, too, try to encourage him to work on their relationship again. She was going to need as much support as she could get.

Decision made, I sat up and dug my phone out of my pocket. Lynn Walker was the real estate agent I'd used to buy this house. I scrolled through my contacts until I found her number and hit *Call.* She answered on the second ring.

"Fox Cassidy. How are you, hun?"

I guess my number had been saved in her phone too. "I'm good. How are you, Lynn?"

"Surviving on coffee and good intentions. What can I do you for, son?"

"Umm... I have a friend looking for a rental, preferably a house in Laurel Lake."

"I don't think there's much in Laurel Lake for rent at the moment."

"What about Hollow Hills? Somewhere near the rink might work."

"Let me do some research. Is it for one person or a family?"

"Just one person."

"What's the budget for the rent?"

Money was the least of my concerns. "There isn't one."

"Any requirements, like a big yard or certain number of bedrooms and baths?"

I shook my head. "Only requirement is it has to be in a good neighborhood and have security. It's for a woman living by herself." Neither this town nor the surrounding towns were unsafe, but when Evie drank, she didn't pay attention to things like locking the door. So a good security system was important.

"Okay. Let me see what I can do, and I'll get back to you in a jiffy."

"Thanks, Lynn."

After I hung up, I stayed out on the lake a little while longer, second-guessing whether I was doing the right thing. But when I walked into the house and found Evie burying a bottle in the garbage can at nine in the morning, I felt better about what I'd set in motion. Now I needed a time when she was actually sober enough to break the news.

"Do you think you could not drink today? I want to sit down and talk later."

"About what?"

"About us."

"What, like how you don't even kiss me anymore?" Evie's eyes filled with tears. "You don't even like me, do you?"

I could smell the alcohol on her breath. This wasn't a conversation I was going to have with her drunk. I might have to wait a while, but I thought it was important for her to understand how I'd come to the decision I had to make.

"Evie—"

She started to undress, pulling off her top first and then reaching for her pants. "I bet you'll fuck me though, right?"

I wasn't sure where this was coming from. We hadn't had sex in weeks. "Evie, stop."

She didn't listen. She reached around and unclasped her bra. "Oh, come on. Let's just do it. It's the only reason you keep me around and you know it." Half dressed, she walked over and threw her arms around my neck, pushed up on her toes, and pressed her lips to my chin. "Come on. Touch me."

"Please stop."

She grabbed my hand and brought it around to her ass, forcing it on me. "Grab it. It'll make everything better."

I shook her off and took a step back. "No, it won't, Evie."

"Fucking touch me!"

I swiped my car keys from the hook and headed for the door. Evie continued to scream at the top of her lungs as I walked out. She followed with barely any clothes on as I marched to the car.

"Go in the goddamn house, Evie!"

"No! Come in here and fuck me!"

I shook my head and got in. As I pulled out of the driveway, I saw Mrs. Craddox across the street peeking through her blinds. *Great.*

I rolled down the window and screamed from the car. "Get in the goddamn house, Evie!"

She flipped me the bird, but turned around and stomped back inside at least.

I didn't know where the hell to go, so I went to the place where my head was always the clearest: the rink.

Ten hours later, I was lying on my back on the bench in the penalty box. I'd sat in the office most of the day, then once the arena closed, I'd laced up and skated some aggression out. Now I was tired and wanted to go back home, but the thought of sleeping on a twelve-inch-wide wooden plank in the penalty box was actually more appealing. *Maybe I'll go to my mom's.*

I hated to drag people into my business, but I didn't have the energy for more Evie tonight. I pulled out my phone to call my mom, but then Evie's name started to flash on the screen.

I sighed and debated answering. By the fourth ring, I decided if I didn't, she'd only keep calling back. So I swiped.

"Hello?"

She cried into the phone. "You...you're kicking me out?"

I sat up. "What are you talking about?"

I could barely make out what she was saying, her words so slow and slurred. "The real estate lady... She came by."

Oh fuck. "Evie, let's talk tomorrow when you're sober."

"We can't," she sobbed. "I don't want to wake up tomorrow."

"Don't say that, Evie."

"But it's true."

I stood. "Evie, just sit tight. I'm coming home."

She sobbed harder.

"Evie, talk to me."

She steadied herself with a big breath and whispered into the phone. "I gotta go. I'm sorry, Fox."

Something about the way she said it sent chills up my arms. She sounded so desolate.

"Sorry for what? *Evie!*"

"Goodbye."

"Evie—wait!"

The line went silent. I called back, but it rang once and dropped right into voicemail. I called again while running through the rink and out to the car. When she still wouldn't answer as I started the car, I dialed 911.

"Nine-one-one. State your emergency."

"I need someone to go to my house. Forty-four Rosewood Lane."

"Can you tell me what's wrong?"

"I think my fiancée is in danger."

"Is someone going to hurt her?"

"No. I'm afraid she might hurt herself."

CHAPTER 32
The Coward
Fox

"You've got to be freaking kidding me..."

"Took you long enough to open the damn door." Opal brushed past me.

My mother at least had the decency to look like she felt bad showing up unannounced. She kissed my cheek before walking in. "Sorry we didn't call first. But this is necessary, Fox."

I wasn't happy, but I stepped back and held out my hand for her to walk in.

She smiled sadly. "Thank you."

I stole a glance next door before shutting myself inside with two women I was in no condition to talk to. No sign of Josie.

In the kitchen, my mother was already fixing a pot of coffee, and Opal was cleaning up the mess I'd made over the last two days. This wasn't good. They were already synchronized and had a plan of attack. Meanwhile, I felt unbalanced. The food I'd eaten sometime in the middle of the night was threatening to make an appearance, and my head was already starting to pound, though I wasn't quite sober yet. I was no match for these two in my current state. But it wasn't like I could sober up fast, so I went the other direction. I swiped the fifth of whiskey from the counter, twisted off the cheap plastic cap, and swigged back as much as I could get down.

Opal shook her head. "At least buy the good stuff. That crap will kill ya."

"Next time, bring it with you. Or better yet, don't come at all."

With the table clear, Opal motioned to the chairs. "Why don't we sit down?"

"Do I have a choice?"

"Not if you want us to leave anytime soon."

I frowned and pulled the chair out.

Mom stayed at the coffeemaker, waiting for it to finish brewing.

"What happened?" Opal asked.

"Ray said something that pissed me off, so I hit him. Cops came."

"Not that. We don't care about Ray. Someone should've walloped that snake a long time ago. What happened with Josie that set you on a tear?"

I shrugged. "It should've never happened. The woman sends Christmas cards to strangers because she believes in some fantasy that doesn't exist. I'm no knight in shining armor."

"Well, that much we know. Because as far as I'm aware, there aren't any knights named Sir Surliness or Lord Grumpalot. But that's beside the point. Josie is a smart woman. She knows exactly who you are. Yet for some insane reason, she still cares about your ass. So tell us what went down, and we'll try and help you fix it."

I raked a hand through my hair. "There's nothing to fix."

The coffeemaker beeped. My mom had been leaning against the counter watching Opal and me, but she turned and opened the cabinet above her head, the one where I kept mugs. She froze with one in her hand, looking out the window to the yard. "Where's the kayak that's always in the same spot on the dock?"

When I didn't cough up an answer fast enough, Mom turned. "Fox, where's the kayak?"

This wasn't going to end unless I gave them something. Might as well be what they came for. I closed my eyes, because I knew the reaction my answer would garner. "It sank in the lake. With Josie and me in it."

The room grew quiet. I imagined the glances being exchanged before the looks of pity were directed at me. Eventually, there was a rattling of dishes and the sound of the chair next to me scraping along the tile floor. When I opened my eyes, I was surprised to find there weren't mugs on the table—there were shot glasses. Mom took the bottle of whiskey in front of me and poured a round. The three of us knocked them back in silence. Two ounces seemed to have a much bigger effect on me than it should've. It seemed to reactivate my drunkenness. My head spun, and I slouched over the tiny glass.

Mom reached out and rested her hand on my forearm. "I know it's scary, but you can't let things from your past keep you from having a future."

"I'm not scared. I'm doing Josie a favor. I helped her with some work around the house. She took that as meaning more than it did."

Opal rolled her eyes. "She wasn't seeing things that weren't there. She was seeing what was written all over your face. We all saw it. You're head over heels for that woman. You have been since the first moment you set eyes on her."

I scoffed. "You don't know what you're talking about."

"I saw you smile, Fox. Not the evil one you flash when an owner thinks they can stiff you and get away with it, but really smile, the kind that starts on the inside and spreads to the outside, making your whole face light up."

"I think you need glasses."

She shook her head. "I've always admired your smarts. But right now you're being a dumbass."

I needed to move. This town had too many people in your business, and everyone knew where you lived to drop by and share their opinions. I had no doubt Porter, Rita, Frannie, Bernadette and Bettina—and everyone else in Opal's speed dial—would be by soon enough. I was definitely disconnecting the doorbell as soon as I got them out the door.

I huffed. "Are we done?"

My mom looked disappointed, but she nodded. A few minutes later, I walked them to the door. Opal walked out first, but Mom lagged behind.

Again she kissed my cheek. "I hope you come around. Because that lady next door is something special. But if you don't, you at least owe her some closure. Have a conversation and set her free. You aren't the only one who fell hard."

Her words hit like a punch to the gut. But she was right, so I nodded. "Alright, Mom."

◦ ◦ ◦

Thursday morning—at least I thought it was Thursday—I woke at the ass crack of dawn, still buzzing from the night before, my feet hanging off the couch I didn't fit on. I looked around in the dark, trying to figure out what the hell that pungent smell was. Then I lifted my arm and sniffed my pit. *Damn, it's me.*

Forcing my dragging ass up, I stopped in the kitchen for some breakfast of champions—three Motrin and a palm full of tap water cupped in my hand from the sink. I debated whether I should wait until my head stopped pounding to shower, but I was pretty sure that's what I'd done yesterday and never made it. So I sucked it up and headed upstairs.

Warm water sluiced over my slumping shoulders. What normally felt good was like needles pricking my skin today. Everything ached—my head, my shoulders, my neck. Though the biggest ache came from inside my chest. It fucking hurt, felt like an elephant had parked his fat ass on my ribs for a few days. But I deserved it.

By the time I washed the stink off of me, the sun was up. An annoying ray streaked through the blinds and cut a rude path across my bleary eyes. I squinted and reached for the wooden slats. Before I could flatten the offending pieces, I saw her. It took my damn breath away. Josie walked into the yard, carrying her duck in her arms. She set it down on the grass and took a few steps back. But the thing ran right to her, nuzzling against her legs. *Yeah, I know, buddy.*

She bent to scratch its head and smiled, but it didn't reach her eyes. It made me feel like someone had shot a dart and pierced right into my heart. I stayed there watching her on the sly for another ten minutes, feeling like I deserved every ounce of the pain it caused, until she finally scooped up the duck and went back inside.

My mother was right about one thing—Josie deserved better than I'd given her. So it was time I manned up and had a conversation. The sooner she moved on, the better for both of us.

Twenty minutes later, I stood outside her front door. My palms were sweaty, and I debated turning around and having a shot or two before knocking. Before I could shit or get off the pot, the door swung open.

Josie jumped back. "Shit. I didn't expect anyone to be there."

"Sorry."

She wasn't smiling, but I saw something spark in her eyes. I thought it might be hope. "How are you?"

"Okay. We need to talk."

Her eyes met mine. She was on guard, but seemed to soften. I hated that she trusted me so easily. "Sure." Josie stepped aside.

The duck was now perched on its dog bed once again, watching TV. I lifted my chin, gesturing that way. "You found him."

She smiled. "Her. And she found me. The other morning she just showed up at my front door."

I stuffed my hands into my pockets and nodded. "That's good."

There was a moment of awkward silence. It broke when we started to talk at the same time.

We exchanged hesitant smiles. "You go first," I said.

"No, you. Please."

I nodded and cleared my throat. "I'm sorry about the other day. Disappearing and all. I shouldn't have done that."

Her face softened. "It's okay. I spoke to Porter, and he filled in the blanks. I know about the lake...about Evie."

My jaw tightened.

Josie took my hand. "It must've been so hard on you when it happened. I'm sure you've been keeping a lot in for a long time. But I want you to know, I'm here if you want to talk about it. I was never a person who discussed my feelings either, but sometimes it really helps."

Fuck. I should've had those shots before I came over. Here I was ready to rip her heart out, and she was trying to console me. I felt like the biggest piece of shit on the planet. But I needed to rip the Band-Aid off, even if it stung.

"Josie, listen...I think you should go back to New York."

She blinked a few times. "You mean to stay?"

I nodded.

"By myself?"

I nodded again.

Her hand had been resting on my arm, but she pulled it back like she'd just realized she was touching a hot stove. "You're serious right now?"

"I should've never let things go as far as they did. It's not what I want." The last few words tasted bitter, even as I said them. Probably because they were made of *shit*. I fucking wanted her. Yet I shook my head. "I'm sorry."

Her voice rose. "You're *sorry*?"

"Look, Josie, you have every right to be upset. I—"

She cut me off. "*Of course I have every right to be upset*! I came here to heal, to find myself again. I wasn't ready to start something new. When you pulled back after the weekend we went away, I was sad, but I figured it was for the best. I didn't want to get even more attached if it wasn't what you wanted. But then you sucked me back in. I trusted you."

"I know." I raked a hand through my hair. "I fucked up. I'm sorry. I shouldn't have let things go so far."

Her eyes flitted around, like she was trying to absorb everything I'd just said and make sense of it. But it didn't even make sense to me, and the words had come out of my mouth. Eventually her gaze met mine again. "Why?" she chirped.

"Why what?"

"Why isn't what we have what you want? What about it don't you like? What's wrong with us? Or better yet, tell me what you *do* want."

"I...I like not being tied down."

Josie kept shaking her head. "Ridiculous."

"I'll finish whatever you need done in the house."

She frowned. "No thanks."

I didn't know what else to say, so I thumbed toward my house. "I should go."

"Yeah, you do that."

The vulnerability in her eyes when she'd opened the door was gone now, shuttered over with anger and sadness.

"I hope we can be friends," I said.

Josie opened the front door in response. I guess I should've been grateful she stopped shy of telling me not to let it hit me on the ass on the way out. She didn't speak again until I was out on the porch.

"We can't be friends. I don't like cowards. Goodbye, Fox."

CHAPTER 33
Pity Party
Josie

"Hey, Josie."

I forced a smile and pushed my sunglasses farther up my nose. "Hi, Bernadette."

The next day, I'd debated going to the grocery store to pick up a container of coffee instead of stopping by Rita's when I realized I'd run out. Now I was kicking myself that I hadn't.

She pointed behind her. "You heading to the Beanery?"

"I am." She had a brown apron tied around her waist, so I figured she was working at her sister's place. "Are you helping Rita out today?"

"I opened for her. She's the class mom at her kids' school and went for some bake sale this morning. But she's back now, so I'm going to Bettina's for some lunch. You up for joining? Bettina made chicken pot pie, so there's plenty."

"Thank you for the offer, but I have a lot to do today."

"Another time, then?"

"Sure."

"Saw Fox last week when I went to pick up Opal from work. Her car was in the shop for new brakes." Bernadette shook her head. "The woman drives for a month after hearing the sound of metal on metal, yet is surprised when she needs her rotors shaved down every time. Anyway, I went into the office because I was a few minutes early, and Fox was there. The man *smiled* at me. You know how long it's been since I saw that man's smile? I wasn't sure he even had teeth anymore."

I guess word hadn't gotten around that he'd dumped me yet—not surprising since Fox hated everyone knowing his business. But I wasn't about to ignite a gossip fire. Plus, if I had to say the words out loud, I'd probably wind up crying again. It was bad enough that I had to hide behind dark sunglasses today because my eyes were so puffy. Luckily, my phone rang, giving me a perfectly timed excuse. I pulled it out of my purse and held it up as evidence without even checking the screen to see who it was.

"Sorry, Bernadette. I need to answer. I've been waiting for this call. But it was nice seeing you."

"You too. Enjoy the weather today."

I pushed the Ignore button, yet brought the phone to my ear as I walked away, waving. "Hello?" Once there was enough distance between Bernadette and me, I stopped pretending I'd answered and lowered my phone again. A few strides later, it beeped, letting me know I had a message. There was also a second message from a call I must've missed while I was in the shower earlier. I pressed play as I walked the rest of the block to the coffee shop.

"Hi. This message is for Josie Preston. My name is Florence Halloran, and I'm calling from Rehnquist University. We received your resume for the adjunct professor position, and I was calling to set up an interview."

My heart sank. I'd completely forgotten I'd submitted an application online. It felt like so long ago, but it had only been four or five days. Yet so much had changed. Should I bother to call the woman back? Would I even consider staying in Laurel Lake now? I really liked it here. Life was simpler, and the pace was nothing like New York. And I'd made a lot of friends—not many my own age, but I was sure I'd meet plenty of younger people if I got the job at Rehnquist. I felt a true connection here—to nature, to the community, to my dad. The only thing people in Manhattan were connected to were their phones. But *could* I stay here and see Fox next door every day? The thought of pulling into my driveway while he walked another woman into his house after a date made me feel sick.

Oh God. Imagine if I heard them going at it through an open window?

The rest of the message from the woman at Rehnquist had finished playing, though I didn't absorb it because I'd been too lost in thought. But it didn't matter what she'd said since I wasn't in the right headspace to make a decision about calling her back, so I kept the message, scrolled to the next one, and hit play.

"Hi, Josie. This is Lauren Cahill from HR at Kolax and Hahm. I sent you an email the other day to confirm you'll be returning on the tenth, at the conclusion of your medical leave. I didn't hear back, so I thought I'd check in. Please give me a call when you have time. Two-one-two—"

I swiped up to stop the message as I arrived at the front door of Rita's. Everyone seemed to want a decision from me today, but I'd be lucky if I could pick the coffee I wanted. I tossed my phone back in my purse and decided to concentrate on that first. Caffeine would make facing the day easier.

"Hi, Rita."

"Hey, Josie. What can I get you today?"

I stared up at the menu above her head. I read the first few coffee choices, but none of them seemed to sink in. I sighed. God, I was really indecisive today. "You know what, I'll have a large black coffee, please."

She winked. "Fox orders the same thing."

My teeth clenched. "On second thought, I'll take that first special coffee listed up there."

She turned around to check the board. "The caramel macchiato?"

"Yes, please." I didn't have a clue what a macchiato was, but I didn't care. "Plain coffee is too boring."

Rita smiled. "Coming right up."

After, I stopped at the grocery store. Today's outing was bad enough. I didn't want to have to do a second one later and talk to more people. While I was there, I picked up a pint of ice cream—I'd actually put two in my basket, but forced myself to put one back. Then I grabbed a bottle of wine and a box of frozen Bagel Bites—all the makings of a pity party in bed. I was going to allow myself one more day of it. Then I'd kick my own ass and finish the work left on the house. Whatever I decided, that needed to be done.

I'd been in the house for all of two minutes when the doorbell rang. I hated that my heart started to race, hoping it might be Fox. But when I opened the door, it was only the postman with an express envelope.

He held out a handheld computer. "I just need you to sign here, Josie."

"Oh, okay. Thank you, Tom."

I hadn't ordered anything lately, so I wasn't sure what it could be. Back in the house, I tore open the pull tab. Inside was my passport and a letter-sized envelope. I frowned, seeing Noah's familiar handwriting on the outside in blue ink.

> *Josie,*
> *I'm taking a leap of faith. I'll be on that flight to Aruba. Give me a chance to show you I've changed, and meet me on it. I love you.*
>
> *Noah*

I sighed and tossed the package on the kitchen counter. Today was the day that just kept on giving. Maybe I needed that second tub of ice cream after all.

CHAPTER 34

Heartsick and Homebound
Josie

A week later, I stood at the kitchen window, watching Fox's truck pull into the driveway. We'd had no contact since he'd walked out of my house. I was embarrassed to admit it, but at first I think I was hanging on to hope that he'd come around, realize he'd made a mistake and apologize. But as the days went by, I felt like an idiot for considering that was even in the realm of possibility. The man was cut and dried. He liked his life neat and orderly. But at least one good thing had come out of me trying to pretend I wasn't waiting on him—I'd kept myself super busy.

I looked around the house. Fresh paint, the living room had an *actual* ceiling, new flooring, appliances, lighting fixtures, hardware, and decking. I'd gotten a few windows replaced, the house power-washed, the driveway sealed, and today I'd replaced the last of the tattered screens. It was almost unrecognizable as the house I'd walked into two months ago. Feeling proud, I snapped a few pictures and texted them to Nilda. A few minutes later, my phone rang, and I smiled at the screen.

"That is *not* the same house," she said when I answered.

"It is. I have the dent in my bank account and pain in my back from all the lifting to prove it."

"It looks amazing. I can't believe you did all that yourself."

I hated to give the jerk credit, but I couldn't lie to Nilda. "Actually, I didn't do it all myself. Fox is a contractor, and he helped a lot."

"Oh, how wonderful! Mr. Grumpy Hothead who is thoughtful, fiercely loyal, and devastatingly handsome is also handy! Sounds too good to be true."

Truer words were never spoken. Too bad I'd fallen for his act—hook, line, and sinker. I sighed. "Turns out he was, Nilda."

"Oh no. Are you okay?"

I didn't like to lie, but I didn't want her to worry. She had enough on her mind with her upcoming move. "I'm good. He wasn't my type after all." I took a deep breath and soldiered on. "When are you leaving for South Carolina?"

"Four days. The day after tomorrow is my last day with Dr. Preston, and I leave Tuesday morning."

God forbid Mom give her some time to breathe after twenty-five years of employment. I bet she wasn't even doing anything special for her last day. Nilda deserved a party.

With that, a light bulb flicked on in my head. She *does* deserve a party. Everything was done now here. There was no reason I couldn't drive back and throw one.

As quickly as the thought struck, I turned to look at the house next door. But I forced my eyes away and inwardly scolded myself.

No.

No, no, no.

I'm done here. I'm done wallowing. And Nilda's departure was important. I'd let a man turn me upside down *yet again.*

"Will you have dinner with me on your last night?" I asked.

"I didn't think you'd be back until after I left?"

"Change of plans. I'm coming home."

"It would mean the world to me to spend my last night here with you, Josie."

I smiled. This was the right decision. "I'll see you Monday night."

"Safe drive home, sweetheart."

After I hung up, I got to work. I called the only auto-repair shop in Laurel Lake and made an appointment to get my oil changed and tires checked. Then I called a real estate agent I'd met at the party Bernadette Macon had thrown when I first arrived. Lynn Walker had been elementary-school friends with my dad and owned one of the two agencies in town. She said she'd stop over tomorrow to look at the house and discuss renting it again.

With the big things out of the way, after dinner I decided to pour myself a glass of wine and sit down and write out a to-do list of what needed to be done before I left the day after tomorrow.

Three tasks in, my phone rang.

Opal.

I figured it was safe to answer. I might have believed Fox had fallen for me, but I was certain he was not spreading gossip. So I swiped.

"Hi, Opal."

"I'm going to kill that man!"

Uh-oh. Apparently, I'd misjudged more than I thought about the man next door. Yet I pretended to not know what she was talking about. Just in case... "Who are we talking about?"

"That jackass boss of mine. I *knew* there was a reason he's been particularly hateful the last week and a half."

I sighed. I supposed it would get out sooner than later. Though I would have preferred the later to be *after* I was gone. "He told you..."

"I put two and two together. He fired three subcontractors this week, can't put anything down without slamming it, and looks like he hasn't slept in a month. He tried to play it off to Porter as being stressed over one of our jobs going long. But then Regina Watson called me."

"Who?"

"I don't think you've met her yet. Regina bowls with Bob on Friday nights. She's a really good bowler. Whoops all the men's asses."

I was lost. "Okay..."

"Bob is Bob Walker. He's married to Lynn, the real estate agent you're talking to about listing the house for rent. Lynn mentioned it to her husband, who mentioned it to Regina at bowling tonight, and Regina called me. Now it makes sense why the boss is extra grumpy. You're leaving. And my guess is he did something to cause that."

Oh, Jesus Christ. I couldn't keep up with the game of telephone these people played. But the cat was out of the bag. I exhaled. "I am leaving. But Fox didn't do anything to me. Not really. He just...we're not looking for the same thing."

"When are you leaving, sweetheart?"

"The day after tomorrow."

"Well, then we'll need to have the party tomorrow!"

"That's very sweet. But I don't want a party, Opal. I don't really feel up for it."

"If you'd rather keep it small, I can do that. How about just a few of the girls then?"

It wasn't lost on me that a woman I'd met only two months ago was ready to jump in and throw a party for me on a day's notice, yet my mother wasn't even taking Nilda to dinner. Laurel Lake was a special place. It wouldn't be right if I snuck off without saying goodbye to some of its special people.

"That sounds perfect, Opal."

"Great. I'll call the gang and set it up and get back to you with the plans. But let's say seven tomorrow night?"

"Okay."

"Goodnight, sweetheart."

"Goodnight, Opal."

* * *

A *few* turned out to be twelve. But it also turned out to be exactly what I needed after a full day of packing. Opal had arranged dinner at an upbeat Mexican restaurant two towns over, one with a lively mariachi band and a long list of margaritas. When I'd walked in, she'd hugged me and whispered, *"The jackass hates these types of places. He'd never step foot in here."* That went a long way toward helping me relax and enjoy the evening. Everyone had gone now, and it was just me and Opal at the table, eating fried ice cream.

"Thank you for pulling this together. You have made me feel like family since the moment I arrived, Opal."

"You are family, sweetheart. Your daddy grew up here, and we take care of our own. But that sounds like it's an obligation." She shook her head. "With you, it's an honor."

My eyes welled up. So much of me didn't want to leave here. After two months, this place felt more like a home than my own house ever had. Opal reached across the table and covered my hand with hers.

"He's crazy about you," she said. "I know he is."

"He has a funny way of showing it."

"The man can keep skating after taking a stick to the head. He's the toughest guy I know. But he can't seem to move on from what happened."

That might be true, but I'd promised myself I'd never settle for a man who wasn't willing to give me back what I gave him. "I can't stick around waiting for something that might never happen. You know how he is, everything is black and white. I don't exist anymore to him."

"I think you're wrong there. He might not be knocking on your door anymore—in fact, I'd wager that dumb oaf keeps his head locked straight ahead when he comes out of the house because he won't allow himself to catch a glimpse of you—but you're in here..." Opal tapped over her heart. "He can pretend all he wants, but you exist in a place you can't ignore forever. Maybe he'll come around."

"I can't wrap my life around a maybe."

"Of course not. You have to do what's best for you."

"Take care of him, will you, Opal?"

"You know I will. Whether the grumpy idiot likes it or not."

CHAPTER 35
Happily Never After
Fox

Why does doing the right thing always feel shitty?

I stood in the guest bedroom on the second floor, watching her through the mostly closed blinds as she packed up her car. It felt wrong for a thousand reasons. Josie had just loaded a box into the backseat. She stopped halfway to the door and used the back of her hand to wipe sweat from her forehead.

"Why don't you open the blinds?" she yelled while looking straight ahead. "It's less creepy."

Shit. I jumped out of the window's view, my back flush to the wall next to it. My heart pumped like a criminal who'd just gotten caught red-handed. *Fuck.* Maybe I was one. After I caught my breath, I leaned forward and chanced a quick look outside. Josie was walking out of the house with another box, and it looked like she was struggling to carry it. Halfway to the car, it fell, toppled over, and the cardboard busted. Shit started to roll down the driveway.

Fuck. I can't watch this. I jogged over like some kind of hero and started to scoop shit up with her. Josie held up a hand, without looking up. "I got it."

"Just let me help."

"You've done enough."

"Jos..."

She looked up and narrowed her eyes, like they were loaded with daggers she was trying to shoot at me. But it was the things she couldn't cover up that made my chest ache. Her eyes were swollen from crying and rimmed with dark circles.

"No," she snapped. "You don't get to *Jos* me, like I'm the one being ridiculous. *You're* the one being ridiculous. You haven't looked my way in two weeks, and then today you run over here like I'm some sort of damsel in distress. I'm not. I don't *need* your help, and I don't *want* it. You only want to make *yourself* feel better."

I stayed kneeled down next to the box while she hastily tossed shit inside, not knowing my next move. But the next move wasn't mine, apparently, it was Josie's.

She stood, smacked dust from her hands, and marched into the house. Since she didn't slam the door behind her, I took that as a sign she was coming back out. For all I knew, she might be getting a bat to hit me over the head, and part of me hoped that was what she was doing, because I deserved it. But what she came back with hurt much worse.

Josie held out a check. "I looked up how much all the work you did around the house would have cost. This should cover it."

When I didn't lift my arm to take the check from her hand, she waved it around as her voice climbed a few octaves. "Take the damn check."

I stood. "I'm not taking the check, Josie."

She shoved it into my chest. "Take the damn check!"

I held my hands up and took a step back. "I'm not taking the damn check. I did that work because I care about you and wanted to. Not because it was a job."

"You care about me." She laughed maniacally. "You mean car*ed*. Past tense."

"It's not like that."

"No? Then tell me what it's like, Fox. Because one minute we were spending a weekend at a bed and breakfast and you were making love to me, and the next I was tossed to the curb like garbage."

I dug both hands into my hair, yanking. "This is what's best for you."

"Best for me? You don't *get to decide* what's best for me."

There was nothing I could say that she wouldn't toss back at me. She didn't understand how things worked out with a selfish bastard like me. Evie hadn't known either. I hung my head. "I'm sorry."

She softened. "I am, too. Will you please take this check?"

"I'll take it, but I'm not cashing it."

That seemed to pacify her for now. I shoved the check into my pocket, and she marched into the house again. When she came back out, I leaned forward and snuck a peek inside. The house was empty—even the cards on the walls were gone.

Josie shoved the box into the backseat and closed the door. She walked around to the rear of the SUV and slammed the hatch shut, turning her attention back to me. "I gave away all the furniture or threw it out. The real estate agent said it will rent better unfurnished. But I'm leaving Daisy's house in the back. Would you at least keep an eye on her for me?"

I pushed my hands into my pockets. "Of course."

"Thank you."

"When are you leaving?"

"Before the sun comes up tomorrow morning."

I swallowed. "Okay."

She stayed quiet until my eyes lifted and met hers. "Goodbye, Fox."

Fuck. It hurt more than any bone I'd broken in my twenty years of playing hockey. It felt like all the air had been squeezed from my lungs. Eventually I managed to mutter two syllables.

"Bye, doc."

         ◦ ◦ ◦

I stood at the front door at four AM, watching the taillights fade away down the block. I hadn't slept all night. Couldn't manage to close my eyes long enough to try. Even after the car turned the corner and there was nothing more to see, I kept standing there staring, lost in thought. At six, the garbage trucks rolled down the street. I looked to the curb next door and saw no cans had been put out. She had to have garbage after packing up the last of the house. So I walked next door to double check.

Both cans were packed, so I wheeled them down to the end of the driveway, just as the sanitation guys approached the house.

"Morning, Fox."

I nodded. "Hank."

Hank swung open the attached lid from the first can and heaved the contents into the back of the truck. I couldn't get my feet to walk away, so I figured I'd help him out and peeled the top back from the second one.

Hank tossed the first can back on the curb and grabbed the handle to the second. As he lifted, the contents caught my eye.

I put my hand up. "Hang on a second."

Hank stopped, setting the can back down. "Something wrong?"

It was dark. I thought I might've jumped to the wrong conclusion, so I reached inside and scooped out some of the contents of a box that sat open inside the can. Sure enough, they were Christmas cards—all the ones she'd had on her walls, all from people here in Laurel Lake.

Jesus Christ. I'd fucked up so royally that she no longer believed the fantasy she'd been carrying with her for fifteen years.

o o o

My face heated. *"You're fired."*

Opal's response was to cackle. She waved me off and sat her fired ass down behind her desk. "Oh please. Your idea of typing is pecking at the keys ten words a minute with two pointer fingers, you don't know how to use any of the software, and *doing payroll* is signing the checks after I figure out all the taxes and deductions. The last time I had a day off and the printer ran out of ink, you drove forty minutes to the nearest Best Buy and bought a new one because you couldn't figure out how to change the cartridge yourself." She shook her head. "I'm not fired. In fact, I think I deserve a raise."

Porter had walked into the office halfway through Opal's rant. The fucker tossed me a pity smile. "Grumpy because Josie left," he said.

"Get the fuck out!"

"He's miserable," Opal said. "Biggest mistake of his life, and he knows it."

Porter nodded. "I still regret breaking things off with Stacey Krans when I was twenty. Thought being tied down was stupid when I was that young. Now she's married with a kid and owns an exercise studio. Looks better than she did then."

Was this seriously my life? These two idiots... I took in a deep inhale of patience and blew it out. "What do you want, Porter?"

"Tile guys on the job over in Two Lakes said they weren't going to be able to finish tomorrow. Gonna need another two days, so we're going to have to push back the appliance deliveries."

"*Bullshit.* Tell them to get extra workers here by this afternoon and don't go home until it's finished. They're finishing on time."

Porter looked to Opal. She nodded. "I'll call the delivery company and have it moved to Thursday, just in case two days turns to three."

"Thanks, Opal."

"No problem, honey."

I tossed my pencil into the air as Porter walked out.

"What the hell do you think you're doing?" I growled. "I run this company, not you."

"Well, then get your head out of your ass and do it. Will Rupert is the tile guy on that job. His mother was put on life support last week, and his thirty-three-year-old wife is in the middle of her second round of chemotherapy for breast cancer. They've got two kids under five, too. There's no good reason we can't push the appliance delivery and cut him some slack."

"Fine," I gritted out between clenched teeth.

Opal sighed and stood, then sashayed her ass over to my desk and parked it on the corner.

"Listen, honey. I get that you're hurting. You did something dumb. You let that woman leave yesterday, and you're lashing out because you think it's going to make you feel better to make other people hurt. I've been there myself a time or two. But you know what? It doesn't work. You'll just wind up hating yourself more."

My jaw clenched as I glared at her. I could almost feel steam billowing out of my nose.

"You love this girl. I know you do." Opal pushed up off my desk and strolled back over to hers. She opened a drawer, pulled out her purse, and lifted it onto her shoulder. "So stop being a coward and figure out how to fix yourself before it's too late to get her back."

CHAPTER 36
My Only Friend is a Duck
Fox

"Yeah, I hear you..."

The damn duck looked just as sad and lonely as I felt. I could've sworn it just sighed. The last few nights, I'd taken to sitting on Josie's back porch. The first evening, the thing scared the crap out of me. It had waltzed out from the dog house, snuck up behind me, and bitten my finger. After that, he was friendlier. He seemed to be waiting for my nightly appearances. I figured he wouldn't be around now since it was midday, but he'd showed up about five minutes ago and joined me. Misery loves company, I suppose.

"What do you think she's doing right now?"

No answer. Daisy—the *male* duck with the girly name—stared at me like I was crazy. Maybe I was. After all, I did let the best thing that's ever happened to me walk out the fucking door. No. I shook my head. I didn't let her go, I'd *pushed* her out.

The duck rested his yellow beak on my thigh.

The sound of a truck pulling up interrupted my staring into space. From where I was sitting, I could see diagonally across to my driveway. Nothing was there except my pickup, so I figured it must've been across the street. At least until I heard the sound of footsteps brushing along the grass. I turned to find Porter walking toward me.

"Hey, what are you doing here?" he said.

"I live here. What the hell are you doing here?"

He lifted the key in his hand and gestured to Josie's back door. "Came to pick something up."

I squinted. "From here?"

Porter nodded. "Josie forgot something."

"Why the fuck is she calling you?"

Porter smiled. "You have no idea how bad I want to say she left me the key and we keep in touch, just to piss you off. But I've seen you knock out guys twice my size with one punch. So I'm not risking it, no matter how tempting."

I had zero patience for this shit. "What the fuck are you doing here, Porter?"

"Josie gave Opal a key for emergencies before she left. She called this morning and said she realized she left something behind that she needs and asked Opal if she would mind grabbing it and overnighting it to her. Opal's cat swallowed a small pigeon, so she called me and asked me to grab it and get it to the post office so she can go to the vet."

"What did Josie leave?"

Porter shrugged. "I don't know. An envelope on the top shelf of the closet in the upstairs left bedroom." He motioned to the cardboard six-pack holder next to me. Five were left. "Can I get one of those?"

I wasn't much in the mood for company, but I'd been a giant dick to everyone the last few weeks, so I slipped a bottle from the holder and held it out to him.

"Thanks."

I nodded. I'd hoped he'd take the thing to go, but no such luck. He sat down on the other side of Daisy and twisted off the cap.

"This your only friend?" He pointed his beer at the duck before bringing it to his lips.

"Yep. Doesn't talk much. You should follow his lead."

Porter stroked the animal's head and looked out at the lake. A family of swans swam up. They slowed as they got in front of us and looked over. Daisy wasn't liking that too much. He stood and jumped off the porch, flapping his wings and quacking as he ran toward the edge of the lake. Swans didn't usually scare easily, but they got the memo from Daisy. Work done, he waddled back to the deck.

Porter chuckled. "Opal mentioned that Josie took in a duck a while back. I guess this is him?"

"Yep."

"She named it something, right?"

"Daisy."

Porter's brows drew together. "You know that's a male, right? Males are raspier. The female's sound is softer."

"Yep."

We sat quietly for a few minutes while Porter finished his beer. Once it was gone, he tucked the empty bottle back into the cardboard holder.

"I liked her," he said. "Josie, not the duck."

I drank my beer while staring straight forward. Porter still didn't take the hint.

"I thought she was good for you. You deserve to be happy, boss."

"Yeah? Then you should hightail it out of here. That'll go a long way in getting me there."

The idiot smiled and got up.

I held out my hand. "Give me the key. I'll get whatever she left and drop it at the post office."

"Oh, no. It's okay. I got it."

"Wasn't asking, Porter."

He hesitated, but when he saw the look on my face, he relented and dropped the key into my palm. "Alright then, thanks. Post office closes early on Saturday, though, so you need to go soon. Opal will kick my ass if it doesn't get out today."

"I got it."

He nodded and waved. "Have a good weekend, boss."

I waited until I finished my beer and heard his truck pull away before getting up and going inside. One step in, and I already regretted taking the key from Porter. The place still *smelled* like her. I didn't know how that was possible after a week, but it did. I took a deep whiff of torture in and closed my eyes.

Fuck. *I missed her.* Missed smelling her. Missed seeing her smile at me even though I never deserved it. Even missed the cards hanging on the wall. It felt like a punch in the gut being in here. But I freaking deserved it.

I tormented myself some more in the kitchen, imagining her standing at the coffeemaker wearing my shirt from the night before, dumb Christmas cards hanging all over the walls behind her. She smiles at me as she reaches up to grab mugs, revealing her bare, perfect ass. *Fuck, I'm really an asshole.*

Upstairs, I opened the door to the left bedroom— Josie's room—and stopped two steps inside. It was empty. Another blow to the gut. I stared at the indents in the rug from where the bed used to be, imagined it still there. I'd *made love* to her in that bed. Hadn't done that in years. It had been so long that I hadn't even remembered there was a difference between *fucking* and *making love*. But there was, and the difference had left a gaping hole in my heart.

I forced myself to the closet. It was empty too, not even a hanger to be found. Reaching up, I felt around on the shelf for what she'd left behind. It was one of those USPS envelopes, about as big as a piece of paper. The return address was a place in New York City. I thought about not looking inside for about half a second, but quickly justified being nosy by telling myself I needed to make sure something was even in there. It would be stupid to send an empty package.

The first thing I pulled out was a passport. Opening it and seeing Josie's smiling face landed a one-two punch. I stared down at it for way longer than necessary. Luckily I had to get this thing to the post office before it closed or there was no telling how long I'd sit here. Walking out of the closet, I went to stuff the little book back into the envelope. But when I did, I realized there was more inside. There was no reason I needed to take the rest out—obviously the envelope wasn't empty—yet I did it anyway.

And my heart stopped when I read the note.

Josie,
I'm taking a leap of faith. I'll be on that flight to Aruba. Give me a chance to show you I've changed, and meet me on it. I love you.

Noah

This is what she needed fucking overnighted? I ripped the papers out of the envelope and unfolded them. My eyes could barely read the printed words because my hands were shaking the page so hard. But I picked off the important parts.

Ritz Carlton Aruba 9/12-9/19
Delta Airlines 6:00 AM departure – JFK airport
on 9/12

My heart raced out of control. She was going away with that fucking asshole? In two days. *Like hell I'll be mailing this shit.*

But after a few minutes of boiling, my blood pressure reduced to a simmer. I shoved my hands through my hair. What right did I have to keep her from doing anything? I'd fucking kicked her to the curb so she could be happy. But was this douchebag Noah really what would make her happy? The asshole had cheated on her. It felt wrong, against every instinct I had to send the envelope. Yet I gritted my teeth and went back downstairs, locking the door behind me.

The entire drive to the post office, I continued to debate it.

She can be with any man she wants. I'm sending it.

Fuck that asshole. He doesn't deserve her. Maybe even more than I don't deserve her. I'm not sending shit.

I hurt her. If this is what it takes for her to be happy... I'm sending it.

That douchebag will only hurt her worse. Nope. Not sending it.

Then it dawned on me. Maybe she only wanted her passport and had no intention of going on that trip.

Yet she needs them overnighted and the flight is in two days.

I flip-flopped back and forth for the entire drive before pulling up to the post office ten minutes before closing. I wasted another five debating whether to go in. Ultimately, I concluded that Josie was too smart to take that asshole

Noah back, and that she'd asked to have the passport over-nighted because it was safer than sending it regular mail.

Yeah, that was it. At least that's what I convinced my-self as I stepped up to the counter. Frannie, the government's grand gossip, scowled upon seeing me. Guess everyone knew now.

"What can I do for you, Fox?"

"You got one of those overnight envelopes?"

She reached down and grabbed one, slipping it across the counter. "We close in four minutes. Step over there while you fill it out so I can take the next person."

I looked behind me, thinking someone had come in after me and I hadn't heard them. Nope. Completely empty. Whatever. I moved to the little counter in the corner and picked up a chained pen. But when I put the point on the envelope to write, I realized I didn't know Josie's damn address.

Great. Just great.

I scrolled through my contacts until I got to Opal's name and hit call. Her greeting was as warm as Frannie's.

"What do you want?"

I shook my head. "Need Josie's address in New York."

"What for?"

"I brought what Josie wants shipped to her to the post office. Realized I didn't have her address."

"Why didn't Porter bring it?"

I sighed. "Can I explain that to you another time? The post office closes in two minutes, and Frannie is *not* going to stay here three for me."

"Fine. Give me a second. It's in my purse, and I'm holding Ernestine at the vet's office."

She disappeared and came back on the line a minute later.

"It's Two-twenty East Eighteenth Street. New York, New York, One-zero-zero-zero-three."

"Thanks."

I went to swipe off my phone and then thought better of it and lifted my cell back to my ear. "Opal?"

"What?"

It took a few heartbeats to choke out the words. "Is she really getting back together with Noah?"

There was a long pause, especially long for Opal who thought it was her duty to fill the air with words nonstop. Her voice was quiet when she finally answered. "Yes, she is."

Fuck.

Fuck. Fuck. Fuck!

My chest squeezed so tight, I wondered if I was having a heart attack.

"Closing in thirty seconds," Frannie yelled. "If you want to send something, get a move on, Cassidy."

I swallowed and walked to the counter in a daze.

Frannie stared at me. "Well? Hand it over."

I lifted the envelope to the counter and slid it over to her side. She went to take it, but I couldn't seem to let go.

"You have to actually *give* me the envelope to ship it."

I stared at her, or maybe through her, because I wasn't actually seeing anything but my future disappear.

Frannie frowned. "Now or never, Cassidy."

I blinked back to the moment. "You know what? On second thought, I'm going to deliver this myself."

CHAPTER 37
Coming to His Senses
Josie

I reached for the light switch and turned back to look at the empty lab with a sigh. Had I ever been happy here? I'd thought I was at one time. But maybe I'd mistaken success for happiness. Lord knows my mother taught me they were one and the same.

I flicked the switch off and pulled the door shut. I'd been back a week now, and it hadn't gotten any easier—not going to work, not going home to my empty apartment, not the ache in my heart. I took the elevator down to the ground floor and pushed through the turnstile door, dumping out onto the busy Manhattan street. As much as everyone being in your business in Laurel Lake could be a lot, there was something nice about walking around and everyone saying hello. I missed that. Here, I felt invisible.

The walk from my office to home was a little more than a half hour. Usually I hopped on the subway, but tonight I needed the fresh air. I stared down at the concrete like half the commuters, avoiding eye contact, lost in thought.

In the short time I'd stayed in Laurel Lake, it had become my home. Here all I had was four walls, brick, and beams. I'd lived in the same apartment for seven years and didn't have half as many fond memories inside it as I did in the house on Rosewood Lane. Sure, a lot of those were with Fox. But I liked the *me* I'd become while living there. The me who appreciated the beauty of a sunset, spent time listening to stories told by my dad's seventy-year-old friends, and planted in the dirt. The me who took on construction jobs—sure, at times I'd bitten off more than I could chew and needed help—but at least I *bit*. Here I didn't bite into anything. I went to work. Came home to my overpriced apartment. Maybe went to dinner or drinks with a friend once or twice a week. *Wash. Rinse. Repeat.*

Could I leave New York and make Laurel Lake my home? Or would it be too painful to be so close to the man next door?

Fox. Every time I thought about him, it felt like I'd gotten the wind knocked out of me. Like there was an emptiness in my chest that I yearned to fill.

I missed him.

I missed the way he only spoke a few words, yet said so much.

I missed the way he was fiercely protective of the people he cared about, even if he pretended they got on his nerves.

I missed the way he couldn't help but be a gentleman, even though it made him grumpy. Like when I'd hit his mailbox and realized I was locked out of my house the night I arrived, yet he still carried in my luggage.

I missed the way he *wasn't* a gentleman in bed.

I walked in a fog, somehow maneuvering through throngs of people on the sidewalk and not crashing into any of them. When I finally came upon my building, I realized I didn't remember half the trip home. In the elevator, people got on and off. Faces were familiar, and some had probably lived here as long as I did, yet I didn't know any of their names.

How many people did I get to know in Laurel Lake? Opal, Frannie, Bernadette, Bettina, Rita, Porter, Hope, Tommy, Rachael, Sam, Reuben... after only two months I bet I could rattle off two-dozen names without having to think long.

I exited the elevator on the thirty-first floor with a feeling of dread. My apartment had become a daily reminder of how empty my life was. But halfway down the hall, movement up ahead snapped me out of my daze. My heart, which had been sitting in my chest like a deflated football, suddenly filled and started beating wildly—beating like it was making up for lost time.

I froze twenty feet from my door. "Fox?"

He'd been sitting with his knees bent next to my door, but now he climbed to his feet. When our eyes met, I had to focus on remembering to breathe. *In. Out. In. Out.* Fox looked tired and stressed, his clothes were crumpled, eyes rimmed with dark circles like he hadn't slept so well lately. But even with all that, he was breathtakingly handsome.

"Why are you here? And how did you even get up here?"

He dragged a hand through his hair. "Doorman recognized me from my playing days. I told him I was visiting a friend and wanted to surprise her. He let me come up after taking some pics and signing an autograph."

"But why are you here? In New York?"

He nodded toward my door. "Do you think we can go inside and talk? I really need to use the bathroom. I drank too much water on the drive up, but I was afraid if I left, the night doorman wouldn't let me back in and I'd miss you."

"The night doorman? What time did you get here?"

He shrugged. "Maybe three hours ago?"

"You've been sitting here for three hours?"

He moved back and forth from one foot to the other. "And now that I stood up, I *really* gotta go." He motioned to the door again. "Would you mind?"

"Oh. Sure." I took my keys from my purse and unlocked the door. "Down the hall, first door on the left."

Fox disappeared into the bathroom, which gave me a few moments to collect myself. I took a deep breath and shut the door, then focused on slowing the blood pumping through my ears. Though when he walked back out, it felt like my body hit the gas on all its inner workings. My heart and mind raced, blood hurtled through my veins, and questions swirled around like a tornado taking form.

I cleared my throat. "Feel better?"

He smiled. "A lot. Thanks."

"Well, that makes one of us. I need a glass of wine before I'll feel better. Would you like one?"

"Sure."

I walked to the kitchen and poured myself a very full glass. Unfortunately, it only left enough for a regular pour in the second glass. I'd normally give a guest the better offering, but I needed it more than he did. He'd known he was coming.

I slid the half-full one to the other side of the counter. "Sorry. You're getting the crappy pour."

"I'm just grateful you didn't break the empty bottle over my head for showing up like this."

I brought the wine to my lips. "You only just got here. I haven't ruled it out yet."

After a healthy swallow, I maneuvered around the counter and into the living room. "Why don't we sit in here?"

My apartment was a decent size by New York standards, but it suddenly felt really small with Fox in it. I took a seat in a chair I rarely used, a protective distance from the other side of the coffee table, where Fox would be forced to sit on the couch.

Once he was settled, he blew out an audible, shaky breath. "I'm really sorry for showing up like this without calling. I was afraid if I called, you might tell me not to come."

My head would've wanted to, but my heart would've overruled it. "What are you doing here, Fox?"

"I came to give you this." He reached into his back pocket and pulled out a folded USPS envelope.

"What is it?"

"The envelope you left at the house. The one with your passport."

"You came all this way to deliver my passport? When you could've dropped it at the post office a half mile from your house?"

"It's not the only reason I came."

"Okay...well, what else then?"

He took a deep breath and pointed to the cushion next to him on the couch. "Do you think you could sit over here?"

"Why?"

"Because I'm freaking the hell out and need you near me to calm down."

I debated his sincerity, afraid to read into what he was saying. "Why are you freaking out?"

"Because I don't think I've ever had more on the line than I do in this moment." He looked into my eyes. "Please, Jos. Just come sit next to me, even though I don't deserve any kindness from you. I need you so fucking much right now."

It was impossible to think straight with his beautiful green eyes searing into me. But when I tried to look away, I saw his big hands shaking. That did it. I got up and moved to the couch, sitting with a fair amount of distance between us.

Fox inched his way over until our knees were touching, then closed his eyes. "Thank you."

I waited, watching the rise and fall of his chest until he opened his eyes again.

"I'm here because I finally realized that I threw away the best thing that ever happened to me."

My heart raced with hope, yet I was still afraid of misunderstanding what I thought he was saying. I needed to protect myself. I swallowed. "What are you saying, Fox? I need you to be very clear with me."

He looked down. After a long time, he reached over and took my hand. "Is this okay?"

I nodded.

"I need to start from the beginning, if you don't mind bearing with me for a while."

"I'm listening..."

He took yet another deep breath. When he spoke, his voice was soft. "You know that my brother died in an accident years ago. I was nineteen, and Ryder was seventeen. He was driving home the day before his eighteenth birthday. But what I didn't mention was that he had been drinking. He fell asleep at the wheel and wrapped his car around a tree."

"I'm so sorry."

I could see pain etched in Fox's face. It made me want to stop him, but it also looked like whatever the full story was, he needed to get it out. So I squeezed his hand, trying to offer silent support.

Fox smiled sadly and continued. "It was a Friday night, and I was away at college. Out with a girl. He'd called me a half hour before the accident, but I didn't pick up because I was having too much fun. I didn't even realize he'd left me a message until the day of his wake. If only I'd answered. His words were so slurred. It would've taken two minutes to tell him not to drive."

"Oh, Fox. It's not your fault."

"I think that's debatable. But anyway... Years later, I met Evie. At first everything was great. We were both Olympic hopefuls. After my brother, I'd pretty much pulled away from anyone and everything except for hockey. Somehow I let my guard down when it came to Evie." He stared off for a while before continuing. "Her mother was a former figure skater and her manager. She was also a drunk. I couldn't stand being around the woman. I think because it reminded me of my brother and how he died. It's also why I rarely have more than a glass of wine or two. Long story short, Evie didn't qualify for the Olympic team. She wound up going back home and going on a bender with her mother. She was already one of the oldest trying to qualify. She wasn't going to have another shot, so I understood why she would spiral for a little while. But the spiral became something more. I thought things would get better without her mother's influence, so I asked Evie to move in with me. She did, and things seemed to smooth out, at least at first. A month after she moved in, we got engaged.

"But there was a lot I didn't know. It turned out Evie's struggles with alcohol weren't new. She had been a closet drinker since..." He shook his head and went quiet for a moment before swallowing. "Since she was nine years old."

"*Nine*?"

He nodded. "I know. To this day, if I look back, I have no idea how I missed seeing it. But she was a binge drinker, and I traveled a lot with the team, so we weren't seeing each other every day, even after she moved in."

"Wow."

"Anyway, Evie went in and out of rehab a few times. She'd be sober for a month, and then I'd come back from an away game and she'd have fallen off the wagon. The doctors in rehab put her on antidepressants to treat the root problem, but it just compounded her issues because she'd drink while taking them, and the alcohol would hit her harder. After a while, I couldn't do it anymore. I decided I would be there for her as a friend, but I needed to end things. I'd contacted a real estate agent to find her a place of her own to live and had planned to sit down and talk to her when she was sober. But the real estate agent stopped by the house when I wasn't home, and Evie put two and two together. She got really upset and took a bunch of pills. I called the police, but by the time they found her, she was floating in the lake."

"Oh God."

"When I pulled up, they were zipping a body bag on a gurney." He shook his head. "The night of the funeral, I got myself loaded. Fell down a few of the stairs in my house, twisted wrong, and blew out my knee. Career over, too. Some people never learn their lesson. I didn't pick up the phone when my brother called because I was too busy having fun, and I wanted to cut Evie loose because she was too much work. I should've been there for the both of them."

I might not have known Ryder or Evie, but I felt a profound loss, nonetheless. Not just for the two humans who died, but for the loss of faith and trust in himself that Fox had suffered as a result. Tears streamed down my face. "You've experienced unimaginable tragedy. But you can't blame yourself for decisions others made."

"Two people who loved me needed me, and I wasn't there for either of them. I didn't deserve a second chance. Certainly don't deserve a third." He reached out and wiped my tears with his thumbs and swallowed. "But I'm so goddamned selfish, I want it anyway, Josie."

I looked into his eyes. "Are you saying what I think you're saying?"

He shrugged. "I have no goddamn idea. I suck at words."

I laughed through tears. "You're doing pretty well today."

"Then I'll keep going. If what you got out of everything I said so far is that I'm madly in love with you and will do everything in my power to make up for hurting you if you'll just give me another chance, then maybe there's hope for me after all."

"You love me?"

Fox cupped both my cheeks. "Sweetheart, if you'll let me, I'll spend as long as I have to and do whatever it takes so that you never doubt that again."

"Whatever it takes? So you're going to move here to Manhattan?"

Fox froze. It looked like he might shit his pants. I should've kept him on the hook for a lot longer after the hell he'd put me through, but I cracked and smiled. *"I'm kidding."*

He blew out all the breath he'd been holding, and his shoulders shook with quiet laughter. "You're going to make me pay long and hard for screwing up, aren't you?"

I twisted my lips like I was considering it. "Not too long. I'm guessing the women of Laurel Lake have been doing that for me since I left."

He groaned. "You have no damn idea."

I smiled. "That's what family does. They stick together."

"How come you're family after only a few months, yet I've lived there my entire life and I'm getting the cold shoulder?"

"Because you *deserve it*, jackass."

"True." Fox's face had lightened a bit, but he grew serious once again. "But what I don't deserve is you, doc. Don't deserve you one bit."

I smiled. "I am pretty spectacular."

Fox's lip twitched. "You sure are, sweetheart. You sure freaking are."

◦ ◦ ◦

It was the middle of the night by the time we finished talking. Fox, man of normally very few words, had really opened the floodgates. We spoke more about Ryder and Evie, about what it had been like for me coming back to New York and saying goodbye to Nilda, and even about how he had struggled to find his way after his injury had forced his retirement from hockey.

I was emotionally and physically exhausted as we slipped into bed. Fox had driven twelve hours straight, too, so I couldn't imagine how his eyes were still open. I lay with my head on his chest while he ran his finger over my shoulder, tracing a figure eight in silence in the dark.

"Do you still love him?" he finally said.

I felt my eyebrows reaching toward my nose. "Love who?"

"The douchebag."

That was the name he'd bestowed on my ex. But he couldn't be asking if I was in love with Noah after all we'd shared tonight. Could he?

"Who's the douchebag?"

"The guy you were going to Aruba with."

I pushed up to look at him. "How did you know Noah and I had a trip to Aruba planned?"

"There was paperwork for it in the envelope I brought you, along with your passport."

"Oh. Yeah, that's right. But why would you ask if I still loved him?"

Fox's forehead wrinkled. He looked as confused as I felt. "Because Opal said you were getting back together." As soon as he said it, he closed his eyes. "Crap. She was just trying to get me off my ass, wasn't she?"

"Is that why you came here? Because you thought I was going to Aruba with Noah?"

"It's not the reason that matters, but it might have had something to do with why I drove ninety miles an hour through five states clutching the steering wheel."

"And here I thought you'd missed me so much, you finally came to your senses."

"I did miss you."

"Yet it took poking the green-eyed monster to get you to act on it. Heck, if I would've known that, I would've told you I was going home to sleep with Noah before I left and saved us both a lot of heartache."

Fox's eyes flashed. "Don't even say that."

"Say what?" I grinned. "That I planned to *fuck* Noah?"

Quicker than the blink of an eye, I was flipped over and flat on my back. Fox hovered over me, looking smolderingly possessive—a look he wore unapologetically, like all his other moods. "You think this is amusing?"

"Why, yes. Yes, I do."

"Why did you need your passport overnighted if you weren't leaving the country tomorrow?"

"There wasn't really any rush. When I realized I'd forgotten it, I called Opal and asked her to grab it before the realtor started showing the house to potential tenants. She said she'd overnight it so it was trackable."

He hung his head. "I'm so damn gullible."

Minutes ago I'd been exhausted, but with Fox hovering so close, my body found its second wind. I figured poking the bear a little more might be fun. "I don't know. Between the paperwork and Opal telling you I was back with my ex, it seems logical to think I might be sleeping with him again, *fucking Noah...*"

Fox's eyes blazed. "You really need to stop saying that."

I leaned up so we were nose to nose. "What's the matter? Does the idea of another man *inside* me bother you that much?"

"You're *really* enjoying this, aren't you?"

"Maybe..."

Fox gathered both my hands in one of his and pulled them up and over my head. He whispered in my ear with a rasp. "There's only one way for me to get rid of the jealousy I'm feeling right now."

Goosebumps peppered my skin, and my nipples hardened to peaks. "Oh yeah? How is that?"

He lowered his lips to mine. "I'm going to fuck all thoughts of any other man right out of both of us."

I liked the sound of that a lot.

His mouth moved to my neck, and he kissed his way to my ear. When he spoke, the words vibrated on my skin. "I'm going to apologize in advance for how hard I need you." He trailed his knuckles down the side of my body. When he reached my panties, he tugged and they ripped away.

I gasped.

"You'll get my soft later."

"I don't care how I get you, as long as I have you."

"Oh, you have me, sweetheart. By the balls."

Fox aligned himself with my opening and sealed his mouth over mine as he pushed inside. I scraped my fingers over his back, digging in when he sank deep. My body felt full, but so did my heart. It felt like...coming home. Like the relief of pulling into your driveway after a long trip. The two of us were tucked inside a bubble, and I never wanted to come out. Each time he withdrew, I grew desperate for more. Another hard thrust, another deep plunge. My body greedily clenched, the climb toward orgasm already begun.

"Fox..."

"Fuck," he gritted out. "I'm gonna fill you up so much, my cum will be inside of you for days."

That did it. The desperation in his voice sent me flying over the edge. My body thrummed through an earth-shattering orgasm. Fox grumbled a string of curses, pumping and grinding until I started to go slack. Then he sank deep and let go. And all felt right again, as if the Earth had been spinning off its axis for weeks and now gravity had forced it back into place.

Later, my head rested on Fox's chest while he stroked my hair.

"I really am sorry for what I put you through the last few weeks."

"I know you are."

Fox lifted his arm, showing me his thumb. I hadn't noticed the Band-Aid wrapped around it.

"What happened?"

"Your duck bit me."

I laughed. "Are you serious?"

"It was a few days after you left. But we worked it out. We're friends now." He shook his head. "Even a bird figured out I was a dumbass before me." He paused. "He misses you."

"I miss her, too."

Fox was quiet for a while. "I want it all, doc."

I tilted my head to look up at him. "All what?"

"You. Kids. A duck. A dog. Fenced-in yard where they can all run around. Maybe even a stupid minivan. And I want it soon, sweetheart."

My heart raced so fast, I thought it might jump out of my chest. "Are you sure?"

"Never been more sure about anything in my life. You don't want to come back to Laurel Lake, I'll move here."

I had a sudden vision of Fox walking down the streets of Manhattan, standing head and shoulders above most, looking like he wanted to rip the head off of everyone in his way. I chuckled. "You? In Manhattan?"

"Why not?"

"Oh, I don't know. Have you ever been on a subway?"

"No."

"Taken a public bus?"

"No."

"Do you know what alternate-side-of-the-street parking is?"

"No."

"How do you feel about street meat?"

"Huh?"

I smiled. "You'd be miserable in Manhattan, Fox."

"What about somewhere right outside the city, then? So it wouldn't be too long of a commute for you. They have places like that near here, right? Jersey or Long Island?"

I looked back and forth between Fox's eyes. "You'd really move here for me?"

"I'd do anything for you, Josie."

My heart melted. "It means the world that you would give up so much. But you don't have to move to New York. I'll move to Laurel Lake."

"Really?"

I nodded. "I love it there. It's the only place that's ever really felt like home."

Fox blew out a breath. "Oh, thank Christ."

I laughed. "Relieved a little?"

"You have no idea. But I really would've moved here if you wanted to stay. Laurel Lake is where I live, but when you left, I realized none of that matters. Where you are is my home."

EPILOGUE
The Ultimate Christmas Card
Josie

Three months later

"Why did you let her go? I don't think we've gotten a good one yet because you were scowling the first few minutes."

Fox grunted and shook his hand out. "Damn thing just bit me. Again."

Daisy bolted across the lawn. Opal chuckled. She was standing a few feet away trying to take our holiday picture. Fox's mom, Hope, was next to her. Neither had stopped smiling since they arrived an hour ago.

"Uh, boss. I think she did more than nip at you." Opal gestured to Fox's shirt. "You might want to look down."

Fox groaned. "Jesus Christ."

I tried not to look amused. "Some people would say that's good luck."

"How the hell is a duck shitting on you lucky?"

"Well, we're lucky I couldn't decide which shirt I liked better for the picture and bought you two, aren't we?"

"I didn't need *one* flannel, much less two," he grumbled.

"I disagree. Go change. We'll let Daisy run around for a few minutes so she's happier when you come back."

Fox mumbled something under his breath I didn't catch, but stalked to the house.

Hope watched her son disappear. "I can't believe you got him to wear a red plaid flannel."

I didn't think it would be appropriate to tell her what I'd had to promise to get him to do it, but hey, I didn't mind. The Paul Bunyan look really worked for me.

"So how many cards are you going to send out this year?" Opal asked.

"One-thousand four-hundred and eighty-eight."

"That's pretty specific."

"I'm doing the entire Laurel Lake phone book. I just finished entering all of the names and addresses into a database."

"So *every person* in this town is going to get a picture of Fox wearing a red flannel and holding a duck with a matching bow in its hair?"

"Yep."

She smiled. "*My, oh my,* how times have changed for the bossman."

And they had. But they hadn't just changed for Fox. A lot had changed for both of us. After Fox drove up to New York, I'd quit my job, packed everything I owned, sublet my apartment, and said goodbye to anyone who meant anything—all in a week's time. I'd even taken Fox with me to my mother's house when I went to tell her I was moving. As expected, she wasn't happy. I got a lecture about throwing away my career for a man. But then late in the day, something *unexpected* had happened.

After we'd finished eating, I was antsy to leave. Fox asked if he could talk to my mother in private before we took off. I knew he was tough, but my mother was a pro at cutting people down to half their size. So I was nervous when the doors to the study closed. They didn't come out again for *ninety minutes*. And my mother was smiling and laughing when she emerged.

Talk about a shocker.

Fox hugged my mother goodbye like they were old friends, then went to wait in the car, giving the two of us a few minutes alone. I'll never forget what she said.

"I made a lot of mistakes in my life. Many of them with you, Josephine. But the one thing I did right was marry your father. Something about Fox reminds me of him. There's something pure within. Hold onto him and don't ever take him for granted. Life is too short."

Tears had stung my eyes as I threw my arms around my mother.

Maybe her approval shouldn't have meant so much to me. But it did. We weren't ever going to be best friends, but we spoke every few weeks now.

Opal interrupted my thoughts. "When are your new tenants moving in?"

I smiled. "Nilda and her sister arrive next week."

A month after I'd relocated to Laurel Lake permanently, Nilda and her sister came to visit. They fell in love with the little town as quickly as I had, and they'd decided to move down together. It just so happened that I was going to start looking for a tenant soon, since I'd finally agreed to move in next door with Fox. So everything seemed to be falling into place. I'd even interviewed at Rehnquist University a few weeks ago and had a second interview on Monday. If things went right, I'd be an adjunct professor of pharmacological sciences come January.

Fox walked out the back door of his house, still tucking his flannel in.

"Daisy is over there with her friends." I pointed. "I'm just going to give her a few minutes more. If she doesn't come back on her own, I'll grab a treat."

Fox shrugged. "Whatever."

"Honey?" his mom called. "Do you think you could come by one day this week and pull my tree out of the basement?"

Fox looked at her, but didn't answer. His mind was obviously elsewhere. So I nudged him.

"Your mom asked you a question..."

"She did?"

I nodded.

He lifted his chin to Hope. "What's up, Ma?"

She repeated the question. But a few minutes later, Opal asked him something about a job and the same thing happened.

I had to nudge him a second time. "You okay?"

"Yeah, why?"

"I don't know. You seem distracted all of a sudden."

Fox shrugged. "Fine."

I chalked it up to him being more miserable than I'd thought taking the holiday card picture, so I figured we should get it over with. "I'm going to get a treat for Daisy, and then I'll grab her so we can get the photo done."

I lured Daisy away from her friends with a baby carrot and picked her up. I went to hand her over to Fox, but he shook his head. "Why don't you hold her?"

I'd had my heart set on a picture of us in front of the lake with Fox holding Daisy for our Christmas card. He looked so damn adorable when he held her. But at the moment, he looked more miserable than anything. So I didn't argue, and we got into position in front of the lake with Daisy in my arms.

Opal held up her phone and smiled. "*Rolling!* Ready when you are, bossman."

Rolling? As in a video? I was just about to tell Opal I wanted a photo, not a recording, when I felt Fox moving around next to me. I glanced over, and my heart stopped.

He was down on one knee.

"Oh my God!" My hand flew up to cover my mouth. But the screech I'd let out had already spooked Daisy, and she started flapping her wings all over the place. I would've dropped her if Hope hadn't run over.

She smiled. "I'll take her."

I couldn't breathe. *Is this really happening?*

No wonder Fox seemed so distracted! Though at the moment, my giant Paul Bunyan looked more nervous than anything. It was forty-eight degrees out this afternoon, yet he had a sheen of sweat covering his forehead. He wiped it with the back of his flannel sleeve and took my hand.

"Josie, since the minute you ran over my mailbox, you've been the center of my universe. I tried to keep away, but something about you pulled me back like gravity. I just needed to be close to you, even if it meant hanging sheet-rock on weekends and acting like having a wild duck for a pet was normal."

"Hey." I smiled. "It is normal."

"Doesn't matter. I'd have a flock of birds if it made you smile the way you are right now."

I covered my racing heart with my hand.

Fox looked down for a long time. When he looked up, his eyes were brimming with tears. "You brought me back to life, Josie. And I want nothing more than to spend the rest of my days with you. I want to be in your stupid Christmas card, and have dumb holiday cards hanging on my walls in March. I want you to be the last thing I see every night before I close my eyes, and the first thing I see when I open them every morning. You make me a better man, and you make me want to strive to improve each day, because every one I spend with you outshines the last. So, please tell me you'll be my wife." He looked over at Opal and his mother, both of whom beamed with camera phones pointing at us. "If not because you love me, then to save me from having to move, because those two are recording right now, and their videos of me getting rejected will be all over Laurel Lake within thirty seconds."

I laughed and leaned forward, pressing my forehead to his as tears streamed down my face. "I would love to marry you, Fox Cassidy."

Fox slipped a beautiful emerald-cut diamond ring onto my finger and climbed to his feet, lifting me off the ground as he came to full height. He pressed his lips to mine. "I love you, doc."

"I love you, too. But you do know this is going to be our Christmas card, right? You down on one knee. It's like I've come full circle. I dreamed about a fairytale life in Laurel Lake since I was a little girl. Now you've given it to me."

"I'm pretty sure it's you who's given it to me, babe." He winked. "But I'll give you something even better later."

THE END

(But turn to the next page to see how their Christmas card photo came out!)

ACKNOWLEDGEMENTS

To you – the *readers*. Without you, there would be no Vi Keeland. Thank you for more than a decade of support and enthusiasm. I'm honored so many of you are still with me and hope we have many more years together!

To Penelope – Because of our friendship, I cry a little less and laugh a lot more! Thank you for always being there to catch me when I'm about to fall off the deep end.

To Cheri – Books brought us together, who you are made us true friends!

To Julie – Thank you for your friendship. I'm ready for something new from you!

To Luna – Thank you for your friendship through thick and thin.

To my amazing Facebook reader group, Vi's Violets – 26,000 smart ladies (and a few awesome men) who love books! You mean the world to me and inspire me every day. Thank you for all of your support.

To Sommer – Thank you for figuring out what I want, often before I do.

To my agent and friend, Kimberly Brower – Thank you for being my partner in this adventure!

To Jessica, Elaine, and Julia – Thank you for smoothing out the all the rough edges and making me shine!

To Kylie and Jo at Give Me Books – I don't even remember how I managed before you, and I hope I never have to figure it out! Thank you for everything you do.

To all of the bloggers – Thank you for always making time for my books and years of support!

Much love,
Vi

OTHER BOOKS BY VI KEELAND

Something Unexpected
The Game
The Boss Project
The Summer Proposal
The Spark
The Invitation
The Rivals
Inappropriate
All Grown Up
We Shouldn't
The Naked Truth
Sex, Not Love
Beautiful Mistake
Egomaniac
Bossman
The Baller
Left Behind
Beat
Throb
Worth the Fight
Worth the Chance
Worth Forgiving
Belong to You
Made for You
First Thing I See

OTHER BOOKS BY VI KEELAND & PENELOPE WARD

The Rules of Dating
The Rules of Dating My Best Friend's Sister
The Rules of Dating My One-Night Stand
Well Played
Not Pretending Anymore
Happily Letter After
My Favorite Souvenir
Dirty Letters
Hate Notes
Rebel Heir
Rebel Heart
Cocky Bastard
Stuck-Up Suit
Playboy Pilot
Mister Moneybags
British Bedmate
Park Avenue Player

VI KEELAND is a #1 *New York Times*, #1 *Wall Street Journal*, and *USA Today* Bestselling author. With millions of books sold, her titles are currently translated in twenty-six languages and have appeared on bestseller lists in the US, Germany, Brazil, Bulgaria, Israel, and Hungary. Three of her short stories have been turned into films by Passionflix, and two of her books are currently optioned for movies. She resides in New York with her husband and their three children where she is living out her own happily ever after with the boy she met at age six.

Connect with Vi Keeland
Facebook Fan Group:
https://www.facebook.com/groups/
ViKeelandFanGroup/)
Facebook: https://www.facebook.com/pages/Author-
Vi-Keeland/435952616513958
TikTok: https://www.tiktok.com/@vikeeland
Website: http://www.vikeeland.com
Twitter: https://twitter.com/ViKeeland
Instagram: http://instagram.com/Vi_Keeland/